PRAISE FOR *THE LAST 8*
A 2019 International Latino Book Award Winner

"*The Walking Dead* meets *Alien* in this expertly plotted debut. Teens will want to follow Clover on her next adventure!"

—Zoraida Córdova, author of the Brooklyn Brujas series

"A fantastic plot following a fierce young woman and an ending that was such surprise I couldn't stop thinking about it for days."

—Bethany Wiggins, author of *Stung* and *Cured*

"A brilliant exploration of humanity and what it means to be alive when the world around you is dying. Between the aliens, the characters, the apocalypse, and the constant surprises, I couldn't tear myself away from this beautifully crafted, heart-stopping book until the very last page."

—Kaitlin Ward, author of *Where She Fell*

"A sci-fi romp with ample intergalactic twists to keep readers satisfied."

—*Kirkus Reviews*

"A diverse and immersive science fiction… From its dialogue to its action, the story is fluid, maintaining irresistible momentum through to the emotional, unpredictable ending. With its powerful world building and emotional twists, *The Last 8* is a beautifully fresh take on the idea of an alien apocalypse."

—*Foreword Reviews*

"This debut is, at times, both joyful and heartbreaking... Pohl's characters are tough, funny, and brave as they manage to persevere despite the debilitating weight of grief."

—*Booklist*

THE FIRST 7

ALSO BY LAURA POHL

The Last 8

THE FIRST 7

LAURA POHL

sourcebooks
fire

Published by Sourcebooks Fire, an imprint of Sourcebooks
P.O. Box 4410, Naperville, Illinois 60567-4410
(630) 961-3900
sourcebooks.com

Library of Congress Cataloging-in-Publication Data

Names: Pohl, Laura, author.
Title: The first 7 / Laura Pohl.
Other titles: First seven
Description: Naperville, Illinois : Sourcebooks Fire, 2020. | Sequel to:
    The last 8. | Audience: Ages 14-18. | Audience: Grades 10-12. | Summary:
    After leaving Earth, now devastated by an alien attack, and exploring
    the galaxy, Clover Martinez and her fellow teen survivors return home
    find crystal formations in the soil threatening to destory their planet
    and a colony of survivors who are not who they seem.
Identifiers: LCCN 2019033750 | (hardcover)
Subjects: CYAC: Extraterrestrial beings--Fiction. | Survival--Fiction. |
    Friendship--Fiction. | Mexican Americans--Fiction. | Science fiction.
Classification: LCC PZ7.1.P6413 Fi 2020 | DDC [Fic]--dc23

LC record available at https://lccn.loc.gov/2019033750

Printed and bound in the United States of America.
MA 10 9 8 7 6 5 4 3 2 1

To Dad,

for showing me the stars even when I was scared of them.

PART I

WAITING IN THE SKY

CHAPTER 1

The sky out here is never the same shade of blue as home.

The levels of oxygen, nitrogen, and ozone don't match in the atmosphere, reflecting directly into the darkness of space, or some strange psychedelic color that makes me feel like I'm inside a video game. Sometimes, on one planet or another, I look up, and there's a shade in it that reminds me of the cloudless summer sky. A second later, I blink, and it's gone.

I really shouldn't be thinking of anything other than the Arc as home.

"You ready?" Rayen's voice sparks behind me, and I turn around from the Arc's command. "Everyone's already waiting."

I nod. I turn around to check Sputnik, who is wearing a

glass helmet and trying to lick the surface to no avail. I pat the helmet, and the Bernese mountain dog barks.

"Come on," I say to her, and we leave the Arc together, Rayen by her other side. The Arc's ramp closes behind me.

The sky, of course, is nowhere near blue.

It's a pinkish glow of stars and lights, and there is no visible sun. The atmosphere is thin, and for the first couple of seconds, my lungs shrink, and the air seems empty. But then it settles, and I breathe normally again. A beach stretches from the edge of the cliff, the Arc sitting in sparkling silver above it.

The beach looks like a collection of small universes put together, a quilt woven into the fabric of the planet. Colors and noises pop out of different tents, easily standing because of the low gravity center of this planet. There are aliens floating in pools of clouds, and a transparent walkway marks the path for those who can't fly. A hundred different species of aliens wait on the beach, where the ocean is made of something that looks like shining butterfly wings, coming and going with the moon that glistens above us like a giant pearl.

It's a spectacle that never ceases to take my breath away.

I follow Rayen to the beach along with Sputnik, weaving between the species of aliens that are beyond any human's imagination. There are insect-like aliens with ten arms or tentacles, furry aliens with huge, glass-like eyes, aliens as tall as houses, aliens that look like houses. No one pays attention to us as we cross the beach looking for the others.

Out of the beings that circulate the universe in these parts, humans don't call attention. We don't have extravagant colors, and we aren't especially tall. We don't have more than one set of arms or legs. If anything, others note that we're ugly and scrawny, which I'm fine with. I'd rather look like this than like the 1 percent of the Hostemn alien genes that run inside my cells. I spot our blanket, lodged between two magnificent tents, small compared to the others. But that's exactly what we want—to go unnoticed.

I see Flint sitting on the blanket, and I wave over to him. Sputnik pads over to Flint, wagging her tail. I let go of her leash, and she runs to him.

"Don't let that dog go anywhere," Flint calls out. "I'm not ready for another God-Sputnik mission."

"You gotta admit it was funny," I tell him.

Flint shakes his head. "I'm done with aliens worshipping dogs and then trying to kill us for wanting to take Sputnik back. Once was enough for me."

I pat his shoulder, sitting down on the blanket beside him.

"Where are the others?" I ask.

As soon as I say it, I see Brooklyn and Avani weaving through the crowd, hand in hand. Brooklyn is wearing her usual black, her dark-brown hair now reaching her shoulders. Avani wears her hair pinned up, her pastel-pink skirt blending in perfectly with the beautiful colors of the beach. They wave to us, and Sputnik barks again, belly up for scratches. Avani kneels down on the ground next to her, rubbing the dog's belly through the special suit.

"Good parking spot," Brooklyn says by way of greeting me. She sits next to us on the blanket and looks up at the sky.

"So what are we doing next?" Rayen asks. "After this."

"There are a couple of options," Brooklyn says. "Diving on the Klurian Sea. There's this weird space coffee that I'm dying to try out. This alien over at space Hot Topic recommended it to me." We all sigh collectively. "Oooh, I know. There's a space race in the rings of Ndonya. It's very *Mad Max*."

"Damn, that shit sounds wild," Flint says, taking a sip of his drink. "Y'all be safe."

Brooklyn glares at him. "You don't have an option. You're coming with."

Flint sighs. "That's the worst thing about the end of the world. I can never tell people 'my mum won't let me' and stay home instead."

I laugh. "I'll take you."

"As long as you're not driving," Brooklyn says.

"I have a clean record in space."

"No, you don't. You crashed the Tesla."

"You said it'd be just like driving a spaceship."

"Clover, you crashed the *only* car in space. The only one. Ever. Congratulations."

While some things had changed since we had been in outer space, some definitely hadn't.

More than a year ago, spaceships arrived on Earth. One week later, the invading species had easily decimated more than a third of the population on Earth. I'd survived because

I was invisible to them, and I spent six months wandering around traveling, and that's when I'd found Sputnik. After six months, I heard a message on the radio calling out for other survivors.

I'd run as fast as I could to Area 51. There'd been tension at first—I wanted to fight back, and the other survivors didn't. We set up a trap and caught one of the aliens, but things went wrong, and Adam, one of our own, was killed because of it. Area 51 hid a lot of secrets, too, including a whole spaceship in the basement. With the captured alien, I started putting two and two together only to find out that the last surviving members of our species were hybrids. Our friend Andy was a Universal, an alien capable of changing the windings of the universe, and the Hostemn were after her power. Putting the lies aside, we'd decided that there was only one thing we could do: fight for Earth.

After Andy used her power to destroy the Hostemn fleet, we'd been wandering space for the last seven months. We'd been to the edges of the Milky Way, visited black holes and red dwarves, seen nebulae eight times the size of Earth, surfed along the stars, and seen things I hadn't even imagined were out here.

The Arc took us anywhere we wanted to go. Anywhere but the place we'd left behind.

This stop on the edge of the Shrofina complex was just another one of our destinations. Brooklyn had managed to find a file in the Arc with the most amazing phenomena to be seen in the universe, and we were crossing out each stop, one by one. This time, there was a giant supernova that scientists had predicted was going to burst in only a couple of human hours. All the aliens gathering at the beach had been waiting for weeks—or maybe seconds according to their own time—for the single moment when the energy would dissipate.

"I think it's about to start," Avani says. "Should we call the others?"

I frown. "Yeah, where are Violet and Andy?"

Brooklyn shrugs. "I don't know. Getting drinks or something."

"Brooklyn," I say in a warning tone. "You know you're not supposed to leave the two of them alone."

Brooklyn rolls her eyes. "They're not children. They can take care of themselves."

Rayen and I exchange a look. It's not a problem, usually, but both of them together call more attention to themselves than is warranted. Andy tries to pass as human, but Violet's another thing entirely—she doesn't survive out here like we do since she's not a hybrid. She has to wear a full-on space suit, and though we've found one as discreet as possible for her, which wraps around like silk over her skin, she still has to wear a helmet to breathe.

"I'm gonna go find them," I announce, getting up and brushing my pants. Sputnik barks, following me, and I get her leash.

I move through the tents and blankets that crowd the beach. Most of the aliens are looking up to the sky, waiting for the supernova to burst. It's worse than the year my grandparents decided to go to LA to see the New Year's Eve fireworks, where there wasn't breathing room for bodies as we waited for the spectacle to start. Some things don't seem to change, no matter where you are in the universe.

I finally spot Andy and Violet almost opposite from where we're sitting, and I make my way through to them.

"Hey," I say when I arrive. "We're all back at the blanket already."

"Okay." Andy nods. "I was just getting myself a drink."

I look at her drink, and it looks good enough to try out. Behind her, there's some kind of improvised bar, and I see all types of aliens ordering something.

Maybe it's going to bite me in the ass, but maybe it won't. Andy says we're supposed to survive everything, so space food and drink are definitely on the list. I lean against the improvised bar, waving to the bartender. Some things definitely don't change when you leave your planet.

"Get me one of those bubbly drinks," I say, gesturing. I'm not exactly terrible at speaking in the common alien language, but Brooklyn is the best of us. She picks up languages as easily as I drive a spaceship, and for all I know, I could be telling the alien to go fuck himself.

"Where are you from?" the alien asks, looking at my weird, gangly limbs. I've heard arms described that way more times than I can count.

"Earth," I say.

"I've not heard of it."

"It's mostly harmless," I reply. "Thanks for the drink."

"Enjoy the supernova!" the alien says. Or maybe the alien says something else entirely. I'm assuming the best.

I grab the drink in my hands and move over to Andy and Violet, who looks at it wistfully.

When we turn around to go, our path is blocked by another alien. Kreytian's smile stretches big when they spot Sputnik.

"Oh, there's the most beautiful creature in the entire universe!" they exclaim, looking up to me. "Oh, there's your pet, too. When are you giving this magnificent being to me?"

"My dog is not for sale," I tell them flatly.

Kreytian shakes their head. "A marvelous thing, a dog. So few of them up in space. Evolution has not graced many planets with this gift."

Their skin is a tanned brown, their robes a polished gold, and they wear a blue eyeliner over their eyes. Their hair is combed back, and if not for their four eyes, they would almost look human.

They finally turn to see Violet and Andy standing next to me.

"Andromeda."

Andy nods back in acknowledgment. "Kreytian. Come to see the supernova, too?"

"Well, I've seen hundreds, but I grow bored," they reply. "We all have to entertain ourselves in some way, don't we?"

Kreytian stretches their mouth into a smile, but it's tense.

They're a fixture at the Blssian market, one of Brooklyn's favorite spots. They gather as much information as possible, and that means that seven newcomers in a ship of Universal making don't go unnoticed by them.

"Yes," Violet replies. "We all do. If you'll excuse us—"

"Just a moment," they say, stretching out their arm.

Nobody dares to move. I exchange one look with Violet, and the light reflects on the glass surface of her helmet. We've been through similar situations. That's always been our number one rule—we don't call attention to ourselves. If there's trouble, we run as far away from it as possible. Don't let anyone spend more than a second thinking about these tiny humans and what they're doing here.

"I haven't had the opportunity to speak to a lot of humans," they say. "And I value dearly all the opportunities for learning. It's not every day you encounter survivors of the Hostemn massacre."

Every single one of my muscles snap in place, tense. I tighten my grip on Sputnik's leash, and she feels the tension, too.

"You know the Hostemn came to Earth," I say. It's not a question.

"I also know they were destroyed there," they reply. "If your friend is the only survivor of the Universals and she now walks among humans, there's not that much to guess. The Burst is not something that goes unnoticed. Especially when it's not only used to destroy."

Kreytian gives one look at Violet, and her shoulder tenses.

Andy steps forward, shielding her.

Kreytian doesn't seem threatened by it. Instead, they're almost amused. They turn to me.

"Has Andromeda told you about the origins of the Universals?"

I don't look at Andy.

"We know about the war," I say, my lips dry.

"The Hostemn were dangerous," they say. "Planet wreckers. But not the most dangerous thing in this universe by far. Wouldn't you say so, Andromeda?"

"I don't know what you're talking about," she replies.

Kreytian keeps smiling.

"No one likes their species being villains. The Universals loved peace, and they loved knowing everything. I can tell you this because I remember the war, and I remember the day the Hostemn took over."

No one dares to move.

I've seen this conversation play out many times already. We arrive someplace, and then someone recognizes Andy for what she is—it's almost inevitable. The change in her eyes, her skin, her hair. She tries to look human, but there is no hiding what she is. There's nothing that can cover up that kind of power.

"I have seen many wars," Kreytian says casually. "I'm seven thousand years old by the human standard. Young for my species. Young for the universe. And yet I can remember every single battle and war that's wrecked it. I've seen planets blown to dust, vanished into nothing." They glance at

Violet. "Your Earth is just another in the cycle. Not important. Universals never tried stopping a war. We wouldn't help them stop theirs."

"We had rules," Andy hisses, unable to contain herself. "We never interfered. Free will above all."

Kreytian's smile widens. Their teeth shine like mother-of-pearl.

"Benevolent like gods," they say. "That's what you called them on your planet, correct? Gods. Able to mold the universe yet refusing to do anything significant. And oh, how we would plead. We would go to Universali and beg for intervention. Beg for them to descend from their mighty chairs and save us."

They continue without hesitation.

"They never intervened. I watched my planet burn while they did nothing, even though they could have. Your species had the power to change everything, and yet they refused."

Andy's soul is a burning fury, and the temperature around us grows cold, chills climbing my spine. There's a burst of energy around her, the same energy I saw back at the Hostemn ship. I hadn't seen it since that day, and her power flutters to the surface, rippling across the galaxies.

It grows and expands all around us, echoing, until Violet pulls Andy back, grounding her. Around us, some of the other aliens have stopped talking, eyeing Andy.

I feel the energy still, though, like it has expanded throughout the universe, a burst of light that has gone from inside Andy and been let out freely.

Kreytian ignores Andy's outburst.

"There won't be a people who miss the Universals," Kreytian says, "but there will always be those of us who remember what they did not do."

"Enough," Violet snaps. "That's enough. Let's go."

"You feel it, too, don't you?" They turn to her. "You don't forget what happened to your planet. What happened to you. You should be careful, human. You may not be the same as you were before."

There's a flash of something in Violet's eyes, almost like she's ready to break. Like she's ready to come undone. I think back to that one moment, seven months ago, when Violet did the unthinkable to stop the rest of the universe from ending. When she sacrificed herself so Andy was free to use her power, to rewind the universe and kill the Hostemn.

It burns a hole in my stomach.

"Not everyone will welcome Andromeda," Kreytian says.

"Is that a threat?" Violet asks, her voice calm.

"No. It's a warning." They look again at Andromeda, and there's pity in their eyes. "There's not a single place in the universe you're going to be safe. We don't forget that easily. She's not welcome here."

Andy steps back.

"Let's go," Violet says again, and this time, we listen.

I turn my back.

I know Kreytian's right.

Andy is never going to be safe, no matter where we go.

CHAPTER 2

The atmosphere is tense when we go back to the blanket.

Andy pretends she's not shaken by the encounter. The thing is, it's happened before, and it'll happen again. We can't hide Andy forever. They'll find her. Her enemies will find her.

There are no safe places for any of us.

The supernova is beautiful. It burns vivid, our eyes protected against the worst of it by the planet's atmosphere—and then a blink, and it's gone. Years and years in the making, the collapse of a dying star, its final breath, and it's over in a few seconds.

It is collapse and it is creation, everything at once.

The others can feel the tension as we head back to the Arc, Violet walking quickly back to our home, and no one questions her resolve. Once we're inside, I lock the doors and bring back Earth's atmosphere.

Violet takes her helmet off as soon as she's inside. Her breath comes out in short spasms, and she bends her back, putting her head between her knees.

"You okay?"

She nods. "Just catching my breath."

"You shouldn't have stayed out so long," I tell her.

"Fuck off, Clover," she says, sitting up. She massages her neck, her piercing blue gaze staring right at me.

"I'm just saying, we've talked about this. If your body can't handle it, don't go."

"I didn't ask for plain old human genes."

My skin prickles at the comment. There's a reason why we survive out here and Violet doesn't.

After the Hostemn invaded Earth, I'd survived much on my own before meeting the others. Us surviving wasn't a coincidence, though—we owed it to our special, modified genes. Three percent of our DNA wasn't human, and it allowed us to go undetected by the Hostemn fleet. Violet is the only one of us who doesn't have that DNA. She's the one who can't be here.

"Stop treating me like I'm made of glass."

Andy approaches her. When she's nervous, her eyes change shades quickly, like a nebula unfurling. I step away, taking off Sputnik's suit so she can run freely inside the spaceship as I boot up the Arc so we can go.

Our next destination is a mystery.

Not only because we have no idea which of Brooklyn's ideas will be next but because no matter where we go, we won't be able to find peace.

"Why the long faces?" Flint finally asks, breaking the silence.

I look up from the ship's controls.

"We've encountered an alien," Violet says in the most cryptic way possible. "They had a message."

"A message?" Brooklyn pipes in. "Like what? Seek knowledge?"

"It wasn't a message. It was more like a warning," I say. "They said Andy's not welcome here."

"Anywhere, really." Andy shrugs like it's no big deal. "It's not like we haven't seen this before."

Violet and I exchange another look.

"What exactly did they say?" Avani asks, her eyebrows knitted in concern. "Was it a general warning, or—"

"Just the usual," I reply. "They know about the destruction of the Hostemn."

"They know about me," Violet adds quietly.

We all fall into a deathly silence.

"What do they know?" Avani asks.

"That the Burst didn't just destroy the Hostemn," Violet replies. She doesn't complete the sentence, but we all know.

Andy brought Violet back from the dead.

Andy did the impossible.

"So what?" Brooklyn asks. "Why is that a big deal?"

"The Universals preached no interference," Andy says, not looking anybody in the eye. "We interacted only with our own species because we knew the consequences of interfering in other planets. It's a rule. A rule I broke."

We don't reply.

"They would have exiled me," Andy says.

"Good thing the others are dead, then," Rayen mutters. "Look, it doesn't matter anymore. That's over."

"It's not over," Andy says. "Not as long as I'm alive. Everyone will be reminded of what the Universals can do. Of what *I* can do."

"Andy, you used your power once," Avani says in her soothing tone. "It doesn't make your whole species evil. If they don't understand—"

"You're the ones who don't understand," Andy says. "We have the power of changing anything we like. There's a reason we don't use it. If we use it for ourselves, we're no better than the Hostemn are."

"And if you can help others but you don't, you watch them die either way," Rayen says quietly. "It's a paradox. Damned if you do, damned if you don't. The alien just wanted to upset you."

"Looks like it was successful," Flint mutters. "And if we can't stay here…"

"We don't have anywhere safe," Brooklyn finishes off.

"We do, though," Violet says.

We all look up at her.

"What?"

"Andy's planet," she says. "Universali."

Andy looks up. "No."

"It might be the only place you're safe," Violet presses. "We could find the answers you need."

Violet's right. I hadn't even considered Universali might be an option until now. I don't know how Andy feels about going back to a planet that might be as devastated and as empty as my own.

"I don't think that's the answer."

"It's about the only option we have," Violet says. "We've been everywhere. Maybe—"

Suddenly, the panels on the ship light up, and the engines jolt. Andy falls to the ground, and I barely hold on to my seat as the engines suddenly start up. A siren blasts inside, the sound echoing through the spaceship, and I have to cover my ears.

"What the hell—"

The rest come up to the main room, the sirens blasting at full volume. The panel lights up in red, invading my vision and shining through my irises.

"Shut it off," I shout, "Shut it off!"

Then the room is quiet again, only a red light blinking in the panel. It's a light I've never seen before.

"Is everyone okay?" Avani asks, and we all nod.

I turn to Andy, and her face is drained of color.

"What was that?"

She takes a second to respond. "Distress signal. We were

supposed to have them. You know, in case anyone got in trouble when the ships separated."

The only thing moving inside the spaceship is the insistent red blinking light. I hold my breath.

Before Andy can say anything else, I press the button.

I don't know what I expect. Maybe numbers, maybe a message, maybe just the siren starting again. But instead, I'm faced with the one thing I'm trying to forget.

The little blue planet stares back at me from a hologram.

Violet steps up, her eyes glued to the image. "What is this? What does it mean?"

Andy opens her mouth, shuts it again. Then she says, "It's a distress signal."

"I know. But what does it mean?"

Andy stares at the hologram, unblinking. "That's where it's coming from."

Earth.

CHAPTER 3

No one moves.

I don't think we can even breathe, and the red Earth signal just keeps on blinking.

Avani is the first one to break the silence. "What exactly do you mean by a distress signal?"

Andy mulls the question over, biting her lower lip until a tiny bit of silver blood cracks the surface. "Originally, when we went to Earth, we had more than one ship. More than thirty people. They were supposed to move on to other planets and see if they could hide themselves there."

Andy takes a deep breath. Violet moves closer to her, slipping one hand over the girl's shoulder. Violet gives Andy the strength she lacks, a single human girl and a being who's going to outlive us by thousands of years.

"But I thought you were the only one left."

"I *am*."

My heart drums inside my chest, and I chase away the squirminess and excitement that bubble inside me.

"It's probably just a malfunction," Andy says, voicing what everyone is thinking. "I don't think the signal means anything."

"But what if it does?" Flint asks.

I look up, and I meet his brown eyes in the corner of the room. He shakes his head just slightly.

"There's a possibility…" Flint finds his voice again. "A possibility that something is there."

"The planet was destroyed," Violet replies, her voice so harsh that it reminds me of our days back on the base. "There's nothing there. And that's the end of it."

Violet presses a button, and the red flashing Earth vanishes. Uneasiness settles in the pit of my stomach. I look over at her, but she doesn't meet my eyes.

"We're all tired," Violet says. "We'll get some rest and decide what to do in the morning."

Violet leaves and Andy runs after her, leaving us five in the center of the ship, facing the panel where the Earth was blinking just a second ago.

"Can you get it back?" Rayen says so quietly that for a second, I think I imagined it.

I nod, pressing the buttons again till I find the distress signal in the panel. Although it doesn't make a sound again, there's a distinct red dot that doesn't stop blinking, half a galaxy away.

But it's there. It's as real as it can be.

When I press the button, the hologram of Earth shows up once more. This time, it floats peacefully, a perfect replica of the one I saw only seven months ago.

Seven months here feels like a lifetime. Seven months here means everything I have ever known has changed, and a little blue planet in the solar system means nothing compared to the sheer size of the universe in the fraction that is the spaceship I drive.

"Does anything else show up?" Brooklyn asks.

I look at the screen and the strange markings of the Universals in the panel. I look at it until they start making sense, but there's nothing beyond the name and location of the planet.

"No," I say finally, turning to them.

"There's gotta be something," Brooklyn says, tapping the metal of the panel. "It's never happened before."

"Violet says we should ignore it," Avani replies, standing next to her girlfriend. "It could be a malfunction."

"A malfunction that conveniently selects Earth? That's likely."

"Brook, I'm just saying—"

"I get what you're saying," Brooklyn replies. "It's still weird as hell."

The hologram of Earth hovers in the quiet. Before I do anything stupid, I shut it down and shake my head.

"Violet's right," I say. "We should all go to bed."

There are nods and grunts from the others, but none of them challenge me.

I leave the Earth behind, but somehow, it feels that the Earth hasn't left me.

I give up on sleep sometime in the early morning. Outside, I can see the three moons orbiting the planet as the Arc floats on the border of the atmosphere, and ahead, a red star the size of a golf ball.

I play with the ship's controls, getting *Prince of Persia* to work. The advantage of having Andy as a crew member is the ungodly number of video games she's installed in the ship, and for a few hours, I get distracted with side quests and trying not to get killed. My fingers are used to the ship's controls, but they're not nearly as fast as a video game.

I hear the footsteps only when they are too close.

Andy sits beside me in front of the panel, looking out to the planet and the sky beyond. She looks tiny. Her hair is deep black with waves, her irises a muted purple color. She almost looks human.

Almost.

"Couldn't sleep?" she asks, eyeing the screen, where Prince Dastan is getting beaten up.

"What is sleep?" I shoot back. "What is time? What is the universe?"

"Bringing you guys along is just the worst." Andy sighs and

rests her arm against the panel. "You've all become nihilists." She looks at the screen again.

I get stabbed a second time and die.

Andy eyes me. "You just have to—"

"Shut up," I tell her. "I'm the one playing."

"You're the worst player on the ship."

"Probably."

"Give me that." Andy snatches the control out of my hand, and in under three minutes, she passes the stage I'd spent my last hour on.

"Are you better at it because your brain is bigger?"

"I don't have a brain."

"You're the one saying it."

"Ha, ha," Andy says. "It's just practice. And the fact that I spent eighteen hours straight on this one time."

I shake my head, amazed by her ability to be a huge nerd. I don't take the control back, and Andy keeps playing, both of us watching the screen.

"What Kreytian said back at the beach, was it true?"

Andy keeps playing.

"Andy." Silence. "Andromeda."

Andy bites her lip, and the swell is turquoise blue.

"I don't know," she says. "Maybe something is happening to Violet."

"Something as in…? We're living in a pretty wide reality here. Something could mean she's being devoured inside by an alien or she's becoming a planet or something."

Andy chortles. "No, not that. But something with what happened that day."

She pauses the game and pulls up a record I'd never seen before in the ship.

"What's this?" I ask.

"Read it," she says.

My eyes take a second to adjust to the Universal symbols, but I understand it enough—it's a manifest, some sort of rule.

"The END rule," Andy says. "Energy never dies."

"You made that shit up," I tell her.

Andy laughs. "Yeah. The principle is true, though. You know what Kreytian said about not interfering? The Universals always valued peace because we couldn't interfere. You do it once, you do it twice, there are no limits. Where do we draw the line?"

I don't have an answer for her.

"I shouldn't have brought her back," Andy mutters. "Her energy was going to dissipate back into the universe. She was going to be something else."

"She would have died, Andy."

"We all have to die eventually. We're all made of stardust." She pauses. "Stardust and dead raccoons."

I put my hand on her shoulder. Andy glances at me, her eyes bright like the stars outside. "You don't mean that."

Andy smiles at me. "No, I don't. I know it's wrong. My ancestors spent their lives not using this power for their own benefit, vowing to not use it for evil, for killing, for destruction."

26

I know she's thinking about what happened. She's thinking about the fact that she wiped out a whole species with her will and how many other planets her people could have saved if only they had chosen to.

Andy returns to the video game, and she plays in silence while I watch her.

"It's not a hoax," Andy finally says. "The distress signal, I mean."

I look at her from the corner of my eye. She keeps playing.

"You don't know that."

"That's not how the ship was designed," Andy says. "It's not going to signal if there's nothing wrong."

I keep quiet. Ahead of us stretches space. If I go outside, that's what I'll see. There's infinite space, infinite possibilities, stars, planets, alien species, ships, and things my mind can't comprehend. There are things more dangerous out there, more ways of dying than a single human mind can understand or even fear.

But those are not the things that scare me.

What scares me is turning back. It's seeing what I left behind.

"We could just..." Andy says guessing where my thoughts are going. "We could just take a look."

I turn to her, my lips pursed. "Violet won't like that."

"That's why I'm not asking her."

Her eyes meet mine. She darts back to *Prince of Persia* as if she doesn't want to say what she's thinking.

I'm the one in control of the ship. I'm the one who gets to make that call. But it would be extremely unfair to the others if I just took us back without asking anybody. I can't really make that call without consulting everyone. Without understanding where we'd go from here.

I turn to the video game, my mind racing with the possibilities.

"What do you think is back there?"

We don't look at each other. We look at the space that is ahead, the planets, the stars, the world full of impossible possibilities.

"I don't know," Andy says. "But I think I want to find out."

CHAPTER 4

The first thing I notice when we arrive in Universali is the asteroid field.

They're all over the place, flying in wild directions, moving so fast that I can barely keep track of them. I activate the shields around the Arc, and when a meteor comes close to us, I see that it's not just rock—it looks like a rock made entirely of glass. One crashes against another, and the glass shatters, bits and pieces of crystal flying everywhere, bright blue against the darkness of deep space.

"Are you sure we're in the right spot?" I ask, turning to Andy.

She doesn't answer. Her skin reflects the asteroid field, dark and looming, and the stars shine on her skin like freckles. She blinks and turns to me.

"Yeah, I'm sure."

Flint lets out a low whistle. "This is Universali?"

"What is left of it."

Andy's expression is unreadable as we survey the asteroid field. There is no sign of any star nearby that the planet would orbit. It's just an empty field of rocks, a lot bigger than my ship. I start flying the Arc carefully. I don't want the asteroids to breach the shields.

We didn't need to discuss Violet's point—Universali was a sliver of hope, and we wanted to reach out for it. The only problem was that it, too, is gone.

"I can't see anything," Violet says.

"Hold on," I say as I search the controls. In a second, the headlights light up. "Told you it could be useful to have headlights."

"Yeah, but only when parking," Brooklyn snorts. "We can't see the light in a vacuum."

Flint turns to her. "You do realize you can see the sun and the stars, and they're in space."

Brooklyn goes quiet for a second. "You know what, that makes *so* much sense."

I shake my head, and the lights sweep the asteroid field as I fly around them. There are no signs of life but a whole lot of debris and destruction. I avoid looking at Andy. I know she came to Earth as a child, but I'm not sure how much she remembers from her home planet.

"Why didn't you tell us?" Avani asks, her voice quiet in the vision of the spaceship.

Andy doesn't stop looking at the asteroids. "I wasn't sure. I think a part of me knew, but…"

Kreytian had called the Hostemn planet wreckers. There is nothing where Universali is supposed to be. Only the floating, glass-like crystals that shine across the darkness.

After a while, Flint points to something. "There. That's not an asteroid. Gotta be a dwarf planet or something."

"Hl'lor," Andy announces, and it almost makes me jump. "One of Universali's moons."

I nod in silence and direct the Arc to land. The moon gets bigger as we approach it, but the gravity pull is under control. When we land, I can only see dunes stretching as far as the eye can see. In the sky, the broken pieces of Universali glitter against the atmosphere.

"What are we looking for?" Brooklyn asks when we land.

Andy shrugs.

"Can you be a little more specific?" Brooklyn insists. "I'm not a huge fan of secrets."

"Yeah, because you can't keep your mouth shut," Flint points.

Brooklyn gives him the middle finger.

"We're just looking around," Andy says noncommittally. "People used to say Universali was one of the great wonders of the universe. You're still on track with your list."

Brooklyn rolls her eyes, but there's a tension there. We didn't expect to find Universali completely shattered. I exchange one look with Violet—there was hope that we'd find a place here, for Andy.

The Hostemn left us nothing.

Rayen is the last one to step out of the spaceship. She holsters three different guns on her belt, ready for a fight. She puts on sunglasses even though there's no need, grinning. "Let's kick some alien ass."

"You don't have to say that every time we exit the ship," Flint points.

"I'm in space," she retorts. "I'll do whatever I want."

I shake my head and move ahead while their bickering stays behind me. Violet and Andy are in front of me. I walk faster so I can reach them, walking side by side with them while we make our way through the dunes of the deserted planet.

"Do we have a plan, or…?"

"Just looking around," Andy says.

"Straightforward," I comment, but no one seems to get the sarcastic tone in my voice.

They don't answer, lost in thought.

"What about after this?" I ask.

"Is this about the signal?" Violet asks. She turns to Andy. "Are you ganging up on me?"

"We can't just ignore it," I say carefully before Violet gets even more irritated. She's on edge lately. "We have to talk about it."

"We left. That's all."

"Yeah, but it was kind of in a rush—"

"There's nothing there," Violet says before I get another word out. "Nothing. And no, I don't want to go back there. We can talk about this later."

Andy looks over her shoulder at me in solidarity but doesn't say anything, not wanting to get into a fight. There are many things that haven't changed with her, and avoiding conflicts is one of them.

We walk in silence till I glimpse something on the horizon.

Columns rise from the sand into metal structures, edges pointed toward the sky. I hurry to the top of the dune until I can see the valley below where the bones of an ancient ruined city lie in decay.

"Are we looking for anything in particular?" Brooklyn asks as we enter the city.

Andy shrugs again. "Anything that looks like Universal technology. Maybe we can salvage something out here."

We split into three separate groups, each taking a different part of the ruins. We spend a couple of hours searching until finally, Avani shouts that she found something.

We all run toward her as she and Brooklyn pick up a single box from the debris, cleaning the surface with their hands. On the top of the box, there are scratch marks that look like runes, old and ancient. When Avani touches them, they glow blue.

"Let me see," Andy says, and we part to let her pass.

She makes her way slowly as if afraid to touch it. Her skin has an undertone of blue, her eyes glowing purple.

There's a symbol etched on the top of the box, a circle with waves, and it lights up with a strange blue glow when Andy wipes it.

Rayen and I exchange a look.

"I have a bad feeling about this," she says quietly.

Something lurches in my stomach, and I don't know if it's the survival instinct or something else. I take the alien gun out of my waistband, holding it at the ready.

Andy puts her other hand on the object, and the box starts emitting another glow of light.

"We should just take it back," Avani says. "We can study it in the ship."

"No, just a second," Andy replies. She steps forward, and the box glows again. I can hear faint, distant singing. A single voice.

The hair on my arms rises.

Andy shifts her position, leaving the box on the ground to take a better look, and it's then that I see something else. Something moving across the sand.

A tentacle erupts from a dune, sand flying everywhere. Avani screams, and Brooklyn moves to protect her as the tentacles rise in the air.

"Grab the box!" Violet orders, and Flint dives for it, cursing. The alien in the ground moves fast and dives straight for Andy.

I don't hesitate, and Rayen moves in with me, both of us pointing guns toward the creature as it wraps one of its tentacles around Andy's throat.

Andy, to her credit, doesn't even yell as the slimy thing wraps around her and hauls her up in the air. She chokes, gasping.

"Looks like we got a problem," Brooklyn points out.

"You don't say."

"You know, sarcasm doesn't help, Flint!"

Another tentacle erupts from the sand, and I take the first shot I see. The tentacle recoils, but the rest of the body emerges a moment later.

It's huge.

A monster with twelve wrapping tentacles, black as night, its body shaped like a spider. In the middle, there are spikes like body armor. One of the tentacles still holds Andy in the air. Another one goes straight for Flint, trying to get to the box.

"Protect it," Andy manages to choke out.

And then the deserted plain becomes a bloodbath.

I strike first, my gun sending a pulse that tears through the alien's tentacle. My instincts are on fire as I dodge when it turns back to me. I duck, and Rayen strikes—this time with one of the swords on her hips. The metal slashes through the alien's skin, cyan blood running down. The alien emits a scream, dropping Andy to the ground.

I don't have time to check on her as I signal the others to move. Brooklyn and Avani each have a knife out, and Flint hauls the box across the desert. The tentacles try to reach for him, but I'm too fast. I pull out one of my knives, striking like Rayen taught me, hitting the alien on the side, stopping it before it reaches Flint.

Brooklyn shouts, and I'm running, but Violet is there first.

"I got it!" She says, "Get the ship ready!"

Without looking back, I run. Flint and Andy are with me,

the sand making us slower than usual. It takes about ten minutes to get inside. Sputnik barks in welcome, but I run to the controls, starting up the ship.

"Hold on, girl," I tell her.

I drown out the noise in my head, concentrating on the task ahead of me: getting this ship to fly. I forget about the aliens. I forget that someone might die, that we're in space and everything is uncertain. I've done this hundreds of times with Abuelo. I can do it again.

At the end of the day, a spaceship is not that different from a regular plane.

I press the panel, and the computer starts saying something that I shut off—I don't have time for its usual sassiness.

The motors roar to life.

Alien ships are supposed to be mysterious, but the Arc and I understand each other. We're one of a kind. We're a team.

I slide into the captain's seat, making sure all the buttons are turned on and ready to go. I lift the Arc into the air, and we're zooming in the direction of the ruins. I smile triumphantly as the spaceship flies across the desert and find the others in seconds.

I open the ramp, extending the shield atmosphere from inside to the back.

Brooklyn and Avani are the first to get inside, Brooklyn half carrying an injured Avani, who looks like she has seen one tentacle too many. I look through the window and see Violet and Rayen are still fighting the alien, now damaged with only seven of its tentacles intact.

I flash the spaceship lights at them.

"We're coming!" I hear Rayen roar, even though I'm pretty sure she wants to lift her middle finger at me. I don't stop the blinking, hoping it'll confuse the creature.

No such luck.

Violet is the first to break away as Rayen slashes with her sword again, aiming for the creature's spiked face. Violet runs across the dunes to get to the ramp. The alien falls back, giving Rayen the opportunity to come after her. Cyan-colored blood drips from her clothes and blade.

Rayen steps onto the ramp, but before I can close it, the alien surges behind her, dragging her back by the neck.

I try to close the ramp, but it's already inside, tentacles struggling against the Arc's door and forcing it to stay open.

Shouting echoes as everyone scrambles for their weapons, the monster closing in, tentacles whipping around the navigation room.

"Someone *do* something!" Avani shouts.

"I'm trying!" Rayen says, slashing her sword back and forth over the alien as if she's trying to make sushi.

The motor is starting to shake under my guidance, and I know I have to get somewhere soon. If we just stand here, it might be days till we can get someone to rescue us. The Arc is not made for short distances. It wants to leap to a new destination.

I have to fix this now.

I start jabbing the controls of the Arc, preparing to enter hyperspace, seeing if I can make a jump before we're stuck. The ramp closes, but the alien is still inside. I activate the zero gravity to jump.

Before I can do anything, one of the tentacles wraps around my neck, pulling me back.

The yank is painful, and my neck stings and my back slides against the floor of the spaceship. But this thing has made me angry now. I take out my gun and—

"No guns!" Andy shouts. "It'll hurt the Arc."

Damn it. I try to find a sharp object that might hack it away as it tries to squeeze the life force out of me. But the alien is out of luck. I'm experienced in the art of almost dying, and I don't plan to go out this way.

And apparently, Sputnik agrees. She jumps, biting with all her might. The tentacles whip at her, but Sputnik, stubborn as she is, doesn't let it go. Bright cyan blood starts dripping on the floor and over her fur. Sputnik snarls, but her bite is enough that the creature loosens its hold on my neck.

I quickly twist my way out of the alien's grasp and try to force myself to get up. Everyone is floating as the ship goes higher and higher into space, and it takes a few seconds before we're all in control of our bodies. We've practiced zero gravity before, and I swim in the air, grabbing one of the handles of the spaceship and making myself jump forward to reach the panels.

They're all flashing red now.

We have to get out of here.

"Kill the damn thing!" I tell them. Out of six people, I'm

sure they can manage to defeat a single alien. Sputnik barks as if to reiterate my order.

I grab the handle on the panel, trying to reach the button that will tell me what's happening to my spaceship. But just then, there is a jolt, and I accidentally press the hyperspace control.

I don't have time to warn anyone.

I don't have time to do anything, as the ship is there for a second, and, in the next, it's not.

The Arc wraps a bubble around itself, as if time is going slower on purpose, and then it shrinks. I feel my own muscles screaming as we bend space and time and other concepts the human mind has yet to comprehend, and we're flying, falling, dying, all at once. In a burst that lasts for a millisecond and all of eternity at the same time, we move.

The spaceship reappears.

Everyone falls on the floor with a bang.

My neck hurts, and I roll around to see if all the others are all right. Rayen and Avani are both bleeding. But they all seem alive, groaning, and probably wanting to kill me for jumping into hyperspace unannounced.

The only one up, of course, is Sputnik. She licks my face, and I groan. This dog can't be real. She's got the toughest genes in the whole galaxy.

When I turn, I see the alien stuck with Rayen's swords through its middle.

Slowly, Violet gets up, cracking her neck, and she rolls the alien over with her foot. It takes more than half the space of our navigation room. There is nothing to indicate it has survived the jump.

"A little warning next time, Clover," Violet finally says.

"Is it dead?" Brooklyn asks.

"Yeah, it's dead," Avani says. She touches its blood. "This is absolutely fascinating. Look at this—"

"Babe, don't play with the dead thing," Brooklyn replies.

"I'm not playing. I'm studying it."

"You science people are weird."

"As much as I like that this thing is dead," Andy says, "we've got bigger problems. Flint, did you get the box?"

Flint nods, points to the floor where the mystery box lies.

"Well, at least that's something." Andy sighs in relief. "But I think—"

And then she stops, her face going pale. Her eyes widen, and I follow her gaze.

She's looking outside.

I get up, dusting the dirt and sand from my body, and I look out the window of the Arc. Outside, there are planets and stars and space and everything else I expect.

But there is another planet nearby. We're orbiting it, seeing it slowly revolve. It's green and blue and everything I never thought I'd see again.

Home.

CHAPTER 5

There's so much silence in the room, I think it might burst.

Violet walks up to me and says three words.

"Turn us back."

I look at the others. No one dares to speak the words we're all thinking, and there's a huge conflict of emotion among all of us as we stare at the little blue planet we had lived on our whole lives.

It keeps turning, oblivious. It has done so for thousands of years, and it will do so for thousands of years to come.

Seven teenage lives don't matter to the universe or to Earth. But Earth matters so much to us.

"Turn. Us. Back," Violet repeats, each word punctuated as a sentence of its own.

I open my mouth, but I don't find the words.

It's Andy who says it first. "No."

Violet looks up, her blue eyes like lightning. She has taken off her oxygen mask. Her hair is a matted mess of blond in a ponytail, but she still manages to look beautiful, like an angel ready to rain down revenge.

"What?"

"I said no," Andy says, more firmly this time. "It brought us here. We should at least go and look."

Violet looks at all of us incredulously.

"You can't," she says. "There's nothing there."

"Violet, you can't just think—"

"I do," Violet says firmly, rage turning her cheeks a burning red. "There is nothing there. You promised me I wouldn't have to go back, Andy. You promised me."

Her words break at the end. The tears welling in her eyes are a mix of fury and fear, a mix I know well. I don't reach out to comfort her.

I don't know how to reach out for anyone as home spins at my back.

I realize that this is what I've been waiting for the whole time we've been out there. We spent almost seven months in space. Seven months exploring, meeting new alien races, seeing new planets and nebulae and dying stars. I've seen more than any human ever dreamed they would.

I've known so much more than they ever will.

It has never stopped me from missing it. From missing the

green of the cornfields, the whiteness of the clouds, the color of the sky in the early morning.

I've been running away for seven long months.

It's time to go back home.

"It's different now," I say, and Violet turns her fury to me. "We heard the distress call."

"The distress call is nothing," Violet spits. "It's something wrong with the ship."

"There's nothing wrong with the ship," Avani says.

Flint, Rayen, Brooklyn, and Avani hold their ground. There's longing in their eyes. There is freedom that stretches beyond us, out to space, but we're all tired of running. We need to face the things we've left behind.

"It's time," Rayen finally says. "We just go in there, and then we—"

"We see it's empty," Violet says firmly. "It's fucking *empty*, Rayen. Everyone is dead. Isn't it enough we've all been through this once?"

Violet can shout at her all she wants, but Rayen is not backing down from it. She's not letting Violet win this time.

Violet turns to each of us as if she's reading our thoughts, fury burning through her eyes.

"We're going back there," she says, "and that's all we're going to find. Everything is gone. There is no home anymore. The Hostemn destroyed everything. Didn't you see what happened to Universali? We were the only ones left. What do you all expect to find?" She jabs a finger at my chest. "Home doesn't exist anymore." She gives a small laugh and shakes her head, swallowing back the tears by looking up and pretending they aren't there. "But what do you all care?" she says finally. "It's not like you're human anyway."

Violet stalks off to the back of the ship, her anger unfurling and taking over. Andy makes a move as if to follow, but I hold her back.

When I look up, Avani has tears in her eyes, too, and Brooklyn has a hand over her shoulder, hugging her tight. Flint is shaken, Rayen silent.

I don't let Violet's words get inside my head.

She didn't mean them. I know she's only angry. I know she didn't mean any of it. So I swallow all the anger, all the bitterness, and I forget the feelings. I've never let myself be taken by them before, so I'm not letting them run free now. It's time to get practical.

"All right," I finally say, clearing my throat. "Violet's vote is a no. I need to know all your thoughts before making a move."

No one speaks up. They're afraid of the wrath of Violet.

To hell with Violet.

I want to get down there. I want to be on Earth again, even if it's just for a second.

"Yes," says Rayen first. "I say we go down and look."

Flint nods. "I agree."

Brooklyn looks between me and Avani. "We can just take a look," she finally says. "Check out the distress call. And then we're out of here."

I don't want to think back on the days that started this. I remember the cold metal of my abuelo's gun against my back when I was on the run, the constant fear looming every day. That fear never went away. I only push it back now, more relaxed, but I know it's never going to leave me.

I don't want to be back where I started. I don't want to wonder anymore if it's worth living or not. I don't want to think that dying is the only solution.

I owe it to myself to get down there. I want to face my fears one last time.

"It doesn't have to take too long," I finally agree. "We check it out. And if there's nothing, we leave."

That's all there is to it.

We go back, and we just check it out.

Those are the words I repeat to myself as I start preparing the spaceship for our descent.

CHAPTER 6

I bring up the coordinates of the distress signal.

I pinpoint its exact location, and I'm just a little surprised when it says it's in Wyoming. Out of all seven continents, we're almost back to square one.

Not only that. I'm closer to home than I've been in the past year. Wyoming, near the border. Only a stretch from Abuelo's farm.

Andy and Rayen hang over my shoulder, looking at the coordinates.

"Wyoming, huh?" Andy says, frowning.

"Rocky Mountains," I agree. "I think I can find a place to hide the spaceship as we go down."

"You think it's necessary?" Rayen asks.

"Can't be too careful," I say, and then I start moving the ship.

We don't go down until we've gotten rid of the alien inside, to Avani's deep protests. The descent is slow going at first till I get the controls back in order. I order everyone to hold on and put on their seat belts. I've gotten used to landings, but I still need to hit the right speed to enter the atmosphere smoothly. And then we break through, going down, fast, the fire starting at the top of the Arc, the sparks flying, and I control it quickly, holding it back, starting the descent more easily.

When I see it, the tears come.

There are mountains again, trees in the forest, a river winding down a path, crystal-blue water. It opens up into the mountains, and there's green and blue like I haven't seen in a long time. I slow down, the spaceship following the river between the mountains, and I can distinguish the old roads and abandoned houses here and there. And when I look up, there's the sky.

My sky.

That stretching blue, no clouds, infinite and forever.

And I know I'm home.

I missed this—I missed this place, I miss my grandparents, and I miss Noah and Adam and everyone else who used to be here.

I'm exactly where I belong.

A hand slips onto my shoulder, and I look up to see Rayen. She also has tears in her eyes. She squeezes my shoulder, and I nod to acknowledge that I know she's feeling it, too.

I look at the panel for a place I can hide the ship. I find a cave, and I direct the ship there.

As I get closer to the ground, I notice something strange between the trees, a crystal flashing between the green and brown of the Earth.

The Arc does its descent perfectly into the mouth of the cave, and slowly, ever so slowly, I stop it.

We're back.

I look at the others, gathered now around the navigation room, and wait until someone says something. I don't open the ramp yet. Violet comes into the room, her face impassive. At least she's not refusing to leave, which is better than nothing.

Finally, Flint nods, and it's all I need.

I press a button, and the ramp descends.

I don't run first.

Brooklyn does.

She goes faster than expected, and before I can follow, she's out of the cave, looking down the mountains. I wait for a reaction, but she's completely silent.

I follow her out. My first step is unsure, and I almost stumble. The gravity is different again, of course. But my body, it feels like it's back to the place where it should be. The next step is surer. When I breathe, I can feel the oxygen filling my lungs so completely that my muscles ache, my blood flows more easily, and I'm stronger already. I walk up to stand beside Brooklyn in the mouth of the cave, looking down at the mountains.

We all stand side by side.

It's too much.

It's not enough.

It's everything all at once as we at last get back to the one place we've lived and hated and loved, the first place we've ever known.

"We're home," Rayen finally says.

And then we all break down crying, the tears happy, half laughing at the ridiculousness of it all, the oxygen filling our lungs as we just breathe. Breathe and laugh and cry, all at once.

After we're done being emotional, we go back for supplies before heading out.

I don't know what I expect to find exactly, but it all looks the same. I take the distress signal panel and download it to my GPS, and we begin our hike down the mountain. Every single thing I see is old and new at once, the bark of the trees, the leaves, the roots, and the ground. Sputnik goes with us, always just ahead with her snout stuck to the ground until I whistle for her return.

Everything is calm and quiet. When I look up, I see the birds chirping in the trees, undisturbed, and the ache in my chest is back.

"How long to go?"

I look at the GPS. "I don't know. It's a pretty wide distress call."

I look around the forest, but I don't see movement. My eyes meet Violet's, and I look away.

We keep hiking, going slowly, taking in the animals and everything else around us. The green is vibrant and clean, unspoiled by humans. Sputnik chases any squirrels she sees, happy that this time, she doesn't have to wear a suit to go outside.

As we hike, we don't find any houses. The signal is distant, wavering in and out, and I can't pinpoint its exact location.

"What do you think it is?" Flint finally asks, taking our mind off things. "What exactly constitutes a distress signal?"

We all look at Andy. Her skin is vibrant this morning in a pale shade of purple, and she looks healthier than ever, her freckles reflecting the constellations, going between dark brown and blue. "I don't know."

"What do you mean, you don't know?" Brooklyn asks. "Is it distress like 'help, our planet is dying,' or distress as in 'shit, did I leave the oven on'?"

Andy doesn't rise to the provocation. "It's meant to warn other Universals that someone is in grave danger."

"So we're running right into it," Brooklyn says, her voice happy. "It's not like we just got out of trouble anyway."

The distress signal chimes once again, and when I look at the screen, it stops.

"What is it?" Violet asks.

"It's gone," I say, handing her the GPS. "It's just disappeared."

"Maybe we lost the signal of the spaceship," Avani suggests.

"No way." I shake my head. "The Arc picks up signals from all the way across the universe. It picked up Earth's signal."

Andy snatches the GPS from Violet's hand, starting to mess

with it. Then she does what everyone on Earth is used to doing with things that aren't picking up signals. She puts her hands up and waves it in the air.

"Sure, that's going to work," Rayen grumbles.

"We are in the right place," I say. "We know it's around here."

"How precise is this thing?" Avani asks. "We could be trekking here for days."

"Don't exaggerate," Rayen replies. "We've only been out a few hours. We can go back to the Arc before it's dark."

I wonder what the best decision is.

"We can follow the mountain range," I say finally. I look at the position of the sun in the sky and estimate we still have three or four hours of light. "Go by the river. We can make it back to the ship before it's dark."

Nods of agreement follow. No one can offer a better option, so I stick with the GPS and keep walking. I get distracted easily by the trees, the sound of water, and everything that looks brand-new but that I've seen before.

It's the afternoon when we finally come to a small town.

It's silent and inviting.

As always, I don't have to take the first step. Brooklyn is first, followed by Flint. I mark it on the map and walk just behind them, taking in the houses.

My muscles tense up, remembering the day with Noah. It's been more than a year since that happened. More than a year since he and my grandparents have been gone.

The flashbacks start, and my body is frozen with fear.

I can't move and can't breathe. It looks exactly like last time.

I try to slow my breathing, but it keeps coming in short gasps, as if my lungs have forgotten how to function. I feel dizzy, my vision blackening.

Someone puts a hand on my shoulder, and I look up to see Flint.

"You okay?" he asks. "Put your head between your knees."

I do what he says, and the others walk ahead. Flint stays back with me.

"Concentrate on the small things," he says. "The sound of my voice or the sound of the river."

I open my eyes, focusing on the gurgling water, the curls in Flint's hair that are moved by the wind, and his hand that holds mine. Slowly, I start breathing again. I get up, my knees still trembling.

"Thanks." I clear my throat, not sure how to deal with the sudden panic attack that reminds me so much of what I went through. "It's been a while."

"No problem," Flint answers. He smiles. "It's fine."

"I know."

It's no use thinking about what happened the day of the attack. I shake the thoughts out of my head and keep going.

There are no people here, the houses empty, vines covering most of the walls and the gardens overgrown over the asphalt. Small towns weren't destroyed. It was the way the Hostemn worked—if they sent down a single unit of two, they could have easily wiped out a small town with no setbacks. The bombs and destruction were reserved for the big cities, and those had been wiped off the map, left with nothing but rubble.

Here, the trees and vines creep up the walls, flowing over the houses' rooftops, painting green what had been pure cement. It's a pretty sight—bushes and flowers and vines and seeds over what was only construction, nature reclaiming what humans once took. We walk silently through the town.

And when we leave, we haven't seen a single soul.

It's what I expected, I tell myself.

We pause by the edge of a river to fill up our water bottles again, the fish dancing in the cold, clear water. Sputnik goes in splashing, scaring away the fish. Brooklyn chases her, stumbling into the river and falling on her butt, completely soaked.

Avani pauses next to me as we both watch them play.

"Do you think everywhere will be like this?" Avani whispers next to me.

"I don't know," I answer truthfully. "It's better this way."

"At least the dust has dissipated."

I agree in silence. There are no bodies to see. It's better to see just the trees. It makes me feel less guilty that I survived.

The town turns into mountains once more, and before we know it, we're climbing again. The trees are not silent—there are rustling leaves, the occasional bird and squirrel or rabbit. But there is no sound except that.

It's deafening.

It's suffocating.

"We should head back," Brooklyn calls out. "There's nothing here."

I agree silently, but I don't want to give up at the same time. There is a small part of me that still believes there's got to be something here, that we can't just be back to see it empty.

"Just a little farther," says Andy. "Ten minutes, maybe? Just to make sure we covered everything."

"There is nothing to cover," Brooklyn says. "The whole idea is stupid anyway. Let's go back to the ship. We shouldn't have come here."

Andy ignores Brooklyn's tantrum and keeps walking.

But a few paces in, she slams into something and is sent stumbling back. She falls against a tree and then to the ground.

"What happened?" Flint asks first, looking between Andy and what she just hit.

Which, apparently, is nothing.

"I don't know," Andy complains, getting up. She offers a hand to Violet, and both of them dust off twigs. "I just hit something."

Frowning, I look back at the place Andy pointed to. Slowly, I go toward it and reach my hand out in front of me.

I step forward, but there's nothing there. Until my hand feels it. I push against the air, but it holds me back. I move my hand down, at the exact place Andy hit, and there's nothing. When I force it, my hand is forced back. I stumble, and I can't get through.

We've just hit an invisible barrier.

CHAPTER 7

The barrier goes on for almost a mile.

We walk with our hands stretched toward it as it keeps going, seemingly infinite, stopping us from getting through. I can almost feel it pulsing. The other side is visible and normal, but every time we try to push hard to get through, it sends us back.

We wait to see if anything comes through, and our wait is rewarded. A squirrel crosses the barrier, and more quickly than I can follow, Rayen snatches it. It struggles against her grip, but she's adamant—she pushes the squirrel back toward the barrier, and it tries to run back where it came from.

It hits the barrier again.

Things can come through, but once inside, there's no getting out.

After we walk a whole mile to the north and then one mile back to the south, we know it's not going anywhere.

"We should go back," Rayen is the first to say. "Back to see if it goes all the way around."

"It's weird," Avani replies. "We got in fine. Why should a barrier stop us from going the other way?"

I exchange one look with Violet, who's been quiet the whole time. She now munches a sandwich almost aggressively, her blue eyes sparkling.

"I don't know," I finally say, not wanting to alarm anyone. "The Arc will have answers."

There are nods all around, and we start heading back south, our hands occasionally going to the barrier to see if it's still there. The invisible wall is impenetrable, and although it doesn't sting when I touch it, there is a low hum of energy that buzzes through my fingertips when I try to push through it.

Night falls almost lazily, the sky slowly being painted a darker blue, the stars blinking into view, and the familiar sight pains my chest. Out there, the stars were never the same, and there was never any familiarity in looking up. Here, I can see Orion's belt again, the Ursas, and it feels like greeting an old friend.

When we're almost to the ship, I spot a light in the middle of the woods.

"What's that?" I point.

Heads turn to see the source of light. It looks like the same thing I saw from the ship above, shining in strange colors in a place where there ought to be no light. Carefully, I make my way through the dark.

A crystal formation rises in the middle of a clearing.

Its hue is blue and green, brilliant like I've never seen before. It looks like a precious stone, its edges sharp and cutting, a big rock wedged into the Earth. The crystals rise just above my height, too big to be normal, and emit a strange, radiation-like glow that sets it apart from the rest of the woods.

"What *is* that?" Avani asks, frowning up at the crystal.

Flint is the first to approach it. "Looks like a quartz cluster." Then he frowns. "But they never grow that big. Or in the middle of nowhere."

"I've never seen anything like it," Brooklyn says, crossing her arms over her chest. "So is this, like, normal Earth now? Weird-ass barriers and, you know, penis crystals?"

We all sigh collectively.

"That's not—" Violet starts, then shakes her head. "Never mind, Brooklyn. How can you ruin literally everything?"

"I was just pointing out what it looks like! God!"

I look up at it again. The glow of the crystal feels unnatural. When I look down at the ground, I see Flint examining something.

Thin blue crystal veins spread from the crystal to the ground, stretching their way toward the trees. They are like roots, reaching out for others in the darkness, and the crystal is wedged right in the middle of this strange formation.

I crouch down next to Flint.

"What exactly is this?" I ask him.

He touches the ground, and it comes crumbling off his fingers, as if it's been sucked dry. Sputnik sits next to him, sniffing and then quickly turning away, displeased.

"I don't know," Flint says, shaking his head. "This is definitely not normal. See these veins? They stretch toward the trees. Now look at them."

He points towards one specifically, and in the dark, I force my eyes to see. The trees near the crystal have dull, cracking barks, their leaves faded and twisted, cracked branches.

"So rocks aren't really supposed to do that," I say.

"They're rocks. They're not supposed to do anything at all."

He shakes his head again, biting his lower lip.

"We can get a sample," I suggest. "Analyze it back on the ship."

"It could be dangerous to touch it."

"It's a rock, Flint. It can't be that dangerous."

"I've just…" He shakes his head again but doesn't finish his sentence. "We should be careful with it."

We turn back to the rest of the group, waiting for their reaction. But they're just looking at the pretty crystal as if there's nothing wrong with it.

"So two weird things in a single day," Rayen says. "That's a sign, right? Could it be the distress call?"

"The distress call wouldn't activate with this," Andy responds. "But it's not normal." She frowns up at the crystal, her eyes far away for a second as if she's trying to recall something she has long forgotten. "There is—"

Andy reaches out for the crystal, and before Flint and I can stop her, she touches it, her eyes reflecting the glow, mesmerized.

For a second, nothing happens.

Then Andy stumbles back, falling to the ground. It seems she's all right until she looks up. In her eyes, there are black holes and galaxies, moving too fast and swirling around in her skin and hair.

"Andy?" I ask, hesitant.

She bursts into light.

CHAPTER 8

"Shit!"

I move out of the way quickly, stumbling back as Andy keeps bursting in golden and silver light, her eyes distant and lost. She moves her hand in the direction of the trees, and another burst of light goes through them, and then her body is glowing, growing slowly, the entire universe seeping through the pores of her skin.

She rises in midair, her feet floating, her eyes open but unresponsive. She raises her hand, and Avani screams as another surge of light hits a tree and sets it on fire.

"Andy!" Violet calls out, approaching her. "Andy, listen to me!"

She doesn't even recognize us as we shout her name. She's in an entirely different universe, lost to the incomprehensible.

Violet pulls one of her feet back to the ground, but she's thrown back, an invisible force hitting her. Andy starts targeting the trees again.

She'll set this whole forest on fire if we don't stop it.

Rayen seems to have the same thought as she jogs over, a rifle in her hand. Avani kneels down next to a knocked-out Violet, and Rayen turns to Flint and Brooklyn. Even Sputnik gets in on the plan, barking incessantly. "Distract her."

They both nod, and then they start running, waving their arms to call Andy's attention. She doesn't seem to care much, but Rayen and I sneak behind her.

"What are we going to do?" I ask.

"Knock her out," she tells me. "Can you lift me up onto your shoulders?"

I nod, crouching.

Rayen doesn't wait another second as she climbs. We're already behind Andy's back. She's still glowing, suspended in the air like some kind of wood sprite except with the power to destroy us all if she wanted to. I move, not as fast as I would like, Rayen's weight bringing me down, her legs heavy on my shoulders.

I move faster, Rayen steady, and in one single move, she bangs her rifle against Andy's head.

Andy drops immediately, her glow gone, and I drop beneath Rayen, both of us falling to the ground. Sputnik yelps, touching Andy with her paw. Flint and Brooklyn stand over her.

"Is she dead?"

"Of course she isn't dead," Rayen snaps. "She's an immortal being as old as the universe. I don't even know how to kill one of these things."

I move Andy's head just slightly. Her eyelids flutter but her skin doesn't stop swirling, like a psychedelic hallucination that keeps moving.

"Let's go back to the ship until we figure this out," I say, and they all agree.

It's hours later when Andy comes back to herself.

We are all standing guard outside the cell we put her in, the glass the only barrier between us. I don't know how the Universals predicted they might need a holding cell in their Arc, but I'm glad it's here now.

Her eyelids flutter open, but she doesn't seem altogether there.

"Let me out," she says with a snarl. "You can't keep me in here."

"This cell is going to hold you until we figure out what's happening," I say as calmly as I can.

Andy turns her eyes to me. I see a predator in them, ready to strike. Ready to burst out of what's holding her back.

"You're going to regret this," she says. "You can't escape the power of the universe."

Something glows in her hand, and she hurls it in our direction. The burst of light hits the glass and bounces back toward her. She looks at us, anger and hurt in her eyes, and changes in an instant.

"Let me out," she cries. "I can't be here. Please."

"What's going on with her?" Flint asks.

Andy moves between begging and snarling, her powers uncontrolled as she pushes against the glass, trying to break out. Every time she hits it, her skin changes to a different color, stars exploding into supernovas and then black holes and then beginning everything again in a cycle.

"It's something to do with that crystal," Violet replies, holding a bag of ice over her head where Andy hit her. "We gotta find out what that is."

We all turn to look at Andy, who's now laughing hysterically.

"Is she—" I start.

"Mad?" Brooklyn suggests.

"We can't diagnose it correctly, and that word is complicated," Avani says. "But yeah. She's not behaving like usual."

"Let! Me! Out!"

Slowly, she backs toward the wall, now shivering as if it's cold. She darts her eyes between us, wide and scared.

"Guys? What's going on?"

For a second, she turns back into the normal Andy. Violet jolts, but I hold her in place—it could be a trick.

Andy starts crying and sobbing. "What's going on? Why have you locked me up?"

Avani is the first to approach the glass, standing so near to it that if it breaks, she will be hurt.

"It's okay, Andy," she says in a soothing tone. "We just need to look at some things. Make sure it's safe to come out again."

"I don't want to be here," Andy whimpers. "It's small. And cold. I want to go home."

I exchange a look with Rayen. We're all home, and look where that has gotten us.

Avani leans against the glass. "It's going to be okay."

Andy slams against the glass, rage and fury once more. "It's not going to be okay! *LET ME OUT!*"

She slams against the glass, and Avani stumbles back, surprised. Andy keeps hitting the glass, again and again, but thankfully, it holds. Finally, when she's run out of energy completely, she slumps against the floor, her eyes distant and vacant.

"Stupid humans," she says. "You're going to get what's coming to you."

I look at Violet, but for the first time since we've arrived, she's comfortable.

I realize it's because we're in danger. Violet responds well to danger. She pushes back all her feelings into a deep, dark corner, and then she rages until she's finished.

Her best friend is locked in a cage, and she's not going to stop until we know how to get her out of there safely. Andy mutters something under her breath.

"What's that, Andromeda?" Violet says quietly.

Andy looks Violet dead in the eye and smiles the most terrifying smile I've ever seen.

"You're all going to die."

And then she turns her back to us, and I know she's just waiting for an opportunity to break out of there.

CHAPTER 9

In the morning, Andy's situation hasn't changed.

"Okay, so," Brooklyn starts as soon as we're back in the navigation room and Andy is out of earshot. She yawns, stretching. "We got an invisible barrier, we've got a weird crystal that instantly turns you, well, you know, and now Andy is a full-on megalomaniac alien trying to kill us. Did I get everything?"

"She's not trying to kill us," Violet says.

"She said 'you're all going to die' very distinctly. I don't know about you, but I've got at least forty years left."

I sigh. "Staying here may not get us anywhere," I admit reluctantly. At least Violet doesn't give me a nasty look this time. "We can try and find a cure elsewhere. Maybe the effects will just wear off."

Avani gives me a look like she knows I'm bullshitting them. I am.

"We need a crystal sample," Flint says.

"I ain't touching that thing," Brooklyn says.

"We've got suits and everything else in the back," Flint replies, ignoring Brook. "We can go out there, get a sample, and then have the computer analyze it. That way, we can find something to cure Andy faster."

"We should leave," Violet says. "Get somewhere else far away so we can find a cure for Andy."

"Oh yeah," Rayen says sarcastically. "That's what we need to do, run away."

Violet glares at Rayen.

"We need a sample," Flint insists.

"I don't like that option," Violet says.

"It's the only one we have right now," Flint replies, a little irritated. "I don't like it, either. But we have to do something about it."

I don't tell them what I'm thinking. Turning on the ship's computer, I start pressing buttons.

"Computer," I say, "send drones to map out the barrier."

"What are you doing?" Brooklyn asks.

"I just want to check how far the barrier goes," I tell her.

All is quiet inside the ship as we wait for the answers, and I expand the Earth map I have on the ground. The barrier stretches up to Montana, and then it stops.

The barrier incorporates almost the entire state of Wyoming, and we're stuck here.

"Drones returning," the computer says.

"Send them up to the atmosphere," I tell it.

I wait a few beats, but nothing happens. The computer says nothing.

"Did they get through?" I finally dare to ask.

"Drones returning," the computer says. "Breach to the atmosphere unsuccessful."

I turn to the others, biting my lip.

"So what does that mean?" Avani asks. "That we can't—"

"We can't leave," Flint finishes. "Not until we find out how to take this barrier down."

Violet's face reddens with anger. "I told you all this was a bad idea."

"Yeah, but there is something wrong with Earth," Rayen replies. "This proves the point of the distress call."

"Great," Violet mutters. "I know you love being right."

Rayen puts her hands on her waist. "Don't pull that one on me. All of us like to be right. This is just—"

"Everyone, shut up," I snap. "We have a lot of problems, and we need to figure out how to deal with them one by one. Fighting is not what we need right now. We need to follow Flint's plan and collect a sample from the crystal. Start there."

There's a pause, but finally, Violet stands down and nods.

"All right," she says, "Avani and Brooklyn stay here to guard the ship. Clover, Rayen, Flint, and I go back to get some of the crystal."

We start the preparations.

The great thing about the Arc is that it comes equipped with everything, and when I say everything, I do mean everything. We've got kitchen equipment, food to last for ages, labs, bunk beds for thirty people, shower rooms, and everything else we've adapted to our needs as we see fit. It also has a getaway ship.

The smaller ship is much like an airplane and fits about four people. It's sleek and silver, like the Arc, its wings slightly curved. We don't have a nickname for it yet, and I've only used it once, but I greet it like an old friend. I love driving the Arc. But it's like driving a U-Haul when you're used to a convertible.

Bad analogy, since I can't drive either.

Flint arrives back with a container and antiradiation uniforms that we've swiped from Area 51, dumping them in the back with the other things. It's easier to use the ship even if the crystal is close so we don't have to carry the heavy equipment ourselves. Violet and Rayen arrive together, Rayen carrying a gun. They all sit down, and I'm ready to go, activating the controls, taking my hands to the panel, and then we're out of the cave faster than I can think.

The ship cuts silver through the atmosphere, zooming past the cave, the river, and the mountains. When I approach the barrier to our left, I go slower, trying to decelerate to make sure we don't get hurled back across the sky.

When we exit the ship, we put on the suits before heading to the crystals.

The strange thing about the barrier is that we were able to

come inside. A barrier usually works both ways—to keep people out and to keep people in. This one has purposely led us here.

We climb up the mountain in silence as we head for the crystal formation, the ship hidden within the forest. The suits slow us down, and when I get to the crystal, sweat is clinging to my back.

Flint is the first one to step forward, grabbing one of his instruments to get to the crystal. He makes a precise cut, not touching it, and with the yellow gloves, he puts the sample into the box. We wait to see if there are any other effects, but everything seems fine. Flint doesn't start reacting, so we shove the box closed.

It's simple. Almost too simple, and something sets off my nerves as we make our way back to the ship, sharing the weight of the crystal between us.

When I get to the ship, I have one second to admire the view. From this side of the mountain, a plain stretches, mixed with green and brown as it opens up to the river, stretching beyond till we can see the mountains again in the horizon.

Something is moving. Animals, most likely, but they are going too fast to be grazing and too slow if they are running. I narrow my eyes toward the shapes, and then I finally see it.

It's not animals.

It's humans.

We are not alone.

PART II

WELCOME TO THE HUMAN RACE

CHAPTER 10

My heart seizes, and I can't believe what I'm seeing.

It's humans.

It can't be.

"Is this…real?" I ask, because I want to make sure my eyes aren't playing tricks on me.

The field stretches far, the view between the trees faded. I'm probably imagining things.

The shapes move again, and now I'm certain that what I see are other people.

"It's…" Flint says, his mouth open in awe. "It's other humans."

No one moves.

Then we scramble to the ship as fast as we can, buckling

in and taking off. I keep the ship low, between the trees, not daring to rise higher, afraid we'll be spotted. When we get to the Arc, we're all running, and before Avani and Brooklyn can ask, Flint pants.

"Humans. We just saw other humans."

It's strange how he uses the word *humans* instead of *people*. On any other day, it would make me laugh, but this time, it makes my nerves tense.

Humans mean one thing. They mean danger. Danger for us. We have an alien aboard our spaceship, and the last time we met with aliens, things didn't go so well, and the whole planet ended up dying.

Or so we thought.

If there are people and they find out we have a spaceship, they won't exactly be throwing welcome parties.

Everyone starts talking at once.

"We can just go over there—"

"We have to hide the whole—"

"Andy can't show up there, or else—"

"Everyone, shut up!"

Violet's yell calms everyone down, and we turn to her. She puts her hands on her hips. "We need a plan," she says calmly, "and yes, we'll go to investigate."

"But what about Andy?" Brooklyn asks.

"She stays here, locked up," Violet says. "Flint and Brooklyn stay."

"What?" Brooklyn asks. "Why?"

"Because you talk too much," Violet says. "If we have to talk to people, we don't want someone who'll overshare almost immediately."

"I never overshare," Brooklyn says indignantly.

"Your daily gastritis update," I offer.

"Diarrhea when you went to Thailand," Rayen supplies.

"Zero-gravity lesbian sex," Flint adds.

Brooklyn looks pointedly at us. "That one should just be plain common knowledge. I was doing you all a favor. Come on, Violet, I promise I'll behave."

Violet waits a second before answering. "Fine. But you need to take off that eyeliner. No personal effects that make us stand out."

"This cost me a fortune in space Sephora," Brooklyn mutters. "I can't believe we're coming back to Earth like barbarians."

"Flint and Avani stay back to guard the ship and Andy," Violet orders. "We'll investigate but try not to get too close. We should be back with news in no less than twenty-four hours. Understood?"

That sounds like a plan, or at least the best plan we can come up with under these conditions. But there's a sense of danger that tenses my muscles and that I can't push away. We shouldn't be going there.

But with the barrier, we can't go anywhere else.

"Gather what you need," Violet says. "And stay alert."

We all nod, and I go back to my room. Avani and Brooklyn bunk together, and Andy used to be with Violet, but we each picked whichever rooms we liked. Sputnik follows on my heels as if sensing something in the atmosphere.

I pick up a bag and set it on the bed. It's better if it looks like we've been hiking—and not just arriving from a spaceship. We need to look worn down and like we belong.

The only problem is that I don't know if I've belonged here for a long, long time.

I pick up clothes and supplies randomly from the closet, not stopping to think too much. Sputnik catches what I throw at her and shoves them untidily into the bag. I grab one of the knives and slide it into my boot, but all the other weaponry will stay behind. Nothing alien should cross the cave and go out of the spaceship.

We can't risk anything.

When I'm almost done, I come across Abuelo's gun at the bottom of a pile of clothes.

I stare at it for a long time before picking it up.

It's heavier than I remember. I haven't touched it since Violet shot herself. Sometimes, I still wake up screaming in the night, the nightmares following me.

Sometimes, I shake and cry, and some days, I can't get up, replaying everyone's deaths inside my head over and over again. At least I stopped wanting to hurt myself. Some days are better. Others, not so much.

I'm making it through.

Sputnik barks as if she, too, remembers what it was like before.

"It's okay," I tell her. "Good girl."

She licks my fingers, and I bury my hand behind her ear, scratching it slightly.

I turn around and spot Violet at the door. She's got her hair in a ponytail, her thick blond eyebrows frowning just slightly as her eyes land on the gun.

We have never really talked about her sacrifice.

No, not just sacrifice. Her death. Her suicide.

I bite the inside of my cheek. "Do you ever think there might have been another way?"

Violet's gaze is indecipherable. "Another way to what?"

"To get Andy to use her power. To end them all. I don't know."

"We would have all died anyway," Violet says flatly. "I just did what had to be done."

She doesn't say it as a hero. Violet saved us all. She died not because there was no way out for her but because she saw a way out for the rest of us.

Knowing this doesn't make it less terrible.

I know what it feels like to have that gun pointed to my head. And even if Violet believes in the sacrifice, I know there's a part of her that is like me—just glad it had come to an end.

"Come on," she says. "The others are waiting."

I nod. Violet got a second chance. I'm glad for it. Maybe it was a sacrifice, but there's always something deeper than that.

I leave the gun behind and follow Violet out.

The four of us make the trek down the mountain in silence.

We follow the path, sometimes stumbling in the dirt, stepping over twigs and leaves, seeing the occasional squirrel. We are all tense and not willing to let that tension dissipate. I can't imagine what it's going to be like.

People.

I'm meeting real people, other real people, for the first time in seven months. It has been a lifetime. How did they survive? How did they make it out so the aliens wouldn't get them? How did I never meet any other survivors in my travels before I got to Area 51? I have so many questions that had no answers, and I don't know if I'll be able to ask them.

"How many people were there?" Brooklyn finally asks.

"Three," I reply. "That's what I saw anyway."

"Do you think they'll welcome us?"

I don't know the answer to the question. I don't know what will happen next or if we will even be able to find them again, though I doubt it would be hard.

Finally, we arrive in the open field we saw before. This was a deliberate planting, the rows of corn in their rightful places. They sway in the wind, and when the smell hits me, I almost choke. It smells exactly like home.

I swallow back any tears, and we keep walking. The corn gives way to lettuce and then to wheat, bright and growing. I hear a rustling in the wheat.

I turn around, listening for the sound that I know is there.

I spot the moving leaves, and in an instant, four people have us surrounded.

"Hands in the air!" one of the men says. He's older than us. "Nobody move!"

God, he's a lot older. Almost fifty, his head shaved, his hands and face burned red from staying too long in the sun. The others with him are in their forties and fifties, all with wrinkles already, most with their hands calloused and skin burned.

I can't move, just taking them all in. Two men and two women, eyeing us with suspicion and disbelief.

I put my hands in the air, and so do the others. Rayen throws her rifle to the ground. Sputnik doesn't move, either, staying close by my side.

Relief floods me, and there they are: other humans.

Other people.

They are real. I wasn't dreaming.

And then instead of hugs or questions or anything else, the older man takes out ropes, and one by one, they tie us all up.

CHAPTER 11

They take us directly into what looks like a jail. It's a cabin in a sea of them set up like a village. All the buildings are made of sturdy wood, and when we walk inside, there's an office chair and one open space behind bars. They lock us up behind the metal. They don't separate Sputnik from us, especially when one of them tries to grab her by the collar and she runs, keeping her distance.

On the walk to the building, I spot other cabins with curious children popping their heads out to take a look. Women and men too. There were so many faces.

I can't seem to forget them as we're locked up inside. Sputnik comes in with us, sitting in the corner. No one bothers explaining anything or even saying a word before the door is shut, leaving us alone. There's only one window in our cell.

"Great." Brooklyn finally breaks the silence. "We arrive, and we get put into jail. Awesome."

"Brooklyn, shut up," Violet says. "We show up out of nowhere. They have the right to treat us as dangerous."

Brooklyn gives her a pointed look. "We're teenagers. The least dangerous things in the world."

I can't see anything, and I lean against the wooden wall, waiting.

"They'll come back," Violet says. "None of you tell them anything, understand? Remember our story: we came in from the west, and that's it. Other people are waiting at our camp. Say nothing else."

A man and a woman show up in the doorway. They wear simple cotton clothes, white and gray. The man looks like he's in his late forties, with pale white skin. The woman's a bit older, with dark-brown skin and curly hair. They both eye us.

The man is the first to speak.

"I'm so sorry we must treat you this way, but it's standard procedure," he says, opening with a smile. "We never know who's going to be a danger to our colony."

Violet gives him a tight-lipped nod.

"That's awesome," Brooklyn says. "Can you let us go now? It's stuffy in here."

We glare at Brooklyn, all three pairs of eyes telling her to shut the fuck up before she ruins everything, which, considering all our previous adventures, happens eight out of ten times.

"We're just passing through," Violet says. "We want to go on our way."

"Where are you headed?"

"Washington, DC," Violet lies smoothly. "I understand you're concerned. We just want to head back."

The man meets Violet's eyes for a second, but he doesn't acknowledge what she just said.

"I'm Castor," he says, "One of the leaders of this colony. This is Heidi."

Heidi gives us a nod of acknowledgment.

"What are you going to do in DC?" Castor asks.

"I'm sorry," Violet says. "We're surprised. We didn't know we were trespassing on anyone's territory."

At that, Castor gives a hearty laugh. "Territory? Is that what some other folks are calling it now? Dear lord. No wonder you all look like half savages."

Rayen flinches, and I slide my hand to hers, giving it a little squeeze to tell her it's all right. It is not all right, but I offer her my hand all the same.

"Well, we want to welcome you all, but there's just the slight problem that we don't know where you're from or why you're here. We're just going to ask a few questions."

He says it in the nicest, most harmless way possible. But I know what this means. He's interrogating us, one by one, making sure all our stories match.

Heidi surveys us, and then she points to me.

"You can go first," she says and unlocks the jail.

Sputnik whimpers, but Rayen holds her back as I give her a small wave. Castor picks Violet, and they head out in the opposite direction.

I follow Heidi and her sure footsteps inside the cabin to one of the back rooms. I think for a second that this is going to end in a weird interrogation room with mirrors, tied to a chair, but I realize quickly it isn't that kind of questioning as she opens a door to a cozy room with a chair and a sofa, complete with a carpet and cushions.

I must be eyeing it suspiciously, because Heidi says, "We took it from other houses in the vicinity. Now that no one is using it." She indicates the couch for me. "Sit down, please."

I do, on the edge, refusing to sink back. I look at the door, my muscles tense, and then I look back at Heidi. She's analyzing me.

"You don't need to look so suspicious," she says to break the silence. "They're just simple questions. You answer them if you can."

"I thought the point was to get what you can out of us."

Heidi laughs. Wrinkles form around her eyes when she does. Grudgingly, I admit she sounds nice. Nice doesn't change things.

I want to know what these people are doing here. I want to know how they survived. I want to know every single possible thing about them.

"You're a tough one, I can see that," she says with ease. "What's your name?"

"Clover. Clover Martinez."

"That's an interesting name, Clover."

"Why?" I snap. "Because I don't look like a Clover?"

She shakes her head slightly. "There aren't many girls named after good-luck charms these days."

I don't answer her. I look around the room, searching for something else to concentrate on. I used to be good at staying still, at ignoring people and just being calm. This situation makes me feel jittery, and everything about this makes my muscles tense.

As if she's reading my mind, she says, "You're safe here."

"How is that?"

"We have everything we need," Heidi affirms. "After the aliens left, we lived a life of peace. Trying to connect back to the nature we once abandoned. It does help that it's very hard to start generating electricity again."

I bark out a laugh. "Miss the hot showers?"

"Yes," she agrees. "We have solar panels, but we leave them for emergencies only. Unity is a good place to find yourself in if you're lost."

She doesn't give an indication that that's what she thinks we are—lost. A bunch of teenagers walking aimlessly around, waiting for something to reach out to them.

It's sad that this seems so fitting and not so far from our reality.

"We're not lost," I guarantee her. "Just passing through. We left some of the team back at camp, and they're waiting for us to return."

"Oh, so you knew there were people here."

I don't answer her.

"It's all right. You don't have to answer everything right away. What you say here is private and confidential."

"Are you a therapist?"

She smiles and nods. "It's that obvious, huh?"

I can't help but smile back at her. It's like her kindness is seeping through me and trying to get through my cracks.

I'm not cracking.

"Lots of people needed someone to talk to after what happened," Heidi says. "It's hard to process it all."

"Tell me about it."

She looks again at me, trying to understand. She can't, because I'm too different. I have gone to the edge of the universe and back.

They didn't save this planet.

I did. We did.

"How did you guys survive?"

There's a slight crease in her eyebrow as I ask the question. If she finds the question strange, she doesn't say it out loud.

"Different ways," she answers. "Most of us stayed inside the mountain range, going underground. It was easier. We were too many for them to wipe out after all."

I give her the smallest hint of a smile.

The Hostemn wouldn't have stopped if we hadn't stopped them first. They would have hunted all of us down, one by one, until they found their precious missing needle. Until they burned the whole haystack to the ground.

"Were there many people where you came from?"

I shake my head just slightly. "No."

"Is that why you decided to make your way to Washington?"

I don't answer.

"What do you think you'll find there?"

"I don't know," I answer her honestly. "We were hoping to find something. Anything."

I leave it at that. Meeting other survivors is enough. Just knowing they are here is good.

Deep down, there are other things that bother me. They are not just about knowing how they survived and how they are living out here. It's about asking them more questions than I can get answers for—if they've seen the barrier, if they know about the crystals, and if they know what happened to the rest of the population. If they have any more information.

"I see," she says, nodding slowly. "Neither Castor or I will stop you from leaving. Staying is always an option though. We work for our food, and we have school for the young ones. You haven't been to school in a long time, correct?"

I frown at the question.

There's something strange in it.

Of course it's been long—it's been a year and a couple of months, since the day of the invasion. Six months of roaming on my own. One month in Area 51. Seven months since I said goodbye to this planet.

But the way she asks the question is wrong. She asks it

carefully, as if it's a dangerous subject to bring up, and I know something is amiss.

"You don't have to talk about it," Heidi says, sensing the sudden panic in my eyes.

It's not panic. I'm not panicking.

I just know there's something wrong.

"Unity is a good place. You can be safe here," Heidi repeats. "We just want to know who you are before you are truly welcomed. We don't sense danger from your group."

I look at her, my brown eyes meeting her black ones. She nods her head in encouragement, willing me into saying something she wants to hear.

I look around the room, trying to gather clues, anything that gives me a hint of the overcoming dread I feel in the air—but there's nothing. The cushions and the couch are in good condition, the desk is neat with no papers on it, and even the pictures hung up on the wooden walls don't have enough personality to set them apart.

"When you ask how long," I say, so careful I feel like I'm slipping on ice, "how long do you mean?"

"Since the invasion," she says. "Ten years ago."

CHAPTER 12

Ten years.

I open my mouth to respond, but I can't think of anything to say. It makes sense—we were traveling at light speed, tearing holes inside the universe to get from one side to another. All time is relative. We spent seven months traveling in space, going to new planets and stars.

And ten whole years have gone by.

Which means she probably thinks I was eight at the time of the invasion instead of just shy of seventeen.

"We don't see many people your age. That's why I'm asking," Heidi says with a kind smile. "Our children are mostly under ten, born after the invasion. There are only two other teens in our camp."

With the implication that most small children died in the invasion. Enough that four teenagers showing up out of nowhere makes a screaming difference. Four survivors, either way. A group that's bound to draw attention.

"I don't remember much," I say after a while.

She nods. "Experiences like that can be traumatizing, especially for a young child. I'm glad you're all still here."

Heidi offers me another smile and dismisses me. She guides me back to the jail, where I murmur under my breath, "Don't say anything. Don't mention dates. Don't mention anything at all."

My tone scares all of them off as they look at me wide-eyed. Heidi points to Rayen, and she goes with a lingering look in my direction. I know I've made an impression and that they won't let anything slip. Violet comes back, and Castor takes Brooklyn next. Time seems to trickle down slowly as I wait, sitting down next to Sputnik with her head on my lap. When all of them are back, I watch as Heidi exits the back room, craning my neck to see if Castor leaves as well.

He does, and when the door shuts, I can finally breathe in relief.

Three pairs of eyes stare back at me. "What the hell happened in there?"

I shake my head. "What did you guys say?"

"Nothing," Rayen replies. "You told us to say nothing, so we said nothing."

I nod, relief flooding my veins. "It's been ten years."

Brooklyn frowns.

"What?" Rayen says, all our voices whispers. "Ten years from what?"

"Ten years since the invasion." I slump in my seat. "For them. That's how long it's been. It's why they locked us up. We're teens in a world where kids are not supposed to have survived."

I let that information sink in, their faces twisting in shock and horror as they realize what this means.

It's been ten years since we left, and nothing will ever be the same.

"It can't be," Violet says. "That is so…"

"Wrong?" Brooklyn offers. "It's possible. And if they say ten years, who are we to tell them that it's only been fifteen months?"

I nod, agreeing with Brooklyn, even though it's hard to find words for what I'm feeling.

"Shit," Rayen mouths. "What do we do? We can't leave. Not until we find out what's up with the barrier."

"Do you think they know something is up?"

"They definitely do," Violet agrees. "Castor wouldn't say it, but I could read it in his face."

"You didn't tell him anything?" Brooklyn asks.

"That we arrived in a goddamn spaceship?" she asks, staring daggers. "Have them put us to death because they're still scared of things that might fall from the sky?" She shakes her head, combing her blond hair back into a ponytail, her fingers gathering up loose strands. "I'm not sure where we stand here. We can't tell them anything about our past, and we can't tell them about Andy. At all."

"Well, it's been ten years," Brooklyn says quietly, "Maybe they won't be as scared."

"It's been ten years," I say, "but it's ten years that they've been watching the sky. Just waiting to see if anything comes down."

When the aliens arrived, everything changed. It didn't change for the better. They took us by surprise, hunting us, gunning us down in the street and making bones and skin into the atmosphere for us to breathe. We were nothing to them. We were incapable of defending ourselves, of standing on our own. We didn't have weapons. When it came to the end, we didn't even have our prayers.

But against all odds, these people survived. Maybe others survived, too, if we could only seek them out. Humanity stood once again, defying everything.

Except it would never be the same. For as long as we live, from the invasion forward, we'll be looking at the sky and wondering if others might come for us, too.

Ready to fight or flee once again.

"All we can do for now is stay here," I say calmly. "Figure out what they know about the crystals and the barriers. Find out how long it's been here, find out everything they know about it and what it has to do with our distress signal."

They all nod once again, exchanging looks.

"We need to go back for the others," Violet says. "This is our best chance to understand what's happening, and we can't throw it away."

"We can't trust these people," Rayen says. "We find out what they know and see if we can bring the barrier down, and then we're out of here. All right?"

We all nod together in agreement.

But for some reason, I know deep in my gut it's not going to be so simple.

CHAPTER 13

When Castor comes back, he brings the key and unlocks the door. I hesitate for a second, but then step out. He smiles at me, his brown eyes warm.

"It's all right," he says. "Violet told me you have other people waiting for your return to camp?"

I nod. "Yes. They'll be waiting for us to get back."

"I'll go with you," he offers.

"No need," Rayen says quickly. "If we don't come in alone, they might think it's something else. We want to avoid that."

Castor shrugs. "As you wish."

When we go outside, other people are still looking. They try to pretend they're not, their gazes quickly averting when I meet them. Women hush their children, bringing them closer together, but all of them are still staring.

"I apologize. We're not really used to visitors," Castor explains.

"No?" Violet asks. "When was the last time?"

"A couple of years ago at least," Castor says. "We're just a small colony at the base of the mountains. There just aren't that many people around."

Just our luck.

"Are there other colonies nearby?"

Castor hesitates a little before his response. "Let's just say it's not common to find other people wandering about."

His answer is no answer at all. Castor guides us to the edge of the woods like an escort.

"We serve dinner after sundown," he says. "You're welcome to join us."

It's not just an invitation. He'll be waiting for us to return, either tonight or tomorrow. I nod my thanks and go ahead, Sputnik climbing the hill in front of us. It's steep, and I keep looking back to Castor's location, waiting to see if he'll follow us. But he stands there, and soon enough, the forest around us provides a thick cover for our footsteps, and there's nothing but the sound of birds and squirrels running up the trees.

When the door of the Arc opens, Avani and Flint jump from the seats.

"How was it? Did you find them?" Flint asks.

"What took so long?" Avani shoots.

Violet puts her hands up.

"It's fine," she says. "We met them."

The room is suddenly silent.

"And?" asks Avani, her voice shaking at the end of the question.

"They have a colony," Rayen says, her words masking the strangeness that we're all feeling. "They've offered for us to stay there. They want to know more."

Brooklyn quickly sums up what we've seen and talked about to Flint and Avani and about the ten years we've missed since the invasion. I check the surveillance camera I set up next to Andy's cell, but she's quiet now, no sign of movement.

"What are we going to do?" Flint asks as soon as Brooklyn finishes. "We can't just leave Andy on the ship. Maybe we should go back to space."

"If you think about it, Earth is in space," Brooklyn says, picking at her nose piercing. "So you're still in space all the time."

"Brooklyn, shut up," all of us say at once.

"I don't think we have a choice," Violet says, ignoring Brooklyn's interruption. "They're expecting us. Besides, we have a better chance of finding out what's really going on if we go back."

"We don't belong there," Rayen says.

"I do," Violet says, and her eyes meet Rayen's.

Rayen shifts her feet.

"What do you think?" Avani asks Brooklyn.

Brooklyn shrugs, pushing Avani's smooth, long hair behind her ear.

"Honestly?" she says. "I think it sounds good."

All five heads turn immediately to her.

"Look," Brooklyn says, "maybe this is what we need right now. The distress call came from somewhere. Maybe they know about it, maybe they don't. But we're not going to find out by staying here locked up on the ship."

"She's right," Violet agrees. "We can make a schedule, see what works so Andy has what she needs. Flint, do you have the crystal analysis?"

"It's in the lab," Flint says. "I can check on them tomorrow, no problem."

"Good," Violet replies. "We can't stay at the Arc. We're not getting answers here. Staying in Unity is our best shot."

"It still sounds fishy," Rayen says. "I don't like it."

"You don't have to like it," Violet snaps. "This is what we have right now. You wanted to follow the signal, right? We followed and found this. Now we have to stay here and find out what the hell is going on."

Violet storms to the back of the ship, probably off to get the rest of her things. Avani exchanges a look with me but doesn't argue, and she and Brooklyn vanish as well. Flint, Rayen, and I stand in the middle of the Arc, and I watch Andy inside the cell.

"Something strange is happening," Rayen says. "The distress call, the barrier, the crystals. It can't all be a coincidence."

"I know," I reply. "But Violet's right, too. We won't be able to find out anything by staying here locked inside the ship."

"I don't like leaving Andy," Flint says. "She seems…"

"Dangerous?" Rayen suggests.

Flint shakes his head slowly.

"Remember when you first showed me the Arc?" he asks, turning to me. "And we talked about ancient civilizations and the Universals."

It was all a long time ago. Before we knew who Andy was, before we'd faced the Hostemn, and before we embraced the whole universe, reaching out to it with our fingertips. When things were confined to the Earth and to us and to our loss of Adam.

I wonder what Adam would think. If he'd want to stay, too.

"Yeah," I reply. "I remember."

"We only know Andy," Flint says, "from the Universals. And I can't help but think that maybe Kreytian had a point when they talked about beings that could hold the fate of existence in their hands."

"I'm not sure where you're going," Rayen says.

"What if that's the real Andy?" Flint jerks his head back toward the cell. "What if that's just who she truly is?"

"You don't mean that," I say.

"Maybe not." Flint shrugs. "But as Rayen said, I don't exactly believe in coincidences."

Flint turns to leave, and so does Rayen. I don't like any of our options here. I don't like the idea of going to Unity and staying there like we belong, but it might be the best plan. Study the barrier and the crystals and find out what these people know, how they survived. Investigate the distress signal. If we can leave, we can find a cure for Andy.

I just hope it won't be too late.

I go fetch Violet before we leave.

She's standing in front of Andy's cell. Andy is muttering to herself, lost and isolated in a place we can't follow.

"You ready?" I ask Violet.

She turns those stormy eyes to me.

"I don't have a choice," she says.

Of course she does. We could take off with the Arc and land on the other side of Wyoming. It wouldn't be a problem, as long as we stay inside the barrier. But I don't think that would be helpful, and somehow, living with all of them for the last seven months, I learned when to keep my mouth shut.

"We're going to find out what's happening," I tell her.

"I'm not worried about that." Violet's gaze is fixed on Andy. "You're the one who insisted on coming here," she finally says. "I never wanted to, and now this."

"No need to rub it in my face. This isn't what I'd envisioned, either."

"But you didn't care."

"What did you want me to do, Violet?" I ask, my voice rising just a little bit. "We received a distress signal. I couldn't just ignore it and go on living happily as if I knew nothing else."

"You never had a problem ignoring things before."

Her words hurt more than a slap to my face. I'm not sure if she says them on purpose, but I don't retaliate. Then I see that she's still staring at Andy and that the emotion in her eyes is anger. Pure, white rage.

I'm not sure if Violet is ever going to forgive us for coming here. But I don't think she will forgive us for not wanting to stay, either.

CHAPTER 14

We discuss our stories to get them down to the smallest detail. Lies are based on the truth, so we each take what we can get— Violet and Flint are from Nevada (Flint's mom being British, which accounted for his accent), Rayen came from Arizona, and I'm from Montana. Brooklyn can't hide her accent, either, so we decide that she and Avani managed to make their way out west because of Avani's mom. We found each other years and years ago, but after Avani's mom died, we were left to fend for ourselves and decided to make our way somewhere else.

They're painful lies, lies that remind us that there is a terrible truth lying just beyond them if you look hard enough. At least it makes sense to be distrustful of strangers, and if we're not ready to share our stories yet, others will understand.

Castor welcomes us back the next morning with a smile. We introduce Flint and Avani, and Castor is more than happy to welcome them both. He introduces us to some people, and then our group is separated to be shown around the colony. They don't ask us how long we'll be staying, but with our things packed, we're obviously staying here for a while.

Once more, I am paired with Heidi. I really don't mind her, and her smile makes it easier, but I'm so used to being distrustful with people that I don't let her get through my wall. She shows up with a new set of clothes and takes me directly into one of the improvised shower rooms to change.

"And who is this girl?" she asks, seeing Sputnik by my side.

"The name's Sputnik," I say. "She's been with me a long time."

Heidi nods, smiling again, and I step into the shower room.

The water is cold as it washes my body, but it's a relief. It's different from the synthetic water of the ship; even the smell is different. I wash my hair and let the soap sink in, and when I'm done, I feel like a person again.

"I'm taking you around the colony so you can see how we work," she says. "If you're staying here for a while, you're expected to contribute to all the tasks. Is there anything you can do?"

I pause, not sure how much I could reveal. "My grandparents used to own a farm," I say carefully. "And I can hunt."

Heidi nods. "That's good. Not many hunters around here, so you might be a useful addition. We also have the school depending on how much education you had after the invasion."

I make a face, and Heidi laughs. School for little kids is clearly not my area of expertise.

"We'll have you settled in no time," she says. "And for as long as you need to stay. There is space in the cabins for more people, and we're always ready to welcome more people in."

I nod, looking at the strong wooden cabins. They're all built of large logs, cabins that look sturdy and made to withstand the cold. It almost looks like a setting from a Wild West movie.

"Why not use the houses? There's a town nearby, isn't there?"

A shadow crosses Heidi's face. "Too many memories for a lot of people. It's hard facing a house from a time long gone."

I can get the logic behind that. "Did you live here before?"

She nods in silence, showing me around the encampment. Eight dormitory rooms, the school, the storage for winter and the cold weather, the storage for clothes, the law enforcement office—that's the one with the jail—and an archive room, where all the records are stored.

"So is Castor the leader?"

"Of sorts," Heidi agrees. "We have a council to make decisions about hunting parties and other things we worry about. But in general, we're a very open community, and we like to make decisions that affect us together. Castor helps because he moderates all debates."

I nod. "How many of you are there?"

"At the moment, two hundred and sixty-three."

"Wow."

"We're very proud of what we did here. It's difficult building things when we can still see remains of the old civilization. But everything is a brand-new world now, and we can't just try and make it in its old image."

I nod gravely. I can see why it would be hard going back to the houses and buildings. Better to leave it as it was and forget it entirely. It's not like we can simply go back.

"Do you have any contact?" I ask. "With other colonies?"

She darts a look at me, and I'm fast enough to catch it. She doesn't hesitate to respond, but there's something weird in her voice.

"Not really," she says. "None that we have established permanent contact with."

I don't want to press her too much or give away what I'm thinking with my own questions. The more questions I ask, the more I let her know about what we're really doing here.

I'm sure that she knows something about the barrier.

Heidi takes me around the fields, showing me the corn, the wheat, and everything else they plant to survive. It grows green and fresh because it's the season, but come winter, the storage is really important, and the rations get shorter. The colony functions as a small town, with everyone contributing in ways they can, mending clothes, taking care of children, planting, and sustaining themselves. It's peaceful, and when Heidi takes me to meet the others, I even manage to smile.

I shake hands with over forty people, and all of them welcome me with warm smiles. They take me to meet their children, scared little things with big eyes open, watching me as if I'm some kind of alien. They don't know that I am, but it's fine—they're not staring at me because of my DNA. They're staring because there's suddenly someone who's not as young as them but not as old as their parents. Soon enough, I have a trail of three or four children following me as Heidi takes me around, showing me all the things and what I'm expected to do.

"They like you," she says with a laugh.

"It's just the dog," I say.

The kids play with Sputnik, but they are also looking at me from the corners of their eyes. Suddenly, a pang makes me remember Jacob, Noah's brother. He used to follow me around the house, too.

My smile almost instantly crumbles, and I try my best to hold it inside. When I turn back, Heidi's observing me.

"It's all right to share, Clover," she says quietly. "Everyone lost people they loved back then."

"Are you now my official therapist or something?"

"I can be," she says. "I've got a degree if you want to look at it."

"The world is burning and that's the thing you save? Your degree?"

Instead of anger, she just laughs, the wrinkles forming around her eyes. "I worked very hard for it. Also, it was painful, so I might as well carry it around."

I can't help but laugh with her, the easiness with which she takes my hardened edges and even the way she's trying to make me feel safe. It's as if she can sense it. I don't know if I can trust her. As I look around the colony and the others, I can't trust any of them.

At the same time, I desperately want to.

For the first time in months, I dream about Adam.

The thing about dreams is that they're usually confusing, and one ends up merging with another. Sometimes, I see Noah, and I beg him to run. Sometimes, I beg Adam to run. Sometimes, I'm leaving them both behind and not looking back, telling myself that I did what I had to in order to survive. I'm always thankful that when I see my grandparents, they're both always alive, and I remember them as they were and not when they were gone. It's a small mercy.

In this dream, Adam stands behind me, and it's not Violet in danger. It's me. He takes the blow, and I'm silent, my scream not warning him soon enough, my legs glued in place, and I can't do anything but watch as he vanishes into a cloud of bone dust. I wake up with tears in my eyes, wiping them quickly against the pillow. Sputnik whimpers, wagging her tail, and I pet her to tell her it's okay. I have no idea what time it is when I exit the cabin, but it's early—the sun is rising, painting the horizon a dusty shade of pink.

We need to find a way to make Andy normal again. That's

our top priority. It's wrong to leave her there in the spaceship, but there's no way we can bring her here without causing panic. And there's no way we can find out more about what's going on without staying longer in Unity.

When I hear footsteps behind me, I turn to see Violet. She doesn't look like she's slept well, either, dark circles under her eyes. Her blond hair is arranged in a braid that falls over her shoulder, and her blue eyes are pale in the dark.

"What do you think?" she asks, her voice husky.

"They don't trust us, and we don't trust them," I reply. I know she values my analysis. "It's going to be tough to get answers."

She nods, crossing her arms over her chest, wrapping her coat around her tighter. The cold breeze makes me feel more like home, but she knows nothing of that cold bite of the wind that blows from the mountains.

"We'll have to offer them enough info that they'll rely on us," she says. "But I kind of like it here. It's peaceful."

"Says the girl who didn't want to come in the first place."

She gives me a look. "You know why I didn't want to come."

I meet her eyes. "Do I?"

"Don't start, Clover. I have my reasons. Maybe there would be no people left."

"We would have never known if it was up to you."

I expect her to apologize for what she said back at the ship, but of course she doesn't. Her words still ring in my ears—*it's not like you're human anyway.*

I may not have the same DNA as her. I'm stronger, better, crafted to survive the impossible. I have part of the Universals inside me, people who bent existence to their will. I was chosen as someone who's supposed to survive impossible conditions, to go to space and still be able to breathe and live, because everything in my body conditions me to survive. So no, I'm not human.

But in all the ways that count, I still am.

"Forget it," Violet says, dismissing anything I might say next. "We need to stay here and find out what they know. Get intel on the barrier. Take Rayen to the hunting party."

I nod, and I drop the subject. There's no time for squabbling among group members. It's time we stand together and get our jobs done.

So when the others start waking up and Heidi hands me and Rayen over to the hunting party, I agree to go with them, no questions.

The party consists of five other people, four men and one woman. There's a cart wheeled by horses with them.

Castor is with us, and he welcomes me and Rayen with his usual smile, telling us to hop inside the cart for the journey. Sputnik doesn't hesitate, climbing into the cart first. They hand Rayen and I each a rifle, but they don't hand us the ammo yet, which makes Rayen roll her eyes behind their backs. We find a small spot in the back while the others are still getting ready to leave, organizing the horses. Rayen adjusts the sleeves of her T-shirt, the tattoos on her arms peeking beneath it, on the left arm a wolf, and on the right one a bear.

"What did they ask you yesterday?"

Rayen turns to me. "A bunch of boring-ass questions."

"What did you say?"

"Stared them dead in the eye and dared them to ask another."

"I'm scared of you."

Rayen grins back. "That's the best compliment you've ever given me."

I roll my eyes, shaking my head. Castor at last climbs into the cart, and we're ready to go. We move north, not toward the mountains. Finally, after what seems like twenty minutes, I turn to Castor.

"Where exactly are we headed?"

"Jackson," he replies. "All the best game is there."

"In the city?" Rayen frowns.

Castor nods. "Humans left the city, animals took over. It's how it's been working, at least for us."

I nod, patting Sputnik.

"So how is your dog for hunting?"

"Chickens only," I reply, looking at Sputnik. "But she's very silent and alert."

Castor nods. "That's a good companion, always keeping you safe. I used to have one of my own. I miss her a lot."

"I'm sorry."

He dismisses me with a hand. "It's been a long time. How did you two sleep?"

"Fine," Rayen says, a simple word that comes out like a dagger.

"Thanks for welcoming us." I try my best to sound nice. Rayen is even worse than me with human contact, and I have to compensate, especially if we want them to tell us what's happening. "Do you guys always do hunting parties?"

"Once a week," he confirms. "We do have sheep and some cattle, but it's always good to survey the area in case there's something different."

"And is there?"

Castor shakes his head. "Almost never."

I let it go, not wanting to press it further. When we finally get to the city, I can see what he means.

It's bigger than I imagined, but the buildings have been taken over by weeds and ivy, climbing up the parts where they fell down, and stand awkwardly, covered by green and nature, creating a space when there was only demolition. The houses, roofs, and the bridge that cross the river have bushes and flowers springing from them, vines hanging down. There is a distinct smell of fresh water and grass after the rain, and I breathe in the scent.

"The animals have taken over," the woman says. "They've just spread all over. Now that the humans are gone, they prefer it. Better places to hide."

As we cross the bridge, I spot the birds chirping away on top, colors bright blue, green, and brown. I don't know the names of any species, but it's good to see them.

It's finally realizing that I've come home.

The hunters lead ahead, Rayen and I trailing their steps. She steals the ammo from the cart, slipping it inside her pocket when no one else is looking. Sputnik stays next to me, and if I snap my fingers, she heels and returns to my side. The hunters know their way around the decayed buildings and abandoned houses. Ten years doesn't seem like much, but I can see it in the way the houses are rotting, nature fully taking over. Castor gestures ahead to a specific building, and he opens the door for all of us.

It's quiet, as if nature itself is breathing right beside me.

He motions for us to follow him, and the party splits, each taking a different set of stairs. Rayen, Sputnik, and I climb, our steps soft and breath controlled, careful not to let the animals hear us.

I spot the deer first.

It's grazing in one of the corridors, its head bowed, the antlers rising. As if it senses we're watching, it raises its head, brown eyes surveying its surroundings. No one moves for a second, but it's Rayen who goes first—I can feel her every movement beside me. She takes a deep breath, whispers something I can't distinguish, and takes the shot.

It hits the deer right between the eyes, and it drops.

Castor turns around, and Rayen lowers her rifle.

"Good shot," he says. "But next time, wait for my signal."

Rayen gives him a look but doesn't say anything. We go to the deer, and I put a hand over its warm fur. Rayen kneels next to me and whispers a prayer. I can't understand the words, softly spoken in a language I don't know. When she nods, I know it's time to pick it up and bring it back with us.

Sputnik is not much help in this part, just wagging her tail ahead.

When we meet the other half of the team, they're also carrying a deer and a couple of hares.

The sun is almost at midpoint, meaning the sweat is trickling down my back. I put my hair up in a bun, trying to get it off my neck. We're hauling the game back to the cart when I spot something shining.

At the edge of the forest, its form rises from the ground, green and clear. As I get closer, the sheer transparency of the crystal cluster reflects my face in a dozen different angles. Sputnik's fur rises on her back, feeling the threat.

"There you are," Castor says. "We're heading back."

I jump, looking back at him and then the crystal.

"What is that?" I ask.

He eyes the crystals. "You don't have those out west?"

I shake my head.

"We don't know," he answers. "They're harmless. There are a couple of them north of here, too, and some others in the woods. We think it was left behind by the aliens, but no one knows."

He walks forward, and before I can stop him, he lays his hand on it.

My heart almost stops, and I stare at him.

"See? Nothing there. It's pretty, that's all."

He walks forward again and puts his hand on my shoulder. I look back at the crystal as he guides me. More than one.

It's much worse than we thought.

"Let's go back," Castor says, gently pushing me away. "The others are waiting for us."

We head back to the cart. The others have lifted all the game in, ready to get back to Unity, when a noise echoes above.

I look up, tense, my heart beating fast. But none of the others feel that way except for Rayen, who's also alert. A second later, a single plane zooms across the sky, leaving a trail of small clouds to follow.

"What is that?" I ask, tense. I can't see the plane model from here. It went by too fast.

Castor smiles. "The search party came home."

CHAPTER 15

When we get back to the colony, the sun is lower on the horizon, and it's bustling with activity. Children are laughing and screaming as they chase one another, and parents are hauling stuff from cabin to cabin. I frown at the activity as we make our way back to our cabin. Violet, Flint, Brooklyn, and Avani are already there, sitting on their beds, and they look up as we come in.

"Hey," Rayen says, dropping on her own bunk. "What's going on?"

"A search party returned," Violet answers. "They are throwing them a feast."

"It sounds like we're in medieval times," Brooklyn says and then changes the pitch of her voice to something a lot rougher that vaguely sounds like Gerard Butler. "Our warriors are back! A feast is deserved!"

Avani sighs dramatically.

"It's a good impression," I tell Brooklyn.

"You see, you encourage this kind of behavior," Avani complains. "And then she doesn't ever stop."

The two of them start bickering again, going back and forth about all of Brooklyn's badly done impressions and the inconvenient times she does them, like when she got involved with the alien mafia and almost got all of us killed over her *Godfather* impression. I turn back to Violet.

"So what's this search party searching for?"

She shakes her head. "I don't know. They didn't exactly tell us."

Flint agrees. "I spent all day with the kids at school. They didn't mention barriers or crystals or anything else. And they're kids. They usually can't shut up about anything even if you beg them to."

"Maybe they're hiding it from them," Rayen says. She has her head propped up against her pillow and her eyes closed. "This place is fucked up."

Violet gives her a look. "It's a perfectly normal place. You're exaggerating."

"Yeah," Rayen says, then puts on a cheerful tone. "Here in Unity, we welcome people of all races and types. We live as one together!" She raises one eyebrow, skeptical, to tell us that she isn't buying it.

"Well, no one said anything about us," Avani says, her hand interlaced with Brooklyn's.

"They better not, or I'll kick their asses back to the invasion so fast, it'll rip a hole in time and space," Rayen mutters.

"I don't think it's bad," Violet says.

All of us turn to give her a side-eye.

"Is this one of the clueless white people situations?" she finally asks, and we all start laughing.

Unity pretends to be utopic, or at least it's what they're going for. For Violet, this seems like a community. For the rest of us, it could be a village right out of a horror movie.

"If someone gives me the I-don't-see-color speech, I'm taking them down," Rayen says.

Brooklyn nods with vehemence.

"Actually, about the crystals," I say, wanting to get back on topic. "I saw another one in Jackson today."

"What?" Flint says, sitting up suddenly.

"Yes. Castor said they're everywhere. He touched it, and it didn't do anything to him."

We all exchange looks. Maybe it's just harmless to humans. Either way, we don't have any more answers.

"Well," Rayen finally says, "the sooner we're out of this place, the better."

"We should give them a chance," Violet says.

I can see her point—we're all disgruntled and tired, and all of us have had trust issues with people lying to us for years. Everything about this place is new, and maybe we should give them a chance.

That's what they're trying to give us, too.

When the feast gets started, it's pretty much like Brooklyn guessed it would be.

People gather around a fire, and there's a cold northern wind that blows the leaves toward us, whistling through the woods and the mountains beyond. They laugh and sing songs and share their meal as one. No one dresses up, thank God, but I still stand just a little apart from the rest of them.

This is a feast to celebrate this community. It's not a feast that includes the strange newcomers whose ages don't match the rest of theirs. I spot a teen—he is about fourteen, maybe fifteen, and he stays close to the fire. A little girl sits next to him, probably his sister by the looks of it. He's the only one our age who stands there easily, and the difference between him and us is obvious.

I take my share of the meat, and I go sit far away, next to Rayen and Flint, and we watch the fire. Avani, Brooklyn, and Violet are engaged in a conversation with one of the older women, and Avani keeps motioning for us to join, encouraging us to talk. I really don't feel like talking yet. It's been a whole day, and I'm wondering how Andy is feeling over there in the spaceship, all alone, and if she has improved or gotten worse.

I can't be the only one feeling this, because both Flint and Rayen are also quiet by my side.

"You look like moody teenagers," Avani says when she joins us. "We're not going to find out anything if you guys don't talk."

"I *am* a moody teenager," Rayen states.

"You all are doing a fine job without us," Flint says with one of his biggest smiles. "Please go mingle so we don't have to."

Avani sighs. "They aren't going to trust us if we don't look like we're trying to fit in."

"We're not even staying long," I say. "They know we're moving to DC in a couple weeks or whatever."

"Fine," Avani says. "Be moody, then."

"Thank you. My emo self bids you peace," Flint says. Then he frowns. "I don't think those words fit into the same sentence, somehow."

"Shouldn't it be my emo self bids you despair and tears?" Rayen suggests.

"I hate this world," Flint says, punctuating this sentence with a closed fist aimed directly at God Himself. "We never got the chance for a My Chemical Romance comeback. How is that fair?"

Avani shakes her head, finally giving up on us and joining her girlfriend. She, at least, looks healthier than the rest of us—her brown skin shining, her dark-brown hair arranged in a braid down her back. She's still a lab nerd at heart, and that's why we love her. Brooklyn looks normal, too, even though it's weird to see her without eyeliner and black clothes. She managed to keep her nose piercing and earrings at least. I hope that she's engaging in regular conversation and not another of her conspiracy theory threads.

"I'm getting more food," I announce, getting up. Flint and

Rayen nod in approval as I move toward the fire where the food is being distributed. When I reach the pit, I see Castor and Violet deep in conversation.

Castor is the first to notice, and he beckons me over.

Violet gives me a nod as I join them, forming a small circle, holding my plate like a child, still hoping for seconds.

"Hungry?" Castor asks, then smiles. "The food here is one of the best parts. We have a couple of farmers who know how to take cultivation to the next level."

I smile, tight-lipped, not knowing what to say.

"Violet was just telling me about your journey here," Castor says. "It all sounds very interesting."

"It sure was," I say dryly.

Castor smiles again, friendly. His face is tanned by the days working in the sun, his brown hair cropped short. He's a little on the plump side, his chest large, like one of those friendly neighbors who everyone has in their town.

"So what exactly was in this distress call?"

I almost jump, but I only blink in Violet's direction. She smiles to assure me that she has the whole situation under control. I don't know if I believe her.

"We were just talking about how it came up on our GPS. We use a solar-powered one," Violet explains.

"Satellites still working, that's a true wonder," Castor comments. "I'm glad they haven't fallen out of the sky, though it's not the worst thing to fall out of the sky in the last few years!" He laughs heartily at his joke.

I give Violet a look of pain, and she glares back at me.

"Either way, we really haven't seen anything in the region," Castor says.

"Do you go out that much?" I ask as casually as I can. "What's the range for the hunting parties?"

"The mountains are hard to cross, and no one is exactly willing to face the Rockies. There are bears to hunt as well, but we rarely come across them. They don't venture out where they can see humans, and we don't go out there."

"But what about your search parties?"

Castor pauses. "They're different," he says carefully, looking at both of us. "We look for other survivors. They're gone longer, too. Which is why we celebrate when they're back."

I nod, but even I can see that he's hiding something. Maybe the search parties are not for other survivors as much as for trying to find a way out of this barrier. They are lying, and so are we.

We just need to see who's going to break first.

"It's a good system you have here," Violet says. "I can see everyone is happy, too."

Castor smiles at that. "I'm glad you think so. We know we treated you poorly when you came in, but you're more than welcome to stay here if that's what you'd like. I don't know if there's much left in DC."

"Do you get radio signals?" I ask.

Castor nods. "We try communicating from time to time. Can't afford to spend the energy as much as we used to, of course, but radio is a good way to try and search for other survivors. To see if we can figure out how many of us are left."

He says it with a pain in his voice, and this time, I know he isn't lying. He wants to find other people, too. He wants to know if there's more hope than they've found here.

Humans are sociable animals. Despite it all, we still keep trying to connect with others.

When I turn back to find my friends, I notice someone else looking at me. He stands with the others from the search party. He looks to be in his early forties, but there are not many white hairs on his head.

I frown, and he looks away. A second later, he gets up and walks over to me.

When the man stops in front of me, he's alone.

"Clover?" he asks, his tone filled with surprise and disbelief. "Clover Martinez?"

CHAPTER 16

I don't move.

How does he know my name?

News travels in this small camp. Everyone knows the strangers' names by now, whispers about us moving fast. He has just arrived with the search party, but by now, he already knows who we are.

That's all there is to it.

Nothing else.

"Yeah," I answer finally. "Can I help you?"

He doesn't move, his eyes staring into mine, forehead frowning in confusion, but he shakes his head, coming to a realization of his own.

"No," he says after a second. "I thought you might be someone else."

"I'm sorry, how do you know my name?"

He looks back at where the others are gathered. "They told me yours, and it was the name of someone I used to know. From before."

I search his face, but he doesn't seem familiar at all. He is just as tall as I am but bulkier, age and muscles weighing on him while I'm still lanky. His skin is a lighter shade of brown than my own, wrinkles around his eyes.

"I'm sorry," I finally say. "You're confusing me with someone."

"Yes," he says. "Sorry, kid. I'll see you around."

I nod at him, watching him go. I take a second to check that Sputnik is with Rayen, and then I turn around, stalking back to the edge of the woods, leaving the feast behind to go back to the Arc.

Running was never one of my hobbies before, but I like it now. Adrenaline pumps through my body as I run into the forest, waving branches aside, my muscles powering themselves as I climb uphill. My body is high on the oxygen of Earth where I'd been designed to thrive and live.

In less than two hours, I find the cave again.

It's undisturbed, just like we left it. When I get closer, the spaceship opens, recognizing me. It doesn't bother with a welcome message, but everything lights up. I make my way to the back room to Andy's cell.

She's standing in the corner, bent into herself. Her skin is like a nebula—made of clouds shifting and forming in all different colors. She looks up when she sees me.

"Come to release me?" she asks, her eyes boring into mine. "Or am I too big a monster to be let out of the cage?"

"Don't be an idiot," I reply. "I just came to check in on you."

"Well, I'm just like I was yesterday," she says, her voice full of sarcasm. "Kill me, then, if you're going to leave me here."

"You're sounding like a comic book villain."

"All of them get put into glass cages, you know," she says. "You know what they also do? Break out of them."

A chill climbs up my spine. But the Arc is indestructible. This cell was made to hold the most powerful beings in the universe, and I have no reason to doubt it now.

"It's not meant to hurt you, Andy."

"But it does." She puts her hands to the glass and emits a pulse. The glass doesn't move. "It restrains my powers. Powers that are meant to be unleashed."

"I thought you never used those powers unless you had to."

Andy looks up, sparks flashing in her eyes. They are lightning storms, big and scary, and the clouds around her skin make it even worse. The hair on the back of my neck stands up.

I'm staring at the most powerful being in the universe, and I don't recognize my friend. Only the abyss of power that hides within.

"Andy, this isn't you."

She barks a laugh. "Sure it is. It always has been. You'd rather not see it."

Flint's words come back to me. What Andy truly is. The monster hiding beneath the skin, someone we did not want to believe in.

There is a reason why the Universals are hated, and maybe I'm starting to find out why.

"I remade the universe," she whispers. "I pulled it apart and opened it, I took its fabric and rewove it into existence. I touch something and it changes, giving up its essence to please me. I bring things back from the dead. I remake every edge of creation as I see fit. I take every little line in the universe and write them as I wish."

Something chills me as if the air has grown colder around the ship. We never talked about what happened the day we took the Hostemn down. We acted as if everything had gone perfectly to plan and we'd come out on top.

But it was a lie.

Andy had torn apart the universe to get Violet back, and she'd rewritten reality itself to do it.

"You can't bring someone back from the dead without consequences," she says in a singsong voice, reading my thoughts. "Maybe they aren't the same thing at all."

"Violet is your best friend, Andy."

Andy shrugs. "She's human. Just that."

I shake my head, and before Andy says anything she'll

regret, I press the button to darken the cell, blocking her from view. My breath is ragged, and I'm still scared.

That thing in there is Andy.

That's the worst part. It's not something that has taken over her body, not anything that is completely unlike my friend. It's someone who's been there for a long time, waiting to come out.

Her words ring inside me, and I know that we're not dealing with something simple. It's about dealing with all the consequences and all that we faced back there.

I make my way back to the colony, this time slower. It takes me a few hours to get there, and it must be the middle of the night when I finally am in my bunk bed. No one asks where I've been and what I've done.

There's something on my pillow. I take it in my hands, its texture soft. When I put it next to the window, catching the moonlight to see it better, I can't breathe.

It's a photo of me when I was six, holding out my first fallen tooth in my hand, a gap-toothed smile staring back while wearing my NASA pajamas.

It can't be.

CHAPTER 17

I don't tell anyone about the photo.

I remember posing for this picture, but I don't remember seeing it in Abuela's photo albums, the things she took so much care with, writing down captions in pretty and curvy Spanish calligraphy for every picture in the margins. I'm not sure how it wound up on my pillow, but I know someone here knows who I am.

I can't help but think of the man who knows my name.

The day trickles by fast as I help in the tasks, mostly physical. We aren't allowed to do too much, though, and I don't know if it's because they pity us or because they don't trust us. Either way, I have my afternoon free. When I'm walking back to the dorm to find something to do or take a nap, Heidi waves me over from the porch of her cabin.

I go to her, not wanting to be rude, not exactly willing to have any deep conversations, either.

"Come inside, Clover," she says, waving her head toward the cabin. "We can have a little chat."

Not knowing how to say no, I follow her inside to the same room I saw on the first day. She waves toward the couch again, and she sits in the chair opposite from me. I know this is going to be a long talk.

"Are you really trying to be my therapist right now?" I ask, eyeing her. "'Cause it feels like it."

"I don't see why not," Heidi responds. "We all need therapy, Clover. Even I do."

She doesn't pick up pen and paper at least. It'd drive me up the walls to have someone writing down every little thing I say with the intention of analyzing it, trying to unmake me like a machine.

"I think it would do you good. Especially after everything that you've gone through. I'm sure you could use someone to talk to."

"I have my friends."

"Friends are excellent," she replies. "They really are. But a professional is even better. We have the emotional distance we need to help you figure out things about yourself. Distance that sometimes your friends don't have."

I nod slowly. The worst part is I don't mind talking to her. She seems nice. She's willing to help. She makes everything here sound trustworthy and safe. I think I need that somehow, but I also have too many secrets to share, too many things I can't tell her. So I ask about something else.

"Who was the guy from the search party?" I ask. "The Latino one."

"That's Marcelo," she answers. "He's been here a while. You met him?"

I nod. "He told me he knew someone with the same name as me."

"Imagine that. The world is an odd little place for coincidences."

I examine her. She looks good for fifty, her brown skin youthful with only small wrinkles around her eyes.

"How long have you been here? All ten years?"

She shakes her head. "We've come from all different places. The first person to the colony was Castor and his group, eight or so years ago. They used to live up inside the mountains them. The aliens couldn't get to the Rockies that easily. After they were gone, they came down."

I nod. I wonder how many others survived that day.

"And you?"

"I found them five years ago," she says. "I came from the other side of the Wyoming border and made my way up here, looking for others. My own group stayed here, too, when we found this place."

Still in the same state, still inside the barrier. This is the first clue I've gotten about it since getting here.

"Do you want to tell me about your journey here?"

I hesitate for a second.

"Why do you want to help me?" I ask.

She looks at me. "Because you need help, and you're not sure how to ask for it."

"How do you know that?"

Heidi shrugs. "Call it survivor's instinct. I know what it's like to survive, and so do you. Besides, you walked out here of your own free will. That shows initiative."

"And the fact that I had nothing better to do."

Heidi smiles. "Call it whatever you want."

I take a deep breath, looking around the room for something to anchor myself in. I find nothing. I don't understand Unity, and I don't understand Heidi. I'm not sure of what they are offering or what my place in this new world is.

"Is this going to be like real therapy?" I finally ask. "As in, everything I say doesn't leave this room?"

Heidi blinks and pauses, but then she nods. "If you want it to be. Our resources are limited here, and I can't prescribe any medicine. But you can tell me anything you want to tell me."

I gulp down hard. "We came here because of a distress signal."

Heidi's eyebrows go up in surprise. "What kind of distress signal?"

I shake my head. I'm not an idiot. I'm not going to tell her everything. But if Violet told Castor about the distress signal, I can tell Heidi.

"I don't know, not exactly," I answer. "We followed it here, but then it was gone. That's how we found you. When we were looking for something."

Heidi tuts. "Did you believe it was another survivor asking for help?"

I nod once more, my throat dry.

"What are your plans now?" Heidi asks, and I think her interest is genuine. "If you don't find the signal again. Do you still plan on leaving?"

I don't answer. I'm not sure I know how.

"Plans for the future can be hard when the world is like this," Heidi finally says. "Nothing is certain anymore, and this complicates things. That doesn't mean you can't take small steps to make sure you're in the right place."

I look up. "What do you mean, the right place?"

She shrugs just slightly. "The right place is where you want to be. With the people who love you, and whom you love in return. A place where you can feel safe."

Safe is a word I've forgotten how to use. It's something trivial, almost magical, the essence of which I can't grasp.

"I haven't felt safe in a long time."

Heidi smiles back, but there's sadness in her eyes when she looks at me.

"The world is complicated, Clover," she says. "Even now. But you should never not be able to feel safe."

CHAPTER 18

The next days trickle by slowly, and although I've been keeping an eye on everything, there's no new information to be found. After a week, I'm frustrated by the utter lack of leads. No one is concerned with the crystals because they're apparently harmless, and the signal is completely gone. Each of us has a different job, and everyone around us is doing their best to make sure we are adjusted to the routine.

I pretend the photograph of me is not on my mind.

In the morning, I'm told there's no work for me.

"Why don't you go see what the others are doing?" Lyelle, who heads up farming, suggests. "It's a pretty nice day, after all."

She doesn't need to say it twice. I take off with Sputnik at my heels and walk through Unity.

It's a pretty big community if you consider there are more than two hundred people living in it. The farming fields stretch to the edge of the mountain, and every single cabin is in a line, so there's really only one street where everyone congregates. A lot of the meals are served out in the open if the weather is favorable, and if not, there's a special cabin built like the old Area 51 messroom but warmer. A lot of the cabins are built from logs but with reinforced walls outside because of the cold. There's also the feeling that people are building something here. That there's something meaningful behind this work.

It's about learning to survive when there's nothing left.

I shuffle with Sputnik toward Avani's spot. She was recruited almost immediately by the medical team at the infirmary. I knock on the cabin, and someone stops me.

"The dog can't come in here," the man says. "Do you need something? Are you feeling ill?"

"No," I reply. "I just wanted to talk to Avani."

"I'll check if she's busy."

A few moments later, Avani walks through the door. She's wearing a coat like all the other nurses, and she's clearly part of the team. I feel a sharp pain in my stomach, but I don't know why.

"Hey," she says. "What do you need?"

"Nothing. Came to check on you."

There's a slight crease in her forehead. "I'm busy, Clover. Besides, don't you have something to do as well?"

"I was dismissed," I reply, not letting her annoyance get to me. Maybe she's just having a bad day. "Do you need anything?"

She looks back quickly at the cabin. It's small, and it looks far from a hospital, though there are beds, and this is where people come to get treated if they have a fever or aren't feeling well. I spot only two sick people using the infirmary beds. It can't be that busy.

"No," Avani says. "It's fine."

"Found out anything?"

Avani shrugs. "Same as always. But I like being here."

"You do?"

She shrugs again. She's not comfortable speaking further on this, and I wonder if it's me or if it's something else.

"It's good," Avani says. "I'm learning a lot."

"I thought you didn't want to be a doctor."

"Things change," she says, keeping her voice light. She smiles up at me. "Thanks for coming. I'll see you around."

And just like that, she's done with me. She walks back inside, and a second later, I hear her chatting with one of the doctors. It's not about a sickness or one of the patients, just regular chatting. Exactly what we were doing a second ago.

I don't let her coldness get me down, and I try to find Brooklyn. Unity settled each of us into a category where they thought we'd be most helpful—Flint got a position with the kitchens, Rayen is usually on duty with patrol or hunting, and Violet is helping Castor with the administrative issues. I got stuck with farming, only because I told them that's what I grew up doing. Unity doesn't look anything like my farm, and besides, Abuela was the one who took care of it.

I find Brooklyn with the children in the school. She's helping teach the younger ones to read, and class gets abruptly interrupted when one of the little girls spots Sputnik outside and whistles. Sputnik doesn't know better and comes barging into the classroom, making everyone's day.

"Kids!" Brooklyn shouts. "Hey, look—"

None of them are paying attention anymore. They're all turned to Sputnik, who is loving the attention, wagging her tail while being trampled by over ten kids who can't be older than seven. Brooklyn loses complete control of the class.

I raise an apologetic hand, and Brooklyn steps outside, checking if the kids are still distracted with the dog.

"Sorry about that," I say.

"It's okay," she replies and blinks. "I'm supposed to be showing them how to read and write, and I can barely get them to stop calling each other poop face."

"Sounds tough."

Brooklyn puts a hand on my shoulder. "I am haunted, Clover. Haunted. I've seen things you could never imagine. It's a lawless land, and we all die. You either kill yourself, or you get killed."

"I don't think that's how the saying goes."

She grins at me. She looks a little tired, but a good type of tired. And even when she's talking about the kids, I can tell that she cares a lot about them. I can tell that's one of the things she wants to be doing.

"Have you been talking to Avani lately?" I ask.

"Well, yeah, she's my girlfriend. Pretty sure that's what it entails."

"I mean, I didn't think she wanted to be a doctor," I tell her. I check on Sputnik over my shoulder. The kids are tying ribbons over her ears. I don't know where they got those. "She seems to be enjoying herself."

Brooklyn frowns a little. "Oh, you know. Things change."

"That fast?"

Brooklyn shrugs, puts her hands in her pockets. "They are giving us something to do. Not just be glorified space tourists. Nothing wrong with that, but it wasn't a real purpose."

I don't know what she means about purpose. Before, I had one—I wanted to go to space, be an astronaut. Those things don't mean a lot anymore.

"It was your idea first."

"Yeah, but what else were we supposed to do?" Brooklyn asks. "It's not a life, Clover. You know that."

There's a pause.

"Don't tell Rayen I said that," she says quickly, her green eyes blinking at me. "I know she has her issues with Unity. But I'm hoping she'll come around. She just needs to accept things. She just needs to see that we can be something here."

And it's weird, how Avani and Brooklyn have accepted their new roles this fast, how comfortable they are being here. At the same time, Rayen hates it. I don't know where I am with this.

I want to know what that feels like, to be sure that there's a life out here. To be certain of the future. My mind wanders back to the photograph in my pocket, and I keep wondering if my future will always have to be so connected to my past.

While they're here building lives, I'm putting them all in danger. Someone knows I'm lying. Someone knows who I am.

"I gotta get back," Brooklyn says. "Thanks for buying me five minutes of parole."

"Anytime."

She winks at me and walks inside, bringing Sputnik away from the kids, who all sigh collectively. One of them starts crying, but Brooklyn doesn't buy the fake tears. I watch for a while, and I long for life to be this simple, for it to be this easy.

Maybe it can be.

CHAPTER 19

I keep going back to the photograph.

There's not one second of the day where it's not on my mind, and I think about what Brooklyn said—about belonging and about finding a new place.

I know I can't do this without finding out where it comes from.

My only lead is the man who talked to me that day at the bonfire. It's been more than a week since our first encounter, and when I get to look for him again, I end up finding something unexpected.

It's a Cirrus SRS model. I haven't seen one of these in a while, but its polished black snout stands out from the beige background of the wheat field. I get closer to it, looking around to see if there's anyone else nearby, but I'm alone. I reach out to touch it, the cold metal familiar under my hands. I've driven spaceships now, and yet there's something so familiar with standing here in front of a plane, hoping it'd take me into its wings and let me fly.

"Beautiful, isn't she?" a voice says and makes me jump.

I turn around to see Marcelo staring at the plane and me. He doesn't approach, but I immediately take my hand off the plane and shove it in my pocket.

"Yeah," I say, "she's holding up."

He nods, and I hate myself that I have to ask this question.

"That day of the return," I say, "it was you flying, wasn't it?"

He nods slowly but doesn't move.

"I missed it," he says. "It's not often that I get enough fuel to fly. So I don't do it a lot. And besides..."

"You couldn't after the invasion."

His eyes are the same shade of brown as mine. I hadn't noticed before. Abuelo's shade was darker, almost black, Abuela's clearer and softer. Mine are the color of the earth on a rainy day.

A shiver runs through my spine.

"What are you doing here, Clover?" he asks.

I shove my hands deeper into my pockets. The photo is still there. I haven't taken it out.

"Just wandering around," I reply. "When I saw the plane, I had to come look."

"You have anyone who flew?"

"My abuelo. Before the invasion."

Marcelo nods. Then he gives me a small smile.

"Want to go up there again?"

I hesitate. This could go wrong. I know he shouldn't be wasting a lot of fuel, but at the same time, I miss the familiar sound of an airplane motor with me. I always thought I was meant for space—for moving up there, for reaching the stars. Instead, I miss the simplicity of a sky whose horizon line I know like the lines of my hand.

"Yes," I finally answer. "I do."

Marcelo gives me another small smile, a secret shared between the two of us. I help him prepare the plane and climb into the passenger side. Marcelo finishes preparing and turns the ignition.

The familiar sensation comes flooding in.

I look at the field in front of us, and when the plane rises, my heart squeezes inside my chest until I feel like it's no bigger than a bean. I hold my breath until the sky is open before us and the trees and mountains are down below.

It's familiar and strange all at once.

Marcelo flies with ease, like I once did.

"Do you ever get scared?" I ask. "That they'll come back?"

He looks at me for a second, then he concentrates on piloting again.

"Sometimes," he says quietly.

I lean out the window a little, looking down at the dozens

of little houses that make up Unity and the lake and the edge of the forest. The Cirrus flies steady and sure.

"You lost your grandfather in the invasion?" he asks then.

"Yes," I reply. "Both him and Abuela."

"I'm sorry."

"And you? Did you have any family?"

"I did," he says. "A daughter. She would be twenty-eight now."

Twenty-eight. The age I'm supposed to be.

"I'm sorry," I tell him. They're the emptiest of words. All this time hasn't changed that.

"Thank you," he says. "This world has taken a lot from all of us."

I look out of the window. "Yeah. It has."

I feel him observing me out of the corner of his eye. This could be an opportunity.

"How far out do you go?" I ask. "With the search parties, I mean."

"Here and there," he replies noncommittally. He grips the wheel of the plane just a little tighter.

"You aren't just searching for survivors, are you?" I finally ask. "This is about the barrier."

Marcelo shifts in his seat, suddenly uncomfortable. He's not the kind of guy who's used to lying, I can see it in his face.

"How do you know about the barrier?" he says.

"We crossed it," I reply. "We came over one minute, and the next, we couldn't go back. No way out."

He nods. "Castor sends a few of us to test it. Try to find a breach. We haven't been successful."

"You know how far it goes?"

"Covers the whole state and Yellowstone Park," he replies. "We've been trying it for years. It doesn't give. If there are other survivors in the state, we haven't found them yet."

"How long has it been like this?"

He shrugs. "Ever since I got here. Came to Montana to look for someone right after the invasion, and I kept searching the area. The spaceships left, and then I was the one who couldn't leave."

Ten years at least.

Ten years since the barrier has been here.

Ten years since we left.

That can't be a coincidence.

"So who knows?" I ask. "About the barrier."

"Only a few of us," Marcelo replies. "Which is why Castor and Heidi were so alarmed. Strangers just don't walk here. We haven't seen new people in a long time."

I let that thought sink in. This doesn't answer my questions about the origins of the barrier. I wonder if the rest of the Earth is like this, but there's something odd about Unity, about the signal coming right from here and then us not being able to leave.

We finish the ride in silence. Marcelo circles over Unity and the base of the Rockies, the dark trees covering their base. Among them, the Arc lies hidden. He turns the plane back around, and in twenty minutes, it's over.

It's almost like I have a piece of home back with me. Marcelo lands, shutting down the motor. I sit a few seconds without wanting to get out of the cabin, because there's something I need to say, but I don't know how to start.

Finally, I take the picture out of my pocket.

"The other day, you told me you knew someone with the same name as me," I tell him. My voice is steady. "And then I found this in my bed."

He looks at it for a long time. His fingers carefully pick it up, and then I know, just by looking. It's not just a picture to him. It's treasure.

"You recognize it?" he asks.

"It's me," I reply.

Slowly, he takes the picture and puts it inside his jacket pocket, folding it close to his heart.

"Who *are* you?" I manage to ask.

Marcelo takes a moment to answer, but when he does, he looks straight at me. His gaze is unwavering but emotional, almost like he's going to cry.

"Clover, I'm..." He falters. "I'm your father."

CHAPTER 20

I'm too stunned to react.

"That isn't possible," I say. "I don't have a father."

I realize how stupid the words sound. I didn't have a father before—when I lived with my grandparents. My mother had left me with them and never looked back, and the only thing that had remained were the pictures that Abuela kept. Nothing else.

Logically, I must have a father. Biologically speaking. Like my mother, though, my father was something I never thought about. They didn't matter. My grandparents were the ones who raised me. They were my real family.

I feel a panic attack coming, my breath hitched, short. Clipped. I know I'm not safe here. I have to get away.

"Clover, I know this is strange—"

"This is worse than strange," I say. "This is impossible. You can't prove it."

Marcelo waits. "You're right. I can't prove it to you."

"Then don't speak of it again," I say, opening the door to the plane. All I want to do is get out of there. To have never asked about the photograph at all.

I try to rationalize the possibilities, to organize them in my mind. How it could be possible. How this could be happening, right here.

"Clover, please," he says. "I just want a chance."

"No," I say and step out of the plane. I need to get away and forget this ever happened. My breaths keep coming out shorter and shorter, anxiety peaking in my veins, unable to stop the whirlwind.

I turn around. Marcelo calls my name, but I ignore him. I ignore the wind carrying the whispers to me until I'm deep into the forest and back to the Arc.

The Arc feels unfamiliar and cold when I step in. I know its motors and its panels and its beds, but they were temporary, as if they knew I was always going to find my place somewhere else.

I don't belong in Unity. It's not my home.

But I don't think I belong here, either.

I sit inside one of the labs where the analysis of the crystals is ready but holds no answers. I try not to cry, and I stand still until my breath returns to normal and I've numbed my mind. My fingers stop trembling, and when I blink, I don't see my nightmares. It's hours later when Flint comes in.

"I didn't know you were here," he says.

"Came to check in on Andy," I lie through my teeth. I hadn't bothered to look at her.

"How is she doing?"

"The same."

Two weeks and nothing had changed for us.

"And you?" I ask. "Do you have any good news?"

"Well, the Arc doesn't recognize the composition. The crystal keeps changing, like it's just some sort of energy and not a solid material," he says. "So that's leading us nowhere. But the good news is I made the Arc run a map of the region we have access to and point out all the crystals."

He takes it out and shows me the line of crystals. I see a pattern, almost like a line through the forest.

"What does it mean?" I ask, frowning.

"I don't know," Flint answers. "It looks like a path."

"But to where?"

Flint shrugs. "The analysis got us nothing."

I squeeze my eyes shut. I feel a headache coming. "Did you tell Violet?"

"I did, but she's acting weird," he replies. "It almost looks like—"

"She doesn't want to talk about Andy," I complete. "I know. Has she been to the Arc?"

Flint shakes his head. "Not that I know of. She's the only one who hasn't been here. Everyone else has been sneaking over when they can."

Of course she hasn't. I don't know why I'm surprised. After we arrived in Unity, I barely saw Violet—and barely saw Brooklyn or Avani, either, since they're all busy with the activities. I've been so busy rerunning problems in my mind that I think I'm forgetting half of them, running the same scans over and over again.

I'm bone tired.

"You okay?" Flint asks. "You sound like you're about to explode."

"I'm exhausted, and I don't even know why," I tell him.

"It's okay, Clover." He pushes his glasses up the bridge of his nose. "Do you want to talk?"

I sigh.

"I found a picture of myself on my pillow last week," I say.

Flint widens his eyes. "How?"

I clear my throat. "There's a man here who says he's my father. I don't believe him. But I think he left the picture for me to find."

He takes a deep breath.

"It's not definitive proof," Flint says carefully, "Obviously, you know that. But maybe you should try and talk to him."

"And say what?" I ask. "Hey, I'm actually half alien and not really at all who you think I am, but it's pretty cool you're my dad."

Flint snorts. "You're only three percent alien."

"Thanks for reminding me constantly about this anomaly," I say, and he laughs. I lean against his shoulder, and he lets me rest my head. It's a kind of comfort I only knew with my grandparents and now with them. The Last Teenagers on Earth. "I don't know if I believe him or not."

"You can't believe him if you don't talk to him."

"Why does your advice always sound elderly?"

He laughs and then he says, his voice soft, "Look, Clover, I know this might sound convenient. Maybe too convenient. It's strange. But I'd give anything to talk to my mum and dad again if I could. Anything at all."

He wraps his arm around my shoulder, and I put my own arm around his waist, holding him tight. We sit there for a couple of seconds in a silence that can never transmit enough that we miss what we lost. And he's right, in a way. I lost Abuelo and Abuela, the people I've loved the most in my entire life. And every time I look at the sky, it reminds me of them, of what I don't have anymore.

Maybe this is the way the world is giving something back to me.

The thing is, I'm so used to losing, I'm not sure I know how to accept when I get something.

"You go to bed," I tell him. "I'll stay here with Andy for the night."

"You sure?" Flint asks, raising one eyebrow.

"Get some rest," I order him.

Flint smiles once more but doesn't leave immediately. I watch him work around the lab for a while, and then I wonder if he doesn't know where he is supposed to be standing, either.

CHAPTER 21

I spend the night in the Arc. When I make it back to Unity, it's almost six in the morning. I don't feel tired. My brain is alert and ready for whatever is coming. Sputnik is waiting for me at the porch of the cabin, and she raises her head, thumping her furry tail in happiness.

I sit down next to her and bury my hands in her coat. She seems to notice my mood and turns her belly up for a scratch.

"Lazy," I tell her, giving her belly rubs.

When I look up again, Castor is by the cabin, watching me.

"You're up early," he says, noticing that I'm already clothed.

I decide to give him a partial truth. "I get a lot of nightmares. Don't sleep that much."

He nods in agreement. "They never go away, do they," he

says, but it's not a question. He looks at Sputnik, and she lets him scratch her. "I still have them, too."

I look up to study him. He doesn't look that old. In his fifties, for sure. His skin is pale but burned from the sun, and his eyes are light brown like honey.

"I'm glad you guys are fitting in," he says to me. "It's important to adjust."

"We're not planning on staying," I say just to contradict him. And because it's true—we never intended to stay. We just need to find a way out.

He sighs and then looks at me.

"I think you know why I'm saying this, Clover." His voice has a hint of sadness in it. "Marcelo talked to me yesterday about you."

I jump, looking up. "What? What did he say?"

Castor frowns. "That you know about the force field."

I hold back my sigh of relief.

"Don't spread the word around," he says. "Only a select few are aware of it. We don't want to spread panic over town."

"People have the right to know."

"Why?" Castor asks. "Do you think it'll help, telling them there's an invisible barrier circling us here, stopping us from going out there? What happens if the food runs out, a plague hits, our crops die? What happens if it starts shrinking?" He raises an eyebrow. "Besides, we don't know its origins. How do I tell people who believe they are safe that something strange is happening again?"

I don't have answers to his questions. I hate that in a way, he's right. A barrier means panic. It means losing control.

"Marcelo said it was ten years," I say.

Castor nods. "We hadn't noticed it in the mountains. Spent three years there. Waited to be sure that the aliens had really left."

He sits down on the porch next to me, looking out at the mountains. I can just imagine them. A solid group, trying to survive when all the others didn't. It was smart. The aliens went through the cities first. Here, far out west and at the base of the Rockies, it was total isolation.

"How was it?" I ask. "Living there."

"It was strange at first," he says. "No technology, no access to anything. We had to break into groups to survive, and we could only afford to go out a few hours. Almost no sunlight."

"I'm sorry."

He shrugs, like it's all in the past.

"We survived," he says. "It's a great deal more than the rest."

"You founded Unity?"

He nods, looking over at me. "People started arriving from all over the state. We tried broadcasting on the radio, making sure people would get the message. We didn't know about the barrier, of course, but everyone who survived inside came to us, and they found a safe home."

I almost smile as he says it. I can tell he likes it here. It's his home. It's what he built. Unity belongs to him as much as he belongs to Unity.

"I wanted to build a life," Castor says, looking out to the mountains. "A beacon. I wanted to find myself home again."

He pets Sputnik's head.

"I've lived the invasion once," he tells me. "I don't want to live it again. None of the people here want the memories from it. Most are still trying to forget."

"But we can't forget."

"I know that," he says. "And *you* know that. It's smart of you. But how do you find a reason to live if any minute, something might swoop down from the skies and end your life again? No one wants to fight anymore."

I stay silent, chewing the inside of my cheek, one hand petting Sputnik absentmindedly.

The problem isn't just the barrier or the crystals or Andy. The problem is at my core. I have always been so sure of where I was standing.

Now, I don't know it anymore.

"I don't tell them about the barrier to keep them safe," Castor says. He turns to me, his brown eyes boring into me. "How did you come through?"

I shake my head. "I don't know. We just went through. And then we couldn't go back. The barrier threw us off."

He nods slowly. "Thanks for telling me the truth."

I only nod in response.

"I'm sorry," Castor finally says. "I know you were hoping to get on your own way. But you can find your place here."

"I'm not sure of that."

He gives me a sad smile. "Things won't ever be back the way they used to be. We do our best. And that's really all we can do."

Castor walks away, and I watch him go, alone again.

CHAPTER 22

"I hate this place," Rayen says during dinner after we've been here three full weeks. I turn to Rayen again, and she shakes her head. "Something feels off. Everyone is always so nice."

"Only you would complain about people being nice," Avani mutters. "There is absolutely nothing wrong."

"Of course there is," Rayen insists. "No one is ever nice all the time unless they want something from you. And these people don't want anything from us."

"You're being paranoid," Brooklyn says, chewing on a chicken leg. "And that's *me* saying it. This place is good. We have food. Real food. We have air, and we have people, and we have everything else."

"Yeah, but we can't leave, and we can't find out anything

about those weird crystals in the earth," Flint says. "Doesn't that bother you?"

Avani and Brooklyn shake their heads.

"Clover said they're harmless," Avani says. "She saw it."

"I saw Castor touch it," I correct her. "That doesn't mean anything."

"Maybe the thing with Andy will just wear off," suggests Brooklyn.

Flint gives her a look, like she should know better. I frown, then look over at Violet. She's eating quietly. I haven't really talked to her since we got here, and even now it seems like we never get to be together as a group except at meal times and right when we're about to fall asleep.

"I agree with Rayen," I finally say.

"Clover, you hate *everyone*," Brooklyn snaps.

"I do not."

Five pair of eyes look back at me.

"Okay, fair," I say, "but we should be trying to find out more about the things keeping us here. Personally, I don't like taking care of chickens."

"You just said Castor knew about the barrier and can't do anything about it," Violet says. "Besides, we've hit a wall. No one could decipher the signal, the barrier is a dead end, and Flint's analysis of the crystals got us nowhere. There is time."

"Meanwhile, your best friend is trapped inside a cell because she's gone full-on space dictator," I hiss at her. "Have you even visited her, Violet?"

Violet has the good grace to blush.

I study her, trying to decipher what she's thinking. She didn't want to come here in the first place. Now she doesn't want to leave.

"You're going with me tonight," I say, and I don't wait for her to argue. "No excuses."

She nods, and instead of falling back into our usual conversation, all I can hear is a tense silence between us, as if we don't know how to fit in together anymore.

I can't help but think that Earth has stolen another thing from me.

Violet and I don't cover ground as quickly as I do on my own.

She follows behind me, and I am always a couple of steps ahead of her as we start climbing the mountain that will lead us to the cave.

We arrive at the cave a couple of hours later, and we climb the ramp, heading directly to Andy's cell. When the glass clears, no longer deep black, Andy has her back against it. Her muffled cries are the only thing I hear in the chamber.

Then I see the rest of the cell—crystals, just like the one we saw in the woods, embedded in every single corner of the room and against the right wall. They sparkle in different colors, and it takes my breath away.

"Were these here the other night?" Violet asks, thick eyebrows shooting up.

"No."

We circle back to the part of the Arc with the lab. The crystal sample is still locked tight inside its container. Andy doesn't have it. So how the hell did she get hold of those in her cell?

The last analysis Flint has run is still available to us in the computer, the chemical formula of the crystal exposed in a hologram. I recognize some parts of the formula in the screen—carbon, oxygen, and silicon—but there are several things in the formula that I actually can't identify. As I look, it starts changing, the formula shifting once more.

"It's changing," Violet says. "How?"

We look over at where the crystal stands in the lab tray, unmoving.

"Flint says it's more like an energy," I tell her, "instead of material. Whatever that means."

Violet only looks at the formula, shaking her head. It's odd. The formula changes, but the crystal doesn't. It's like it contains a dozen different possibilities, all folded within the small piece of rock. When we go back to Andy, she has stopped crying, but her eyes are rimmed with red.

Violet blanches at the sight.

Andy moves directly in front of Violet.

"Why didn't you come see me?" Andy asks. "You were my friend."

"I still am," Violet says quietly.

"Friends don't lie," Andy hisses. "You locked me up here. You left me."

"I didn't leave you," Violet says, regaining control. The tone in her voice is that of command. "It's going to be fine. We're going to figure out how to get you back on track."

"I am on track," Andy says. She looks around at the crystals on the walls. "Can't you see that this is perfect?"

"What are these, Andy?" Violet asks. "You know what they are. How did you bring them here?"

Andy doesn't respond. She turns her eyes to me for the first time. Her gaze sends chills down to my bones.

"You think you can stop it," Andy says, her voice calm. "You can't. It's already started. It's too late now."

"What are we stopping, Andy?"

Andy doesn't answer. She looks at Violet.

Then she begins to cry again. Her tears, instead of water, are blood. Violet's face twists in shock, and Andy wails, clutching her eyes as if she's in pain.

Violet, before I can stop her, puts her hands to the glass.

Andy is fast, too fast for me. She puts her own hand against the glass, and Violet's eyes glaze over, white, their shared connection pure energy. Andy smiles.

"I can see you," Andy says. "I can see your thoughts. I can see why you didn't want to come all the way over here. You belong there. I don't. And you like it."

Violet opens her mouth, but her eyes are still white, her hair starting to rise as if she's possessed.

"I didn't abandon you," Andy says. "But you want to leave me here. Maybe you should go back to where I took you from."

Deep black veins start showing over Violet's face, from her eyes to her ears, going over her arms, growing and stretching over her. Her nose starts bleeding, and on instinct, I pull Violet away from the glass with all my might.

Andy's influence immediately disconnects. Violet drops to the floor and takes a deep breath, the veins disappearing and her eyes returning to the usual icy blue. She looks at Andy with widened eyes, taking gasps of breath as her skin returns to its regular color, her nose still dripping blood.

She could've killed her. The same way Andy brought her back, she could've destroyed Violet. A line that she's willing to cross. Maybe uncross—the rule was still present. Violet's energy was supposed to have dissipated into the universe.

Andy broke the rules.

I turn to her.

"I know you're in there," I say. "I know you can still hear me. We're going to get you out of there. I promise."

"Andy's gone," she spits in my direction. "And there's nothing you can do to stop it."

"Stop what, Andy?" I wait for her answer, but she doesn't shift. Her eyes are a deep black, darker than the void. "What can't we stop? The end?"

Andy laughs.

"The beginning."

CHAPTER 23

Violet doesn't speak to me for days after we return from the Arc.

She doesn't tell anyone else what we've seen. I don't insist she goes back. I take over all duties of going to the spaceship and checking on Andy. The crystal wall doesn't grow anymore, but I never try opening the door. Sometimes, Andy cries in the corner. On other nights, she's shouting and hurling insults, trying to break the glass between us. And sometimes, she's quiet, like she's not really present.

And sometimes, for a few seconds, I feel like she's still in there. The old Andy.

She never stays for long.

I share the details with the others, but Flint is the only one who seems interested in Andy's crystals, and he goes back to examine them with me. He prints the different results of the scans, and he shoves them in his pocket, but he doesn't say anything else. It's how he works—he wants to be sure before he shares his findings.

I feel like my friends are distant. I barely see them anymore during the day, when each of us has taken a different duty inside the colony. Brooklyn and Avani are either at the school or helping out at the infirmary, and I only see them at dinner. Even Rayen I see less and less of, as she's on the perimeter patrol. And of course, I'm left with the farming duties.

I don't mind helping. I mind that somehow, every time I get assigned a task, it feels like Unity is tearing us apart on purpose.

The weather has gotten chillier, the cold wind blowing from the north. It's only when they announce that we'll have a Thanksgiving feast that Thursday that I realize that we're in late November.

I'm happy that we get another celebration, because it means I'll be seeing my friends other than just saying good night before we fall asleep. At the same time, I've never really celebrated Thanksgiving with my grandparents, and I don't plan on starting now. Rayen seems to share the same sentiment, giving me one of her usual looks when someone's about to do something stupid and she has no patience for it.

Thursday evening arrives, and I'm happy that it gets us together. I borrow a coat to stay warm, and we get a fire going. Sputnik is happy, too, and she gets a good turkey leg to chew on from the colony's children. It's hilarious to me that they react to Sputnik the same way a species of aliens worshipped dogs and we almost got ourselves killed for rescuing my idiotic Bernese from them.

The evening sets fast and early, but everyone is celebrating together like they're one real family. I stand at the edge of the feast, not wanting to come closer.

"You know," Rayen says, "you'd think that after ten years, people would stop celebrating stupid holidays. They'd start celebrating surviving the invasion or something. But no, they gotta celebrate taking over other people's lands."

"I'm sorry."

She shakes her head, her mouth in a thin line.

I squeeze her shoulder to tell her it's okay that she's angry at something that seems impossible to change and that I'm here for her, too.

Rayen heads to the fire to grab food. They killed some of the turkeys I'd seen walking around in the fields, and I pick one of the juicy legs from the communal plates. The taste of meat fills me whole, and I chew on it happily, glad there's no more weird space food to eat. Sputnik, even though she has her own, keeps eyeing my plate. I spot the others around the fire, and I really feel the difference between us.

Avani and Brooklyn sit together in a circle with some of the other younger people in the camp. They're all in their late twenties, laughing and sharing stories. They don't sit outside the group—they sit there like they belong. Violet is sitting with some of the elders, and she's playing with the children who are trying to braid her hair, thick blond strands falling out of place as little hands try to tame them.

Outside, it's just me and Rayen, sitting like complete outsiders, knowing there's no way we're going back in there. There's no way we're fitting into that picture.

A stab of pain overwhelms me, but then when they open up the circle of stories again, we're invited to join. I end up with a seat next to Castor, who's once again very cheerful and keen on asking how I've been doing lately. He asks me about the corn and the wheat and whether I liked the change of the weather and if we have to do the reaping before the first snow comes. I know he already knows the answers to all these questions, but I appreciate him trying to include me as if I'm a very important part of the camp.

When everyone is quiet, one of the older women rises, approaching the group.

"Today is a day of celebration," she says. "It's a day for giving thanks, for joining our brothers and sisters and being grateful that we are alive and well today. I know for some of you, this holiday might be painful, but it's also a time to think on our new world.

"We have survived," she continues. "By the grace of God or whatever you choose to believe. We have walked across fire and storms and dust, and yet here we still manage to stand, even when all else seemed impossible. On the day of the invasion, many of us believed we would not survive this. Many of us thought that it was the last time we'd stand together. On this date, we give thanks that we found our inner strength not to bow down to any threat. We give thanks that our brothers and sisters are here with us today, and we mourn those of us who couldn't make it."

My throat closes up. I think of Adam. I think of Noah and everyone from my school. I think of my abuelo and his sky, my abuela and her earth.

I look at Violet, who was supposed to be dead and is still alive, and then I see that she's also looking back at me.

"We owe it to them to be strong," the woman finishes. "We owe it to them to be better, to take care of ourselves better, to fight better. We owe it to them to stand our ground. We give thanks."

"We give thanks," almost all the others repeat.

I give thanks, I think to myself. I give thanks. I make the sign of the cross, just like Abuela taught me, and I'm surprised that I still remember how to pray after all this time.

Then someone else gets up and takes the woman's place.

"I give thanks to my family," a man with dark skin says. "To those who survived with me and those who will survive in the future. A long time ago, my ancestors were brought to this country against their will and fought for their freedom. I give thanks to my ancestors who fought hard and taught me to fight and survive like they did."

He throws a piece of wheat in the fire.

Then another woman rises up, taking his place. "I give

thanks to my family. To those who dared cross the sea for a better life, fleeing horrors and terrors and camps in a place where we were not welcome. I give thanks for their courage and their bravery and for teaching me to be brave as well."

She throws another piece, and each person who rises throws something in the fire, and all of them share their stories and their family's stories. Some of them are simple, and some of them are hard to listen to. But all of them come from different places, different backgrounds, different religions, and right now, there's one thing that managed to unite them all.

The aliens may have taken everything from us.

But somehow, the invasion ended up giving something back.

Even the children take their turn around the fire, and although most don't speak, I can see how solemn they are when they complete the ritual. Finally, Castor slips one strand of wheat in my hand, and I get up, stumbling to the front of the fire.

I look at the others, not knowing what to say. Their words were beautiful and brave. I don't have a gift with words. I understand numbers, and I understand planes. But when I look at the crowd, I find the faces of the people I care the most about—and they are all nodding, encouraging me.

They came here with me. All the way to this planet, our home. They came here and walked the first footsteps with me. We were the last remaining of Earth, but now we're the first.

All seven of us.

"I give thanks," I say, my voice a little raspy. "To my abuela, who taught me to love my family and my friends. To my abuelo, who taught me to love the sky and stand my ground. And to my friends, who accept me the way I am."

I throw my wheat in the fire, and I watch it burn.

CHAPTER 24

People start telling stories a little after the ceremony ends, everyone together and sharing as the wind dies down and the fire keeps us warm. I'm making my way to join Brooklyn and Avani, who I spot on the other side of the fire, when a hand taps my shoulder.

I turn around to see my father staring back at me.

It's strange to think of those words together. *My father.*

"It was nice what you said out there," Marcelo says, his eyes meeting mine. "I was wondering if we could have a chance to talk."

For some reason, I nod.

I don't know why, but this time, I let him step a little closer. We walk together, side by side, toward one of the cabins. I put my hands in the pockets of my wool coat, huddling it closer to me.

"I've never been good with people," he says, and I snort out a laugh.

"Me either," I confess.

He nods. "I never thought I'd see you again," he says. "After the invasion, that was all I used to think about. That I had a daughter somewhere out there, and I didn't know whether she'd survived. That maybe she had been taken from me before I even met her."

I look at him. "I'm here now."

"Yes. But it makes me wonder how long you're staying."

I don't answer, my words dying in my throat. I don't know how to have a conversation with a stranger and even worse a conversation that's supposed to be with my father.

What do people ask their parents? How can it be that someone who's supposed to be so close can stand so far away?

"Why didn't you look for me?"

He meets my eyes, and there's pain in them. He gestures to the stairs of one of the sleeping cabins, and he sits down first. I sit next to him, hugging my knees without looking at him directly.

"I did," he says. "After I found out. I didn't know at first."

I wait for him to continue. I don't want to interrupt.

"I met your mother when I was twenty-two," he says. "She was twenty. She was working at a festival in Florida, and I was doing the rounds with the plane. She told me her father flew for the air force."

I nod, a knot in my throat. My grandparents never talked about my mother if they could help it. She'd left and never come back, and that was fine by them. It was less painful than being reminded constantly that she'd turned her back on them and me.

Listening to Marcelo talk about my mother wakes something up inside me. A hunger for information I never knew I had.

"What was she like?"

He smiles. "She was beautiful. Funny, too. She was gone before I realized I'd fallen in love with her." He is quiet for a second before continuing. "Some ten years later, I met her again, another place, another time. And then she told me she had a daughter after we'd met." He looks at me awkwardly. "I looked up the address, tried to contact your grandparents," he says. "And then I gave up trying to reach them and flew to Montana to try and see you. But you were away with your abuelo that weekend."

He nods again, his memory distant, his voice quiet. "I talked to Miriam. I tried to convince her that I wanted to see my daughter. I think she thought I was going to try and take you away."

I hug my legs even tighter. Abuela would have acted protective, of course. And she could be mean-spirited when she wanted to be. But she'd never, ever let someone else take me away. She'd fight tooth and nail for me, for what I wanted, for what I could be.

"She showed me your pictures," he says finally. "Told me to keep some. She told me you liked math and engineering and that you wanted to go to Mars."

My throat tightens even more, and I fight a tear that's threatening to fall down my cheek.

"She said you were the most precious little girl in the entire universe, and I believed her."

This time, the tear falls. I wipe it quickly, not wanting it to turn into full-out crying and the headache that was sure to follow.

Marcelo takes out his wallet. He takes out pictures and shows me. The first is the one I'd already seen, but the others are new. Pictures of four-year-old me sitting on a fighter jet with my abuelo. A Mars diorama I had to do for school, me smiling proudly behind it. There's one of me in my soccer uniform, and Noah is in it, too. And lastly, there's a picture of me and both my grandparents from the same day in Disneyland.

"I have that one, too," I say quietly and take it out of my own wallet.

The photos look almost exactly the same. In one, I'm looking at the camera. In the other, I'm looking at my grandparents, mouth open like I'm about to say something.

"I left, Clover," Marcelo says. "I know it wasn't the right choice or a good one. But your abuela assured me you were in safe hands. That you were being taken care of, and that no matter what happened, they weren't giving you up. That you had everything you could wish for. And I didn't want to intrude on your life."

He stares back at the fire, still far away, the orange flames that rise into the air reflecting back in his dark-brown eyes.

"I still regret that choice," he says. "When the aliens arrived, that's all I could think—that I wanted to find you. That maybe you'd survived. I kept on hoping for it. I came all the way, crossed the whole country, just to get here. I didn't care if the aliens found me. I wanted to see you."

"You got trapped here because of me?"

He nods. "I thought you'd eventually find your way back home."

I did. He looks at me, hopeful, but I can't encourage any of that. He may be my father, but I don't know who he is.

I nod and then get up. "Thank you for telling me."

"I want to be here for you, Clover. You're my daughter. Maybe I don't deserve to get to know you after all this time, but no matter what, I'll be here."

I nod again, my throat bobbing, but I don't have anything else to add. I don't have anything I can say to him that won't sound at least a little fake. *I'm sorry* are not the words I'm looking for, and at the end of the world, I'm not sure I can begin a part of a new life. I'm not sure I have the strength for it.

I had a family before. I knew who they were. The aliens took that from me, but they gave me something new—they gave me my friends. They were my family now.

"Your secret is safe with me," he says finally. "I won't tell anyone."

I look up sharply.

He smiles, tight-lipped. "It's been ten years since the invasion," he says. "I know you're supposed to be older."

I don't say anything. I only stare back at him. Fear rises in my throat and to the edges of my fingers, and suddenly, I'm colder even though the breeze has died down.

He gets up. "I won't tell," he says quietly. "But if you need help, I'll always be here. You probably have been through a lot more than you're saying. I'll be here if you need me."

He doesn't leave. So I do, walking fast enough back to the fire that I don't hear my heart hammering inside my chest.

CHAPTER 25

When I get back, I find that my friends have formed our usual circle. I arrive, and everyone looks up. Then Brooklyn sees my face.

"Clover, are you all right?"

I shake my head just slightly. "Someone knows."

"Someone knows what?" Avani says, frowning.

"Marcelo knows we're lying about how we got here." I get the words out as quickly as I can. "He knows we're supposed to be ten years older."

"Who is Marcelo?" Violet asks.

"Clover's father," Flint answers for me.

They all stare at me, eyes moving between Flint and me. Even Sputnik looks up, blinking with her huge black eyes.

"What do you mean, Clover's father?" Brooklyn says. "Am I hearing this right?"

"I know, it sounds right out of a telenovela," I say, "but it's true. He approached me, and then he showed me the pictures."

Brooklyn and Avani exchange a look, and Violet looks at her hands in her lap.

"He says he won't tell," I say finally. "But he knows, so it's bad. Especially because we don't have an escape plan. And none of us seem keen on finding out what's going on with the crystals."

I give them a pointed look.

"We're trying," Violet says. "I've been spending a lot of time with Castor, Heidi, and the others. They know as much about the barrier as we do."

"We know it's there," Rayen says. "It's enough. We can't leave until we find out what's happening. And isn't it strange? That we conveniently can't fucking leave this place?"

"It's not terrible," Brooklyn says. "It's a good place. They treat us fine."

"And what use is it?" Flint asks. "We can't leave."

"Why would you want to leave?" Avani says so harshly that it makes him flinch.

"Because of Andy?" Flint suggests. "Or have you forgotten about your locked-up friend who's lost her mind over a crystal?"

Avani flushes red. "I haven't forgotten."

"We don't need to fight," I say, but everyone ignores me.

"It sure looks like you did," Rayen snaps. "None of you even go back to the Arc. It's like you're ignoring what's happening outside because you love it here so much."

"And why shouldn't we love it?" Brooklyn snaps, turning to Rayen. "We're all welcome here. We have everything we need. You guys just want to leave because you can't be normal enough to fit in."

Rayen stops, mouth hanging open. The silence is heavy.

"You're not even trying," Avani says. "Rayen is constantly telling people off. Flint only complains. Can't you guys be normal, just for once?"

She storms off, and Brooklyn follows.

Flint looks shaken. He takes out his glasses to clean them, out of habit. I bite my own cheek until it draws blood, the metallic taste filling my mouth with its bitterness.

I look at Violet. Violet stares back at me.

"Are you going to say anything?" I ask.

"I don't think I need to," she says quietly, getting up. "All you need to do is fit in. They're offering us a good place. They're offering us home. And you can't bring yourself to embrace that."

"You didn't even want to come here," Flint says.

"It's like you can't bear it," Violet snaps. "I spent all that time with you, and I didn't belong up there. But this is my place. And all you want is to take it away from me."

She shakes her head, and then she, too, leaves. Flint gives me a tight-lipped smile, getting up and brushing the dust away, and then he walks back to the cabin.

The only ones left are me and Rayen, staring at the dying

embers of the fire. We start walking, side by side. Sputnik pads the ground, following us in her circles. I'm not exactly opposed to storming off on my own, but I'm glad Rayen's here. I'm glad I'm not the only one going through this madness.

We find our path toward the edge of the river to the chasm that opens up to the view. There's a cliff where people can jump into the river, but it's cold now in the winter.

I stare down, thinking of a day when staring down from a cliff would make my mind wander to jumping and dying. I sit, my legs hanging. Rayen sits by my side, the wolf on her arm staring at me.

"This is not home," she says finally, looking down at the water below. "This river, it isn't mine. We had a different river. A different house, a different tribe. These lands are not mine. I know the others don't get it. But it's different for me. This was someone else's place, and I can't forget what happened."

I nod, a lump in my throat.

"I don't think we need to fight," I say. "It's not a bad place."

"Don't tell me you're on their side."

And it's strange, because I wouldn't call it sides. I don't want to believe that we're fighting enough that we're sitting in opposite halves.

Before, I'd be the first to have an opinion. To pick a side. Now, all I want is for us to be united. I can't choose.

I've lost so much to the end of the world. I can't bear to lose my friends, too.

"I didn't forget why we came here," I finally say. "I didn't forget about the distress signal."

"I think they forgot," she replies. "They're right. It's not a bad place. It's just not—"

"Where we're supposed to be."

She agrees, nodding her head slightly. She undoes the bun she's been keeping her hair in the last few days and starts combing it with her fingers. Her hair is so long now. She hasn't cut it since we first left, and it easily falls to her waist, dark brown and silky smooth.

"I don't know where I am supposed to be," I say.

"You've been wondering about your dad."

I nod.

She shoves my shoulder. "Hey, it's not bad. I think pretty much all of us would give anything to be able to see our families again."

"He's not my family."

Rayen gives me a pointed look. "Fine. He's just a stranger who also happens to have a blood tie with you."

I sigh. "He told me he didn't know my mother was pregnant. Which is probably true. From what my grandparents said, she wasn't big on sharing. She wasn't big on sticking around, either."

Rayen gives me a smile in sympathy. She doesn't need to say much. As she braids her hair distractedly, I know she's listening to me. That's all I need.

"I don't even know how to talk to him," I say. "I actually don't know how to talk to other humans."

"Interspecies communications can be very hard."

I glare at her but can't help cracking a smile.

Rayen grins. "I mean, I'm sure everyone who encounters their parents later in life has the same problem. They just haven't lived with you. They don't have anything in common with you. They don't know your tastes, what you're allergic to. The people who raise you know you from the beginning. It's easier for them. Doesn't mean the other people aren't trying."

I nod, letting the words sink in.

That day on the plane, my father tried to connect with me, to offer a bond through the airplane, but I denied him. I wonder if it would feel just like old times, as if I were back in the plane with my abuelo, with the crops beneath us and the wheel steady in my hands. Belonging to the sky once more, for a single second, and not being afraid.

I'd said no. I'm not ready for that.

"I talked to him, and it was strange. It was good. But I feel…"

I can't put it into words exactly. It was as Rayen had said before—I don't want to forget what's in the past. I don't want to replace my home with this place as the others seem desperate to do.

I don't want to shove everything I've been through away just to get that sense of belonging again.

"What if I'm betraying them?" I ask her, turning once more to look at her. Rayen's done with her braid, tying it with her own hair at the end. "What if I'm just doing the same thing the others are doing?"

"You're not," Rayen says simply. "You're not betraying your grandparents just because you want to spend time with your father. I'm not betraying my family because I love you guys."

There's a silence before I answer. I lost my grandparents, and then I found another family. And in a way, I'm desperate to regain a connection from a time before, and my father is a link to that. A link I thought I'd lost.

"I know. I just wish…" My voice dies down, and I can't stop myself from making another stupid wish that won't come true. "I wish they were here to see this, too."

"Yeah," Rayen says. Then she continues, which surprises me. She almost never talks about her family. "My mom was a nervous baker. I'd come home sometimes, and I'd know something was up in the Tribe Council or in politics because the house was filled with that chocolate smell. She was terrible at everything else, though, couldn't cook anything for her life. My dad was a lawyer. He ate all her chocolate cookies so they wouldn't go stale, even though he told me once he hated chocolate."

"Who hates chocolate?"

"Right?" Rayen smiles. "And my little brother was the most annoying person on the whole of Earth. I don't really believe in anything perfect, but you know…my family was."

"So was mine."

"We're lucky girls."

Rayen slips her hand into mine, squeezing it. She's right.

I can open myself a little more to this experience. I don't have to be shut inside all the time. I don't have to replace one thing with the other.

But I don't have to forget.

I never, ever have to forget.

CHAPTER 26

The next day, I go to Heidi's office of my own free will.

She's sorting through papers as I approach her desk.

"I thought you didn't use paper anymore," I say. "Not like other people are actually producing it."

She looks up and smiles. "It's easier to keep track of things that way. How much we produce with the crops, how much meat we're hunting, what other supplies we need. Especially now that winter is turning the corner and we need to know our provisions. Do you want to help me sort this?"

I think of Brooklyn and the others and how they talked about fitting in and trusting them. Being normal for once in my life. Trying hard.

I'm going to try harder.

I sit down in front of her, picking up papers and sorting them into different files.

"What did you want to see me about?" Heidi asks. "Did you want to continue with your sessions?"

Slowly, I nod, but I don't look up from the paper.

"I saw you talking to Marcelo the other day," she continues. "About the planes."

"My abuelo used to be in the air force," I offer but don't add anything else. Even though I like Heidi, I can't exactly trust her. "It'd been a long time since I was up there."

"Do you like flying?"

I nod, and Heidi waits for me to continue.

"There's this one thing my abuelo used to say," I tell her. "Other people have the Earth. My family used to have the sky."

"Until they came."

I nod again. "It was never the same. Knowing what's up there."

I haven't stopped belonging to the sky. Reclaiming things is hard, and it became harder after Abuelo was gone. He was the one who used to tell me my place was up there. It was easy to believe him. I didn't have many friends, and I didn't particularly like interacting with the Earth overall. But I have always loved going up there and losing myself in the eternal blue.

"Do you still have nightmares?" she asks.

I nod once more. "Not as many as before. It's better now anyway."

She looks up to meet my eyes. I force myself to look at her.

"What's better, Clover?"

"The exhaustion. I used to be exhausted every day. And after my family died, I didn't think I deserved to be here. Sometimes, I still think I don't."

Heidi reaches out to squeeze my hand.

"It's something hard to experience," she says. "Not everyone who survived the invasion was left intact. Depression, PTSD, and suicide attempts are more common than you'd believe. You are not alone."

I gulp down, hard.

I don't know how to say this. It was easy telling Violet. It's something else telling a stranger.

I want to get better. I want to be able to let go of the past.

"I thought a lot about killing myself last year."

She doesn't move again to the papers. And I think, what the hell, at least she's a qualified professional. Someone who can understand what's going on and who can help me.

"I kept putting a gun to my head," I say, my voice as neutral as I can, "and thinking, I'll do it this time. And it would happen, over and over again, sometimes when I woke up from nightmares, sometimes when I was just by myself. I thought it'd be easier if I was just done."

She nods, encouraging me to go on.

I don't really know what else to say. There are only my friends who knew what I was going through, the way I'd have to wake up and convince myself that it was fine, that I could do this. It takes convincing.

Every day. Every single day.

"It's better now," I say, clearing my throat. "I don't think about it too much. But sometimes I still wake up screaming and with a lot of pain in my chest like I can't breathe, and there's this one moment where I wonder if it's going to be okay or if it's just better to take the easy way out."

She looks at me then. I can't look back and face her. I start shuffling the papers in the piles.

"Dying is never a solution, Clover," she says. "Never. It's not a way out in any form, and I know you were desperate at the time. But it's a symptom, and you're very brave to have survived this."

"Thank you." My voice is small and quiet.

I thought I was being brave for saving the world. For surviving the aliens, for going out into space. For saving my planet.

No one ever said I was brave to keep living.

I go back to the papers, clearing my throat again, but I'm not sure I'm over talking about all the things from my past. It's like opening up a bottle—I want to keep pouring it out until I'm empty and done with the confusion and feelings and anything else I've been holding inside for so long.

"I saw a lot of people die that day," I tell her. "Including my best friend. The aliens chased us, and he fell down. He called my name. He wanted me to help him, but I couldn't move. I never even reached for him. I just let him die."

Heidi looks at me, her brown eyes filled with understanding.

"I keep replaying it in my mind from time to time, just

rewinding it again and again. I know I couldn't save him. Physically couldn't save him, and I saved myself because I got lucky. But I still wonder."

"It's all right to wonder," she says. "We all wonder. I lost a husband and a daughter on the day of the invasion. I saved a sister and a son. We have to live with the choices we make. What's in the past can never be changed. We don't have the power of rewriting things, no matter how much we wish we could."

Andy had that power.

Andy used it.

"How was it?" I ask finally. "Losing your family."

She tightens her lips, then she looks at me. "It never gets any easier. I loved them very much, and I couldn't imagine my life without them. But I still lived and made my way here. I think of them all the time. But in the end, I'm the one who's here. You have to focus on that, too, Clover. You managed to survive. And you need to figure out what kind of life you want to live."

I nod again.

"That's why relationships can be extremely important," she says. "They ground you in place, be it family, friends, or a significant other. They help you get through the tough stuff and help you shape your life in what you want to be next."

"I don't do the whole romance thing."

Heidi raises an eyebrow, looks at me. "Is that something you've chosen or just something you've learned about yourself?"

"The second one. I think. I went out with a friend for a while," I say, trying to shape my relationship with Noah in a few sentences. I think of the way he made me laugh because he was my best friend. I think of the way he was obnoxious when he was nervous and needy when he was drunk. Of our trips to the lake, of going fishing even though I hated it, of us going to our first prom together. Of the romantic feelings I never had for him, could never reciprocate because I don't think I'm wired that way. I loved Noah as my best friend, but I didn't love him as anything else.

"And then?" Heidi asks.

"I liked him a lot," I say, "always as a friend. But I never had that thing where your heart beats too fast and your legs go shaky."

She laughs. "Love can look like that. Romantic love. But love takes many forms, and it doesn't have to be romantic. If you're not sure whether you loved him or not, in your own way, just think about your memories and whether you miss him."

I miss having a best friend. I miss having Noah.

I also miss Adam. If Adam were alive, maybe I could have understood myself better. Maybe he would have helped me grow past that guilt.

Love takes many forms.

And I don't have to keep feeling guilty for something I might never feel. Something I don't *have* to feel. No one can demand that of me.

"I do," I finally answer Heidi. "I miss him a lot."

Heidi nods, but I still feel like I didn't get everything out.

"Marcelo says he's my father," I blurt out.

Heidi looks up with a frown. "What?"

"He showed me pictures," I tell her. "It feels like too much of a coincidence, but I think I believe him."

"Clover, that's fantastic," she says, reaching out over the table and squeezing my hand. "This is really great. Can you imagine what that's like? It's the world bringing you together."

"I don't know," I say. "I'm not sure how to act around him."

"Are you scared?"

I take my time to answer. "I think I am. What if it changes things? I don't know if I should give him a chance."

"And why shouldn't you?"

"Because it's different. He wasn't there for me. My grand-parents were."

"Clover, you can't go back to the way things used to be," she says. "You must realize that. Every day, things are going to change. And you're going to be scared, because this is a new world. We're facing this together. But you must allow yourself to belong here, in the present. You don't belong in the past."

I look up to meet her eyes. I don't know if that's what I'm scared of. That things will never go back to the way they used to be, which is what is stopping me from moving forward. From just accepting this new world and trying to forge my own path.

I don't know what it takes to forge a new life.

"I don't know what to do."

Heidi smiles at me kindly. "No one can tell you the best

path to belonging or to knowing what will happen from here. If they do, they are lying. You need to come to terms with what happened in the past. You can't dwell on it forever, because the past stays there, and it'll only drag you back. You need to move forward. It's not just about surviving anymore. It's about understanding and being able to heal."

Tears well in my eyes, but I fight them back. I don't know my path to healing or what I'm going to need to do.

"I'll try," I say.

And it's the best I can do.

I keep trying.

CHAPTER 27

That night, I dream of Andy.

At first, it's the Andy she was before the invasion—the Andy I knew who had glasses that were a little too big for her face and who hid herself behind sarcastic comments and computer screens. The Andy who was scared and didn't know how to fight. But in an instant, she changes. Her hair shifts, from the mousy brown to the deep black of the void, her skin flowering into pink and orange, and the dark matter flowing in her veins.

This Andy has no light in her eyes.

"Andy?" I ask, just to be certain.

She doesn't answer. Everything she touches changes beneath her fingers. The earth and plants are slowly replaced by the same crystals I saw in her cell, transforming the ground all around her until there's no sign of the earth anymore. When I walk forward, Andy turns her head to me.

She points her finger, and my heart slams in my chest. There's no mercy and no hesitation, and then I'm dissolving in a second as if I were hit by the Hostemns' guns, and there's nothing but particles in the atmosphere.

I take my last breath to gasp for Andy, to ask her to stop, but when I meet her eyes, I don't recognize anything in them—there's nothing left of Andy there.

Nothing human.

I wake up in a cold sweat. Sputnik shifts on the bed, and she looks up and yawns. I pat her distractedly, and she licks my fingers. I shove the covers off the bed. The others are still asleep, but the sun is already rising. I change clothes quickly and head outside, Sputnik at my heels, her paws padding heavily on the ground. I head straight for the Arc.

When I get there, I check Andy first. She's fast asleep inside her cell. The crystals haven't changed. I don't remember the last time I've seen her asleep or even questioned if she really needed to sleep. It almost seems peaceful, her dark hair falling in waves over the bed, her eyes closed. She almost looks normal, but I can feel the power bubbling beneath the thin layer of skin.

I don't want to admit that I'm afraid.

I go to the lab and find someone is already there.

"Flint, what are you doing here?"

Flint immediately sits up, blinking away his sleep. He pushes his glasses up and passes a hand over his eyes.

"I'm just—" He yawns. "Couldn't sleep."

"Looks like you're sleeping just fine on the bench."

Flint passes his hands through his tight curls, which are longer, falling almost to his chin. He slides his glasses back in place. Sputnik shoves him with her nose, then is off to the rest of the ship, snout to the floor.

I stop next to him.

"What's going on?" I ask.

"I don't like sleeping there," he says. "After the..."

He doesn't finish his sentence. I'm not the only one who's hesitant about wording. I don't want to call it a fight—but what else would it be? We used to have minor fights about stupid things. This doesn't feel stupid.

"Yeah," I agree, just so I don't leave him hanging. "It's easier sleeping on the Arc."

Flint gives me a small smile. "It shouldn't be, though, right? A part of me wants to agree with the others."

"But you don't."

"I don't know," Flint says. "I thought we'd come here after the signal, and now everyone just wants to act like it's all a big coincidence and there's nothing wrong."

I give him a tight-lipped smile.

"So what do you think? You think we ought to stay?" he asks.

"I don't know." I answer him like I answered Rayen the other night. I used to be certain about a lot of things. I used to be sure. Even when the world ended, I knew I had to find a way to survive all this. And I did.

We're past surviving now. This is not living life on the edge anymore.

"We could always go back to space," I say. "Back to the alien dating scene."

"Oh, come on, that was *one* time and because Brooklyn convinced me," Flint complains loudly, shuddering. "I'm not sure we should ever listen to Brooklyn."

"I'm convinced we shouldn't."

"He was nice, but he had tentacles. *Tentacles*. And I was so sure I could just date aliens because of Wookiees. Should've stuck to my ace senses."

Flint starts organizing the desk, and I see the crystal sitting on the table, inside its container.

"So what are you working on?" I change the subject. "Did you get something out of the crystal?"

Flint's eyes spark. It's like I'm giving him purpose, and he's happy to talk about an answer he knows for sure. Something he really understands.

"You might have noticed Andy is quiet today," he tells me. "I sedated her last night. To get a sample of the crystals she's been growing inside the cell."

"You what?!" I exclaim. "Flint, that's dangerous."

"Oh, yes, you're the only one allowed to do dangerous things."

"Screw you."

He gives me a flippant smile. "I got the sample. And here's where it gets tricky—it's not the same crystal."

"What do you mean?" I ask curiously.

"Computer, pull up the analysis," Flint says out loud, and the computer obeys. The screen shows two different compounds.

I recognize them as something organic, but indeed, Flint's right. They've got different elements, and their particles are arranged differently. And the compound keeps changing.

"What's going on?"

"It changes its structure," Flint says with fascination. "It's not from Earth, of course. I'm just not sure where it's from."

"What do you mean?"

"The computer can't analyze it," Flint says. "Literally. I ask for the elements, and it doesn't give me any. Says I can't have access."

I glare in the general direction of the computer and am tempted to call Sputnik back so she can threaten it again. Sputnik and the computer share a mutual dislike, and it's been more than once they've made that dislike known.

"Here is where it gets tricky," Flint says, pointing it out on the screen. "The crystals aren't just, you know, crystals. They're energy, solidified."

"You said that before, but I don't get it."

"That's the easiest way I can describe it," he admits. "I don't know the compound, but the way it works, it keeps changing, like it's holding possibilities within it. Infinite universes. That creation has to come from somewhere, and at the core of it, it's just energy."

"What does it mean?"

Flint shrugs. "I wish I knew. The thing is, it doesn't do anything."

I look at the crystal, at all that energy held inside a small piece of rock. I'm reminded of the talk I had with Andy before flying here—about the rule of Universals for not changing anything. That energy dissipates.

Where is this energy dissipating to?

"But if it does something," I say, "what can it do?"

Flint shrugs again. "I guess it depends on who uses it."

I look at the computer and Andy still sleeping inside her cell. Waiting.

I pat his back. "All right. I'll tell the others. We'll figure out something."

Flint smiles at me, but I can see in his eyes that he doesn't exactly believe me.

CHAPTER 28

When I get back to Unity, most people are busy with the harvest. With winter already knocking at the door, everyone is collecting food and making sure it's stored properly. With the farming stopped, there's nothing much that I can do except wait around all day till the others come back.

We meet around dinner, the place full as always, people sitting down at different tables. When Brooklyn passes with her plate, I gesture for her to come over to our table in the corner, and she nods. I'm nervous, thinking the others won't show up, chewing the inside of my cheek. I shouldn't be as nervous as I am.

I eat my dinner in silence and fast, Rayen and Flint doing the same. When Brooklyn, Avani, and Violet finally honor us with their presence, my plate is empty.

They sit down, and the air immediately tenses.

"Flint found something," I say.

Violet raises an eyebrow. "I thought we were going to start with some apologies."

Rayen sighs. "Really? Maybe you should be the one to start."

I put my hand over her wrist, and Rayen glares at me.

"We were all excited that day," Flint says. "Maybe we shouldn't go deep into this."

"Okay, so those of you who have been to the Arc know that Andy recently started producing the same crystals we saw in the forest," I start. "Inside the ship. Flint analyzed them, and they're similar but not exactly the same."

"Okay, and?" Avani asks, raising an eyebrow.

Flint sums up what he managed to gather about the crystal, making sure he goes through everything.

"So, what, we should be worried?" Brooklyn asks, chewing on her food. "Is this crystal going to transform us into some weird aliens? I thought we already were."

I glance at Violet, but she doesn't look at me.

"So what are you saying?" she finally asks.

"We're saying maybe we should get back on track in investigating and stop with the whole playing happy family thing," Rayen snaps at them. "It means I've been hunting and patrolling and testing the barrier ever since we got here, every day, and none of you bothered to show up even when we asked for help. It means Flint has been working his ass off on all these analyses, and you haven't bothered to look. This whole thing is a trap, and you're all falling for it."

"Just because your skills aren't valued here that doesn't mean it's a trap," Avani replies in a very even voice. "This place is good. It's a future. What do you want us to do, Rayen? What are you suggesting? That we just hack down every single cabin with a machete until we find the answers you want?"

Rayen's cheeks burn a dark shade of red, and her hands ball into fists on the table.

"None of this," I interrupt before this gets any worse. "This is not what any of us want. But Rayen is right, too. We were called here, and we found a barrier that doesn't let us leave, and Andy has been completely transformed by these crystals. They could be a threat. We just need to put more effort into figuring out what happened. If we can decode the distress signal, we can have a hint of what's happening, and maybe we all should help Rayen with the barrier."

"Clover, we've investigated," Brooklyn complains. "We've asked the questions, and it didn't get us anywhere. Flint analyzed the crystals over and over and came up empty."

"Fine," I reply. "I get that, but we can't just give up. Even if Unity doesn't have a secret agenda, I want to know everything. Can we work together on that?"

They all grumble as if an answer is too much. I'm not asking for a lot.

I can't help but think that if Adam were here, none of this would have happened. He would have stopped this nonsense somehow. I miss him so much, I can almost see his laughing eyes, a faint smile in the dark directed at me. Adam wouldn't have let any of this happen. He'd have found a way for us all to stay together.

But Adam isn't here anymore.

It's up to me to figure something out.

"Clover should be less right all the time," Brooklyn complains. "Okay, we will help Rayen with the barrier and Flint with looking at the crystals again or whatever. But that's it. I don't want anyone else throwing it in our faces that we want to stay here."

"I don't get it," Flint says. "This is not your family. This isn't your home."

"But it can be," Avani says quietly.

"How *can* it be?" Flint asks. "They don't even know the truth, Avani. They don't know who we are."

"They don't need to know," Brooklyn replies. "They don't care about the past. They care about the future."

"What future?" Rayen asks, her voice rising a little too high. "The world ended. If there was ever a plan, it's gone now."

"They have a plan *here*," Avani says firmly. "I'm sorry you can't see it. I'm sorry that you just can't look beyond your own concerns to see that they're building something good."

"I can't believe we're having this discussion," Violet says, slamming her hand on the table.

I can see it all around them, what all of us have been thinking. We used to be the Last Teenagers on Earth. We used to be a team.

"I know how you feel about staying here," I say. "I'm not forcing any of you to choose. Once this is over, you can do whatever you want. Stay for all I care." I pretend I don't care, but I think everyone at the table knows it's not true. "But we need to figure this out. We need to understand what these crystals are, and we have to make sure Andy is back to normal. Can all of us agree on that one?"

Slowly, everyone around the table nods.

"Fine," Brooklyn says, and it's another piece that's broken.

It's not just that I don't think their hearts are in it. Flint and Rayen think that the others are forgetting. I don't. I think they know perfectly well what they're leaving behind and what they're willing to do.

I'm not sure we'll be okay after this is over.

I'm not sure we'll ever be whole again.

CHAPTER 29

Things change, at least a little.

Early December arrives, and there's a tension between all of us, although we are working together. Avani looked at the crystals with Flint, but she can't crack their code, either. Violet runs along the barrier with Rayen to test it, trying to pierce it with different materials we have on the Arc, analyzing it so we can figure out how to break it. Brooklyn visits Andy with me, trying to monitor how she's doing, although we can't help much. We don't know what's wrong with her.

It's a routine of sorts, but it's weird because it doesn't make us seem like friends. It makes us colleagues only, and any talking besides what we have to do is forced. Rayen feels betrayed that I won't stand with her, and the others think that Rayen and Flint are both trying to pick a fight they can't win.

I check on Andy at least three times a week. Her crystals are bright, taking over the cell walls, reflecting her in them. She doesn't bother talking to me no matter how much I press her for answers. She seems disinterested.

I make my way back with only Sputnik for company. I look at the trees and the water, listen to the buzz of the insects and the hum of the animals, everything I took for granted my whole life and that I missed in space. These are the things that remind me of what I had before. These were the things that made Earth home and not the Arc.

I don't go to bed. I stand in the cold, looking at the stars. Before I realize what I'm doing, I've already climbed halfway to the roof. The roof is strong and doesn't creak when I climb up. I sit down on top of it, forgetting all the things below me. It's cold, the breeze blowing away the smell of the oncoming rain. But for now, the sky is clear above me, dark, with the stars blinking.

It's the exact color it's supposed to be.

"What are you doing out here?" a male voice asks, and I turn around to see Marcelo climbing up the same ledge I just did.

"Just looking," I reply.

He only stares, not daring to approach. "Can I sit down?"

After a few seconds, I nod.

He sits on my left, his legs dangling over the roof. It's high enough to break something if we fall, but the view under the moonlight pays off. To the east, the mountain rises, the river and all the cabins under a silvery light.

"Looking at the stars?" he asks me.

"I like coming up here," I tell him, remembering Rayen's words. He's trying.

I can't keep losing people just because I've limited my whole world to what I had. Letting Marcelo in doesn't mean I forget my grandparents. Letting him in doesn't mean I forget my friends.

It's not losing anything. It's gaining something I thought I never had.

"My abuelo taught me to watch the sky," I continue, trying to make my voice stronger than I feel. "He said I could always know what it was going to look like the next morning. If it was going to be a good morning for flying or not."

Marcelo nods by my side. "That's right," he says. "I saw the way you looked up. Do you miss flying?"

I don't know if I can miss flying. I did once. But it's like missing breathing—it's so deep a part of me that it's not something I can just detach. It's something that I am.

"I miss the way it used to be simple," I say instead. "Where it was just me and the sky, and that was all."

Marcelo follows my gaze and looks up, too. I study his features—his hair black and full of curls, his skin just a tad lighter than my own, clear of freckles. His unshaven beard is full of little flaws, and there are constant wrinkles around his eyes from where he smiles.

"I miss it, too," he finally says. "But it's never going to be the same again." He looks over at me. "I'm sorry, Clover," he says. "I'm sorry it was all this way. It didn't have to be."

I'm sorry, too.

I'm sorry that he took so long to find me. I'm sorry that he didn't stay that day. I'm sorry the aliens invaded and tore everything apart. I'm sorry that the people I love are dead and I'll never be the same because of it. I'm sorry that I'm still learning to move through these waters and that I'm never sure how to communicate.

"I am, too," I finally manage, my voice choking a little. "I wish it could have been another way."

"There's still time," he says. "Maybe not right now. I know you still need space. But I'll be here when you want to talk."

There isn't so much space for later, for some place after. This is what I'm going to get right now. As Heidi said, I can't move on if I'm always stuck in the past.

"I didn't see my grandparents die in the invasion," I tell him, because I don't know where else to begin. My grandparents, my house, those are my roots. Those are my beginnings, and he needs to understand where I come from. He needs to understand who I was before and who I am now. "I never looked for my mother. They never talked about her. I didn't care."

He waits, wraps an arm around me. I don't push him away.

"In the last ten years, I looked for you everywhere," he says. "I drove all the way to your grandparents' farm, over the state of Montana and here. I kept hoping that by some miracle, I'd be able to find you. Just to have one moment where I'd be able to look at your face and know that you were all right. That you were alive."

Each of us going in a different direction. Each of us trying to make up for something in the past.

"I'm glad that I found you," he says. "I know asking for forgiveness won't ever be enough, because I made my choices back then, and regret doesn't erase things. But know that I'll be here, Clover. I'll always be here."

I realize I'm crying when I'm forced to wipe the tears away.

It's time to forgive. Life can't be just about surviving. After Earth was gone, I found one reason to keep myself alive. I was going to fight back. And then it was always about surviving.

Surviving is not living. It's time I get to do something else. It's time that I get to heal myself.

After a while, my tears stop.

He doesn't say anything. I don't say anything.

In the silence between us, I realize it's not an ending.

It's a beginning.

CHAPTER 30

The next morning, the harvest is finally done, and the rest of the supplies are shut inside the barn, ready for winter. It's an especially cold morning as I stand in the group in the farming field, and both Heidi and Castor are just outside, checking the last of the list. It's been almost two months since we arrived.

Two months and nothing has changed.

When Flint and I make our way to the Arc that night, I hear a set of footsteps behind me in the woods.

I turn around and see Rayen climbing the mountain after us, her hair uncombed, wearing a coat over the set of flannel pajamas.

"Where are you guys going?" Rayen asks. "No one is on duty tonight."

"Just checking things again," Flint says. "I want to keep an eye on the crystal growth."

She nods and follows along as if it was all part of the plan. We go as fast as we can, not stopping until we get to the cave. The path behind us is silent; the animals have started to hibernate. Which is kind of a pity, as it'd be quite a sight to see Rayen fight a bear in pajamas. I'm sure the bear would come out worse for wear.

The Arc lights up when we arrive. I'm the first to take a step in the direction of Andy's cell. Everything looks like before. Tonight, Andy is sitting on her cot, moody, and the crystals glow transparent, throwing a pink light all over the cell. It's now that I notice the difference in the colors, too. The ones outside are all green and dark purple, and Andy's are light, almost pastel.

"Hey, Andy," I say quietly.

She looks up. Her dark hair looks disheveled, and there are circles under her eyes.

"Came to see how your local monster is doing?" she asks. "Just in the cage, exactly how you want me."

"Don't be melodramatic," Flint says behind me. "Andy, what's going on? What are all these crystals for?"

She looks around. Each of the crystals reflects her a thousand times. A thousand fractured faces of Andy.

Andy shrugs. "Something."

Rayen grumbles behind us. "You could be useful for a change."

"You locked me up. I'm not helping any of you." Andy sneers. "Besides, you can't stop it. I told you. It's no use."

"What are we trying to stop?" I ask. "Come on. It's been long enough. You recognized it."

"I did. What about it?"

Rayen bangs against the glass, and Andy jumps. I have to give her credit—she's not scared.

"We just want things to be back to normal," Flint says. "We want to figure out what's going on. We want to help you."

"Help me by letting me out," she replies. She gives us a bloodthirsty smile.

When she points her finger at us, one of the crystals near the glass explodes into dust. Exactly like I'd seen in my dream.

A shiver runs down my spine.

I step away. Andy is not going to help us today.

Together, we move back to the lab, and I pick up the GPS that first picked up the distress signal. The computer system tells me nothing about it—nothing of its origin or how to track it down. Now that it's gone, I can only see the traces of what it once was. I couldn't even figure out what exactly sent the message. Andy said it used to be a signal for survivors. We'd found survivors, but they clearly didn't need our help. It had to be something else.

Flint starts working on the crystal samples again. Rayen sits down on one of the benches, falling asleep almost instantly. I roll my eyes, putting a blanket over her shoulders as Flint and I get to work. The computer analyzes the samples quickly, spouting formulas.

But in the end, it comes to the same results.

"No data found," it repeats.

Rayen jumps, awake again, trying to wipe sleep from her eyes. "What do you mean no data found?"

"Just that," Flint sighs. "No matter how much we try, there's nothing new to be found. All I know is it's not Earth matter."

"You guys mapped it out, right?" Rayen asks. "Can I see it?"

Flint nods and hands her the map where he marked all the crystals. The map stretches through our known area—practically the whole state of Wyoming, catching a side of Montana and most of the Rockies. It's a pretty big area, and the number of crystals is high, too high. There's at least one crystal for every acre.

Rayen taps her fingers against the edge of the map, considering.

"Did you trace all of it?" she asks.

"Yeah, but it doesn't make sense," Flint says. "It's just random—"

"Give me a pen."

I find the pen and hand it to Rayen.

"You're looking at it the wrong way," she says. "Thinking of it like a trail. It's not a trail. It's more like connect the dots."

I find different colored pens for Rayen as she keeps drawing on the map, trying to make sense of it.

"This is the first one we found in the woods," she points. "This one is near Jackson, the other one we found."

She takes the pen and connects the two. Then she starts

working around the map, trying different paths with different colors.

"I've seen this before," Rayen says with a frown. She pushes her dark hair back.

She finishes drawing the picture, working all around the map. And when she's done, there's almost a full circle, all around our area, with an intertwining pattern that looks like a wave. All across the state.

Rayen is right. We've seen this before.

I leave before they say another word, looking for one thing I'd almost forgotten.

I find the box we picked up from the ruins of Hl'lor under a lab bench. I bring it forward, and Flint and Rayen are behind me. The same pattern Rayen just drew in the crystals is staring right back at us, etched in the metal.

When I put my hand over it, it glows.

I can't see a lock or anything else that stops the box from opening. Instead, I trace the pattern of the waves with my fingers, and it's like I can feel something echoing in my bones.

The lid springs open.

"Fuck," Rayen says.

Inside the box sits a crystal.

Exactly like the ones in Andy's cell.

CHAPTER 31

"What the actual fuck?" Rayen asks.

I hesitate a second before reaching into the box. Flint guesses my plan and picks the crystal up with lab gloves. I hold my breath, waiting for a reaction, but it does nothing. The crystal is clearer than the rest of the ones we've seen—it's almost transparent, like a diamond.

Flint flicks a finger against it, and the noise is strange. The echo surrounds us in a single musical note. It's not of Earth.

"Well," he says. "Where does that leave us?"

"Andy said this box was Universal," Rayen says.

"That's great," I reply. "The only problem is the only Universal alive is locked inside a cell, and we can't even ask her."

Rayen lets out a string of foul curses by my side. Flint starts the process of analyzing the crystal, but I know it will yield the same results.

"So we're back to the beginning," Rayen mutters. "Goddamn it. Why can't we get a break?" She slumps on the seat again, rubbing her eyebrows. Sputnik lays down her head against Rayen's thick calves, and Rayen distractedly scratches her ear.

"What now?" Flint asks. "If this thing is Universal, someone brought it over. Do you think the Hostemn...?"

He doesn't bother finishing the question because the answer, as always, is we don't know. We have no idea. Both Flint and Rayen have been demanding action from the others, but it's just because they're feeling so helpless that they want to hold on to something that feels concrete. They think that maybe if everyone helped, we'd have answers.

I'm not sure this is even the case.

All we've hit are dead ends.

The barrier, dead end. The crystals, dead end, too.

The last thing that still remains is the distress signal, but it was gone so fast, I didn't even bother investigating it again.

"Computer, pull up the distress signal," I say out loud, and then suddenly, just like a couple of months ago, Earth shows up in the middle of the lab.

It's exactly the same way it was before. Just the location of our planet, nothing else. I spin it around.

"How does it even work?" Flint asks. "Which system does it use?"

The computer pulls out a series of different signals, starting in its usual superior tone. "The distress signal can be sent from different sources throughout the galaxy. Someone can shine a beacon of light that will reach across the planet or a wave of sound that travels more slowly but still reaches its target. There are several universal codes that work for distress, either for calling for help or rescue."

"Can you send a distress signal for toilet paper?" Rayen asks.

Flint and I both glare at her.

"What about this one?" I tap Earth's hologram, my fingers walking through the empty air and only disrupting the image.

The computer takes a second to answer.

"The distress signal sent from Earth was sent on a special frequency known only to the ancient species," the computer says. "It's automatically decoded in all Universal technology and spaceships."

Flint taps open the computer archives, showing us dates and where it was first picked up. Immediately after we'd left Shofira's shores after the supernova. I start looking at it, examining the signal.

It's not just a frequency like the computer said. Both light and sound are set on different types of wavelengths. It's all waves, traveling across the vacuum, set to different tones.

"The distress signal is repeated," I say. "It has to, to keep sending it out."

Flint nods. "Yeah, that makes sense."

Rayen raises an eyebrow. "What do you mean?"

"If it is repeated, the computer still has the pattern," I say. "Pull it up."

Instead of the beeping Earth, the computer now shows a pattern. A different one. Its codes are small dots, and it is repeated over and over again.

"A pattern known only to Universals," Flint says. "This looks like a child's toy."

"Distress signals need to be simple," I say. They have to be, to be listened by anyone looking for the same frequency. "Why would anyone send out a signal exclusive to the Universals?"

Rayen shrugs. "Maybe it's some old technology that got left behind."

"Not even you believe that."

"No, I don't."

I tap the little dots again, trying to connect them to one another. Trying to make sense of something that's way bigger than I am. Sputnik barks, and I lose my concentration. I shush her with my hand, but then she barks again.

"Sputnik, hush," I tell her. "We're all trying to work here."

She barks.

Then I get an idea.

A distress signal has to work both ways. Someone sends it. Someone receives it. We've only been receiving it, but we need to turn the process around.

We have to send a signal of our own.

"We need to send a distress signal," I say out loud.

"What?" Rayen asks, frowning. "We're not in distress. I mean, we're under stress. Not in distress exactly."

Flint is faster than Rayen, following my logic.

"We send one of our own, and the original source receives it. If it's able to send it, it can receive it."

"Exactly," I say.

"And then—"

"We can trace it the other way around," I finish for him with a grin.

With a couple of taps to the screen, I send out a signal of my own. The inverse of what was sent to us. I wait for a reply, and then suddenly, the computer lights up again.

"Source found," it says like it has regained an old friend.

I smile triumphantly.

"Trace to the original source."

The computer starts working again, this time on its own. My own decoding is amplified, and the computer traces the origin of the signal—it comes closer to Earth, closer to where we are, until we pinpoint it to a single place.

Not a place.

An object.

The source of the signal is oddly shaped at first. It doesn't look like a planet. It doesn't look like a building. It doesn't look like anything I've seen before until the hologram takes shape, and then I'm left staring, stunned.

Rayen opens her mouth, and no words come out.

"Source of the signal located," the computer says happily. "Origin of object unknown."

The signal is not coming from Earth at all.

It's coming from a spaceship.

CHAPTER 32

We find our friends almost immediately after we discover the spaceship, shaking them out of bed in the early morning.

"What the hell?"

"We found some things," I tell them. "The pattern for the crystals is the same one we found on the box on Hl'lor. And there was a crystal inside."

Brooklyn's eyebrow shoot up. "So?"

"That's not all," I say. "I finally figured out the distress signal. It didn't come from Earth. It came from a spaceship."

There's deathly silence around the room as everyone thinks on the implications of this.

"Someone here is not who they say they are," Rayen says.

"They brought us here, probably because they want Andy. They just haven't gotten to her yet."

"That's just a guess," Violet says.

"A good guess," I say. "Either way, whoever owns the ship has to be in Unity. It's probably the same person who brought the crystals over."

"No one said anything about spaceships," Avani says.

"They're lying," Flint replies, his voice already on edge. "Could you just think of the possibility for a moment? Or is it too much to ask, given you're all in love with your new friends?"

Brooklyn crosses her arms over her chest. "You just want to go over this again, huh? You don't have any real proof of anything. After the other day—"

"After the other day, what?" Rayen asks. "Did you just stop believing your friends, who saved your sorry ass a bunch of times and actually saved the planet for these ungrateful fucks?"

"They don't know," Avani says defensively. "You said it yourself, we couldn't tell them where we came from."

"Oh, but you trust them all so much," Rayen says, her tone venomous. "Don't you? Why don't you go and tell them that, then? That you came on a spaceship and that you're actually not human at all! How do you think they'd treat you then?"

"That is not what this is about," Violet interrupts, her voice authoritative once more. "We're not here to discuss the merits of the colony and how they treat us."

"But it's what got us here in the first place," Flint says. "You love it here. You love it so much that you'd rather turn your back on us."

"And whose fault is that?" Violet snaps. "You're so concerned with leaving that you're not allowing yourselves to think that this is a good home."

"This isn't my home." Rayen's anger seeps to her eyes, to her voice. It shields her like armor, every edge sharp. "It's about what this place is doing to you guys."

"It's not doing anything," Avani says. "We *chose* to be here. We chose to come here out of our own free will, and we decided that maybe it wouldn't be so bad if we stayed. Do you want to stay your whole life up there?" Avani gestures wildly toward the sky. "Because it's fun, sure, but it's not the life I want to lead. I don't want to spend the rest of my life up there, wondering what it would be like if we just came home. If I just came to belong in a place where I know I'm supposed to be."

Silence fills the void between us.

All the time I spent in space, I kept wondering if one day I'd be able to come back. If I'd be able to be here once again, to see Earth, and what I would do. The problem was that I never thought ahead of that—I kept running and running, and even my ideas kept running, and I couldn't face what I'd left behind. I couldn't face the fact that I don't know what the next step is and maybe I'm just facing a dark chasm with no bottom in sight.

"It's not about the place," I say instead. "This is about the fact that we're trapped here. Andy is completely messed up, and no one here knows anything. We should've left a long time ago.

Find the answers somewhere else. We found the box, and the same crystals are inside."

"It's just a coincidence," Brooklyn says.

"With the spaceship?" I snap at her. "We can't trust anyone here. Someone set up a trap for Andy, and we better find out who before it wrecks us all."

I look at each of the girls. I don't want to beg, but I'm ready if I have to. I don't want to go on my knees to ask for something that should be obvious.

"We need to get out of here," Rayen says. "We need to get Andy back and get the hell out of here before something else happens."

"How?" Avani demands. "There's a barrier all around us, in case you've forgotten. We can't leave."

"Not with that attitude," Flint snaps.

"We did what we could," Brooklyn says. "Aren't you tired? Why do *we* have to be the ones who figure it out? Why can't we let other people save us for once?"

Her words are prickles in my skin. We were the ones who saved the planet first. We figured it all out together.

But in the end, we're just a bunch of kids. I don't want to have to save myself.

"Take it to the adults," Violet says. "We come clean, tell them all the truth. Let them help bring down the barrier."

"We can't trust them," Rayen hisses. "Haven't you been listening? The signal comes from a spaceship. Someone here is not who they say they are."

"What do you want us to do?" Avani asks.

"Believe us, for starters," Flint hits back. "We need to work together."

We need all of us thinking on the same issue. We need all of us working to figure this out.

We need the Last Teenagers on Earth.

"Well, if you just—"

"Maybe if you'd helped before, we wouldn't be here," Rayen snaps.

"Oh yes, the mighty Rayen wouldn't let us be here," Brooklyn replies, color rising to her cheeks. "Thank God we have you. Or else we're too idiotic to do anything at all."

"By the way you're acting, sure."

"Did you ever think you're the one who's wrong?" Brooklyn said, facing Rayen and looking her in the eye. "That maybe you're just too wrong to fit in here? That the problem is with you?"

Rayen jolts forward, but just in time, I hold her back.

"Hold it," I say.

Rayen pushes my hand away with such force that for a second, I think she might snap my wrist. By the way each of us is staring at the other, I realize that there may not be a good ending to this. That this may just be an ending.

"I'm tired of holding it," Rayen says. "You guys aren't even trying to help. Brooklyn and Avani just want to quit on us because this place is so good for them, and now they're loved. They don't care." She turns to Violet. "You're worse than them," she says quietly. She doesn't need to shout. All the anger, all the hurt, they're all in her words. "You think you're better than us. You think that you deserve to stay here, that this is your place because you're human. I get Brooklyn and Avani trying to forget what they are—but not you. You make sure you parade it every second."

Violet opens her mouth, her eyes wide.

I'm too stunned to try and stop Rayen.

"I know that you want us out of here because we remind you of what happened. That's why you don't want to see Andy," she continues. "That's why you've been avoiding all of us. But guess what, Violet? You can't erase the past. You can't erase the fact that you came here with us." She takes a deep breath. "And you know, you're much more like us than you are like them. That's what's killing you."

Rayen steps back, watching as the words sink in, the silence around us too great for any of us to breach it.

Violet turns around and runs.

I wait for a second as the Last Teenagers on Earth turn their backs on one another and don't look back.

I run after Violet.

I find Violet sitting at the edge of the woods, almost hidden from view. Sputnik nudges her.

"Hey," I say.

"Hi," she says back.

Violet doesn't stand. I don't lower myself to the ground.

Maybe because in a way, I think Rayen is right. It kills me to admit it. Because that means I can't salvage a part of this fracture.

"There's something going on, Violet," I start.

"I believe you," she says.

"Believing isn't good enough," I spit out, crossing my arms in front of my chest. "You know Flint's right. I can't sit back and just watch. I need to know what's going on. What if this spaceship is dangerous? What if Andy is going to be like that forever?"

"Maybe it's meant to be."

I stop myself before I slap her. When I meet Violet's eyes, the usual shade of blue is gone. There is no fierceness in them anymore, no demands, no anything. She's just a lost girl trying to fit in where she can.

"I'm getting to the bottom of this," I say. "No matter what you guys say or think. Because maybe you can't see it, but Unity has torn us apart."

"No, *you* did."

I look up, and I feel the sting of tears coming. I don't want to be having this conversation. This is not what is supposed to happen. We're supposed to be on the same side.

"I get it," Violet finally says. "I get why you don't want to stay. I get why you think it's Unity that's doing all this, and you want to go back to a place where there was just the seven of us and nothing was wrong." She breathes deep. "Except that place never existed. We got together because we thought we were the only ones left, and now we don't have to be. It's easier to want to fight this than accept that maybe we just became friends because of the end of the world. And now that it's gone, we don't have anything left."

I hold my breath, and I feel my feet sinking farther into the ground. I'm not weak. I don't want to be weak.

But Violet's words dismantle me, and the only reason I don't fall is because Sputnik is there by my side, holding me up so I don't lose myself.

"Do you know why I didn't want to come back?" she asks me, meeting my eyes. She pushes a blond lock of hair behind her ear. "You thought it was because I was scared to find any other survivors. It's not true. It was because I was so scared we *would*. Finding that they were different from me."

Sputnik licks her, and I wait for more.

"Andy made me again," she says, her voice little above a whisper. "When you threw me that gun, I knew what I was doing. I knew what I was expecting. I died so you could live. I died so the Earth could be saved. I made my peace with that. It's the price I paid for saving you. It's what I promised. I said I'd protect you, and I did." She swallows. "And then I was reborn, made whole again, and I don't even know. I don't know what I am. I don't know if I'm human. Humans don't get a second chance. We just die. I *died*, Clover."

She shakes her head, still trying to grasp that concept.

I wait. I listen.

"Being here in Unity, I can believe it," she says. "I almost believe I'm normal. Rayen's right. I want to forget. I don't want to be reminded that I died and then came back. I just wanted to pretend I could be like them."

She wipes a single tear from her eye.

"I've been running away from that," she says. "Pretending my death wasn't real. But it was. Every time I see my face, I wonder if there isn't a part of me missing, if I've got all my parts together, all my memories. I don't know that. I can't know what I was like before. So I just keep wondering if I'm really me. Or just a doll Andy created because she couldn't live without her best friend."

She walks away before I can say anything, a shadow of the girl I used to know.

CHAPTER 33

That night, I go back to the Arc.

I'm on my own this time, Sputnik following my trail. I dread seeing Andy, but my consolation is that at least Andy is under the influence of the crystal while my other friends are acting differently for no good reason.

It's not a good consolation, but it's all I have.

When I get to the spaceship, instead of the usual raving and the threats and insults, Andy seems different. She's lying on the floor, staring up at the ceiling with her hands on her stomach.

When the glass clears completely, she looks at me. Her eyes are a mixture of sea green and blue, bursting into star formations, and they look distant, as if she can't really grasp that I'm there.

She's become numb now, exhausted by the effects of the crystal.

I sit down on the floor, watching her. She watches me back.

"Violet doesn't come to see me," Andy says, and her voice is almost back to normal.

"I don't think she's in a good place," I tell her. "There are other things happening."

"I know I said some awful things. I can hear it, playing it back." Her voice cracks. "I don't know what's happening to me."

"We'll figure it out, Andy. I promise."

One tear escapes from her eyes, liquid starlight hitting the floor. "I don't want to stay here forever. I just can't control it anymore."

She doesn't get up from the floor, but she crawls closer to the glass. I lie down next to her, both of us separated by this one sheet of glass. If it weren't for that, our shoulders would be touching.

"So you can't let me out."

I shake my head. "It's too dangerous."

Andy nods.

We both look toward the crystal walls on the ship, sharp and glittering, reminding us of what put us here in the first place.

"Do you miss it?" I ask.

Andy frowns. "Miss what?"

"Your home."

Andy takes some time before she speaks again, looking at the crystals.

"I came here when I was two. Too young. I don't remember my planet." She takes a deep breath. "This here. This is home."

For a minute, I consider releasing the glass. Letting her walk outside. I missed Earth, but I never considered that Andy might miss it, too. That this was the only home she had ever known and she deserved to come back to it as much as we did. She was left here with no one else while her species dispersed, and this was the only place that cared for her.

"We found another crystal," I tell her. "Inside the box from Hl'lor."

Alarm fills her eyes, and she turns sideways to face me. Her hair is wet against her face. She's sweating inside her cell, feverish, and there's still nothing we can do to stop it because we don't know how.

"I thought I'd remembered it," she says. "It's in the back of my mind, but I can't force it. I'm afraid I'll start rambling again."

I nod. What little control she gained, she wants to keep. I don't want to lose her to the other monster, either.

"It's supposed to be from your home," I tell her.

She waves her hand around, and in response, some of the crystals grow. Her eyes glaze over.

"I almost remember it," she says, "how it was before. There were crystal shards everywhere. Our homes were made of glass walls, and they glittered with the two stars of the constellation. There was always light and laughter."

She closes her eyes, starts humming to herself a song that's so ancient, I can feel it echoing in my bones. It's light at first, the melody rising with Andy's voice, and then it turns into the darkness, and I don't breathe. She hums on, light and dark, high and low, each turning again and again till I feel like the power of the whole world is in the song.

The melody doesn't come from her throat. It comes from her core.

It edges on my skin and enters my ears, but it enters my body, too, my cells, like every piece of me echoes it. I've never heard Andy sing anything like it. And as she sings, as the song builds it, I see what Andy sees. I see a new planet, full of crystals in every color. I see the two stars and people who look like me but aren't really me. Their colors are the colors of existence, and they shine brighter than the rest of the galaxy. It's carved out of love, a reality that shines in the darkness of the spaceship and dances in the space between the dust motes.

When Andy finishes, I can't speak.

"It's good," Andy says. "I miss it. I think they miss it, too."

"They?"

"The crystals," she says, her voice far off, and then she turns to smile at me. "They're doing what they know. Taking us home."

She gets up, her feet bare against the metal panels of the cells, and she touches the crystals. They explode in rainbows and colors I can't name.

"What did you say?"

She turns back to me, her eyes wide, like a child.

"You said the crystals were taking us home. What home, Andy? What does that mean?"

She cocks her head to the side. "It means that. They aren't evil."

I sit up. "Andy, please. You're the only one who knows about it."

Andy shivers, then hugs herself, sitting in front of me. She doesn't look me in the eyes. Seconds before, she was still good. Now I know I lost her again to this madness, her eyes unfocused, and I don't even know if she's listening.

"Andy, are we going to die?"

"I don't want to die."

"Me neither," I say, and it's the truth.

I've fought so long against that feeling. The fact that I spent so long trying to die. I'm still not sure how to live without simply surviving, without trying to outrun my own mind. One step in front of the other, never looking back.

She presses her lips together, trying to concentrate as hard as she can. She shakes her head just slightly. "I can't remember." Her voice cracks. "I can't remember anything."

Her eyes are taken over by white light, and there is nothing in them but the brightness of burning ions.

"You'll remember," I tell her. "We'll get out of this."

"You don't know that," she says, her eyes turning back to a bright blue. She sighs, shaking her head. "I always admired you humans. The way you always think it's going to work out."

I stare at her in silence.

"We were the best," she says. "We were the first beings to come into the light, the first to be born in the vast darkness. The first and the last, and still, they got to us in the end. The most powerful beings in the whole universe, made to its image, made to create and destroy. Made with power enough to bring whole galaxies to their knees." She looks back at the crystal. "And even so, I'm the only one left. And the whole universe, in years to come, will forget that we existed. We'll be nothing again."

Her eyes turn to me again, and she shakes her head. Nothing matters anymore. She's too big, too distant, something so strange, I'll never be able to fully comprehend it.

"I am but a small grain of sand in an hourglass bigger than the sun itself," Andy says. "I don't know how you humans bear it. Knowing that."

I don't know how to bear it.

I don't know what it's like to be insignificant, because at one point, I might have been. And I might be again. And we humans keep forgetting. How tiny we are. How small when compared to the whole universe.

But when I look around, I only see what we humans have seen for so long.

That despite everything, we still stand. We survive.

And I think that's bigger than the universe itself.

I get up, putting my hand to the glass. Andy doesn't. She only looks at me, waiting to see if I'll have a reaction. I can't reassure her it's going to work out, that we're going to figure it out.

But I know humans have stood.

And if it's up to me, we're going to stand for a good while more.

CHAPTER 34

I leave Andy in her cell and go back to the lab.

I refuse to leave this ship before I know truly what's happening, before I get the answers we need. We have so many of the elements. We just haven't put them together. There has to be something that we're missing. A link to connect the threads.

I activate the computer, and the screen illuminates. Sputnik growls low out of habit. She comes closer to me, sprawling herself on the ground of the Arc, her fur spreading like a gigantic carpet.

"Computer, pull up the distress signal."

The computer brings it up again. The Earth blinks, and the red dot on Wyoming shows up again. My last decoding of the signal is still up.

A goddamn spaceship.

All our troubles began with spaceships. It sounds almost fitting that they would end the same way.

I tap on the surface of the table. Whoever brought this spaceship brought the crystals along. That can't be a coincidence. The barrier, however... Why would anyone set up anything like that?

"How about the barrier?" I ask to the computer.

"The barrier is a physically insurmountable object," it says in its usual condescending tone. "I cannot analyze its origins, only that no object may pass through it."

Nowhere, as always. No origins, no presence, no anything. It's absolutely useless.

It's strange talking to the computer—it has an odd sense of personality, though it isn't exactly good company. Then I have another idea. "Computer, what can you tell me about this symbol?"

I smoothly draw the same symbol Rayen did last night, repeating the same pattern.

"Data locked."

I glare at it. "Are you serious? You're giving me this shit now?"

"Data locked," it repeats stubbornly. Sputnik raises her head just slightly, ever the opportunist. Hoping that this is finally the time where her aggressive skills will come to use against the computer, and she will destroy it. "Access denied."

"I don't even know what data I'm trying to access here," I say out loud.

I look at the files again. As I see it, we have three problems. The distress signal, the barrier, and the crystals.

The crystal box came from the ruins of Hl'lor. Near Universali. If the computer has answers, those are the files that are going to help me.

"Access the Universal files."

"Access denied."

"Computer, who has access to the Universal database?"

The interface changes to silver. "File access can only be changed by the master species," the computer replies.

"Master species my ass," I reply. Sputnik looks at me, her eyes wide, the same face she makes when she's begging for food. "No, I'm not letting you fight the computer for being species-ist."

The computer blinks red in alarm.

"Okay," I say, more to myself than anyone else. All the pieces of the puzzle are here. The crystal box we found, the fact that the distress signal was gone soon after we landed, and the fact that we can't leave.

This was a trap all along, but it looks too slow for it to be a trap. It's got too many elements.

Maybe the trap wanted someone else.

Someone who hasn't shown up in the colony, someone we locked away before we saw any of the others. Someone whose presence here is unknown. Someone whose power, in the wrong hands, could destroy whole existences.

Andy.

I look at the crystal formulas again, and my brain is a scramble of thoughts that I'm trying to reorder. There seems to be no logic to it, but there's a thread. A thread that will make all the connections clear.

"Computer, pull the analysis of the crystals again," I say, and it obeys immediately. I see the two different crystals hovering above me, each different from the other.

Then I bring up the last crystal, the one we'd found in the box from Hl'lor. The crystals show on the screen, and I recognize the difference. The three crystals are different from each other, but they appear to be essentially the same. There's a slight difference to the crystals from Earth, like they're trying to copy the one we found in the box.

I pull back the recordings of Andy's cell and watch them accelerated. Andy rages in silence against her bonds, trying to break the glass. We come and go, and she sits on her cot most of the time. Suddenly, something changes. She picks up a strand of her hair and tears it off her head. I look on in shock as she threads her hair with her fingers. It hardens against the floor and starts growing until it's crystal-shaped. It latches itself onto the floor and stays there.

I watch the process, again and again, until every single strand she's picked from her head has formed a crystal on the edge of the wall, reflecting her a thousand different times. I check the sample of Andy's crystal again, cross-referencing it with the DNA samples we all have on the ship.

It matches Andy's exactly.

My fingers tremble until I find the crystal sample we took that day in the forest and pull up the analysis against Andy's crystal. The computer isolates the common elements and then separates Andy's DNA strand. Then it isolates the elements of the next crystal, and all I'm left with is a strand of different DNA, something I don't recognize.

But the database in the Arc's computer does. The crystal is easily marked, and it doesn't make a mistake when the answer lights up, identifying the species the DNA belongs to.

Andy isn't the last one.

There is another Universal here on Earth.

PART III

TAKE ME HOME

CHAPTER 35

I don't wait to call the others.

I run back with Sputnik on my heels and go back to the cabin to wake everyone up. Soon, we're all standing outside in the cold in the middle of the night. Sputnik takes her time to go pee in the accumulated snow that fell overnight.

"This better be important," Violet complains. "Couldn't it wait until tomorrow?"

"Andy isn't the last one."

"The last what?" Brooklyn asks between a yawn. "The last one who's still asleep? I wish."

"The last Universal," I say. "Andy was creating the crystals, taking them out of her head. I matched her DNA to her crystal, then I removed it from the other sample."

Rayen stifles a yawn. "What does that mean?"

"It means the crystals here were created the same way," I reply. "There's another Universal here on Earth."

Silence takes over the conversation in a single breath. Our fights seem petty now, unimportant.

"Are you sure?" Avani asks. "I want to check."

"Oh, now you want—" Flint starts, and I give him a death stare. He shuts his mouth.

"Yes," I agree. "We can go there tomorrow, and you check it out. Maybe you can figure out what it is or if you can find out anything else."

Avani nods her head, then pulls Brooklyn with her back to bed. Rayen says nothing, only giving me a look that says we'll talk later.

I stand there with Flint and Violet and wish I could go to bed, too, that my brain wasn't dizzy with possibilities. These crystals can't be meaningless. Andy is putting a part of herself into them. Andy losing her mind over touching the other crystal means something.

"I want to check something," Flint says.

"Be careful," I tell him.

"What do you need to check at this time of night?" Violet asks. "What more can there be?"

"Something that's been bothering me about the crystals," he replies. He adjusts his glasses. Like me, he's fully awake. "Another surviving Universal... This could change everything."

"It's why we were called here," I say. "It was a trap. But not for us."

Violet sets her jaw. "Why would another Universal want Andy?"

"I don't know, Violet. You're the smart one. You figure it out," Flint says.

"You're not helping."

"I'm tired of being helpful," he says. "I'm so tired, all right? You didn't listen to me before because you're out of your comfort zone."

"I don't have a comfort zone. I just didn't think—"

"It was in your best interest to listen to us, fine," Flint says, getting up. "But now maybe it's time to start listening. Or else we'll be facing someone much worse than Andy or God knows what else, because we can't figure out how to stick together."

Flint storms away, and Violet hangs her head in shame. Her blue eyes meet mine. "I didn't mean to," she says.

"That doesn't sound like an apology, Violet."

She huffs. "What should I apologize for? I thought this was what everyone wanted. To stay here. To find our way back home again." She gestures her arms wildly toward the rest of the colony.

"Look around, Violet," I snap, my voice rising. "All you can think is how nice it is to be the perfect person once again, around all the other humans. How nice it is to hang out with people who understand you."

She faces me. "I never said that."

"You did. Maybe it's because we're not human, right?"

Violet's face burns an even deeper shade of red this time.

My bones ache inside me, like I could sleep for a month. The fact that we're not even close to a solution to the problem makes it even worse. The more I dig, the more questions I have.

Violet turns around and goes back to the cabin without looking back.

The anger and hurt swell in my throat, and I'm so frustrated, I could kick someone.

"You okay?"

Marcelo walks out of the cabin and stands next to me on the porch.

"No," I tell him truthfully. "I'm tired."

He gives me a half smile. "Everything is going to turn out okay, Clover."

"No, it isn't. Stop telling me that." I look back at him. "I know that's what you think I want to hear. I don't want someone to comfort me. I don't need it. I need someone to tell it like it is. I need someone to get me some solutions."

I wish I could scream without sounding like a madwoman.

But I am mad. I'm mad in a way that isn't fixable. I have panic attacks. I have depression and anxiety and PTSD and a lot of other things I can't begin to name. I have nightmares and things I'm not allowed to tell anyone, and sometimes I wish I could just get them all out. Get everything that's constantly draining me out, out, *out*.

I don't realize how close I am to crying until the tears are already falling.

Marcelo stands without moving for a moment, then he puts his arm around me. I let myself cry—really cry. Not like I'd done in secret, shed a few tears and move on, but the kind of crying that lets me sob and snot and just let out all the ugly and terrible things inside.

I hug my father back, and for the first time, I think of him as he is. Not just my father but a real, flawed person. Someone who's also trying his best.

"I'm here," he says in my ear.

When I'm done with enough crying to feel like I can talk again, I answer him.

"Thanks, Dad."

And that one word changes everything.

CHAPTER 36

It's the first time we're all together in the Arc since we came back to Earth.

My muscles tense, waiting for someone to jump out from the shadows, but there's nothing. I breathe a sigh of relief as we all gather around the lab. For a minute, I can almost believe nothing here has changed.

Avani starts analyzing the DNA of the crystals, working quietly with Flint. The rest of us are waiting for the results, pacing from one side of the lab to the other.

Violet stays by my side, her fingernails tapping against the table. The crystal tray is right next to us, the transparent crystal sitting on top of it.

"What else do we know about this?" she asks. "Did you get the archives?"

"We can't access it without Andy's authorization," Rayen replies. "Basically, anything that says Universal is off limits for us."

"You guys can't bypass the security system?" Violet asks.

"I've tried, but apparently being a hybrid doesn't really cut it. Just our luck."

Violet keeps tapping her fingers, her blue eyes drawn to the crystal. She frowns when she looks at it. She moves her hand to touch it, drawn to it, but a second later, Rayen slaps away her hand.

"I wouldn't do that if I were you," Rayen says. "The ones in the forest might not hurt humans, but we have no idea what this one does."

Violet nods, but her eyes are still on the crystal, like she can see something that no one else can.

A couple of minutes later, Avani has the results, and everything else is cast aside.

"Okay, so," Avani says in her most professorial tone, "Clover's analysis was raw, but she isn't wrong."

"And…?" Rayen asks.

"Look at it this way," Flint says. "Andy produces her own crystal through her own DNA. The other crystal has to be produced by someone else with their DNA. Thus, someone else is here, making these crystals on their own."

"Can't anybody fake it?" Brooklyn asks.

"Probably. What do I know at this point?" Avani says with a sigh. She wipes her forehead, a gesture I've seen her do a hundred times when she's nervous. "I'm just... This is huge. I don't know. I just don't know."

"Where would they be hiding?" Brooklyn asks. "I'm assuming that we're talking about full-on Universal, skin shifting and shit?"

"It wouldn't be smart of them," Rayen says. "They're probably hiding very well among the humans. Just like they did the first time around."

"Fuck," Brooklyn curses. "Can anything ever be easy?"

"No," we all reply at once.

A shadow of a smile crosses Violet's face. It's just like old times.

"So what do we have?" Rayen asks. "Someone is definitely lying about who they are, and what the hell do these crystals do anyway?"

Something beeps red, and Flint quickly gets to it. He doesn't look like he slept last night, but then he sees something, and his face falls.

"Flint?" Rayen asks.

He takes a deep breath. "I would say good news, but I don't have any," he says. "I went back to the first crystal we found last night. I got a couple of soil samples near it in the woods, because after what Clover said about transforming, I got a hunch."

"Oh, that's never good," Brooklyn says.

"It's really not," he says. "The sample I got is almost entirely made of black veins from inside the crystals, and it's got almost nothing of Earth residue." Flint swipes the screen and points to another sample. "Now this sample is equal parts black vein thing and solid ground. It has a lot of Earth matter still but some strange elements. And our last sample, the one I took farthest away from the crystal, is one hundred percent of Earth, no other alien material."

"So what does this mean?" I ask.

"Well, at first, I thought an alien crystal lodging itself into the Earth was not that bad. We've survived worse."

"Except when it turns friends into psychopaths," Brooklyn points.

Flint nods vehemently and turns again to the screen.

"So what's the problem?" Rayen asks.

"Once the crystal and these strange veins are in contact with the ground, the crystal starts transforming the soil," Flint points out. "It's a slow process. But the crystal itself has no elements known to Earth."

"And then it takes over," I conclude, and we all exchange looks.

"So this means…" Violet starts saying.

"It's a terraforming crystal," Flint finishes for her.

There's a heavy pause in the room while we figure out the implications of this.

"Let me get this right," Brooklyn starts saying. "Terraforming as in…transforming?"

Flint sighs, shrugs a little. "Terraforming is an alien notion.

It takes hundreds of years to be accomplished. It's like trying to create life in a planet that is not habitable, and you need to make sure people are going to breathe and live and thrive. In this case, it's like the crystals are trying to transform Earth into…well, Universali."

He shuts his mouth, leaving a moment for us all to catch up with what it means. "Flint, how do we stop this?"

He looks at us, adjusts his glasses, and then looks back at the screen. A second later, he shakes his head. "I have no idea," he says. "I've never seen anything remotely like this. I don't know how much longer we've got."

"Can they do this?" Brooklyn asks. "Andy said it was against the rules. She's basically using her powers to destroy something."

The END rule. I'm not sure if it applies the same way here, but I doubt that Andy cares. She broke the rule once. She might be willing to break it twice.

"What if we cut it off at the roots?" I suggest. "The veins sprout from the crystal. If we take the crystal out…"

My voice trails off. It's just a suggestion, but even I know we haven't gotten enough facts for this to work or to know the consequences.

"It could work, except we don't know how to dislodge the crystal in the first place," Flint says. "And it's alien. If we damage it, it might just accelerate the process."

Beneath me, it's almost like I feel the black veins of the Universal crystals dragging us down, making the Earth crumble, transforming everything we know. I think about the trees, the water, the buzz of the insects and the animals, and I know that everything will be gone if we don't stop it.

Once it's done, it won't be our planet anymore.

There will be nothing left of Earth at all.

"What do we do?" Brooklyn asks. In the face of this threat, we unite again as a group, our differences in the past.

Right now, we need to save Earth.

"You guys go back to Unity," Violet says. "Keep an eye on everyone. Maybe start trying to figure out the person we want."

"And what are you gonna do?"

Violet exchanges a look with me.

"I'm gonna talk to Andy."

CHAPTER 37

Andy's cell is completely covered in crystals. She sits in the middle of it, her legs crossed and her back straight. She's humming a song to herself, like the last time I saw her, but this song is more powerful—angrier, full of hurt.

"Andy," I say. "Andromeda."

Her eyes snap open, a deep gold. "Yes. I'm listening."

"We know about the crystals. We know what they're for."

Her smile opens up more, sharp edges and teeth like a shark. She looks at me like I'm just a stupid and puny human, just now starting to realize her power.

Then she looks at Violet, and her mask shatters.

For a second, she's vulnerable again, her eyes wide, her mouth open in surprise.

"What are you doing here?" she asks in an incredulous tone. "I thought you wouldn't come."

"I'm here," Violet says in a quiet tone. "Andy, we need you."

Andy recoils, shrinking back into the wall. "Now you need me. Not when you locked me up."

"Andy, you were a danger to everyone else," Violet says. "With your powers uncontrolled, you could have hurt one of us. You hurt *me*."

Andy doesn't blink. "You could've talked. But you left. You didn't come back."

I feel like an intruder in this conversation. I shouldn't be witnessing anything this private, when an inevitable truth is about to come out.

Violet doesn't falter.

"I don't belong up there, Andy," she finally says. "I can't go back there with you. I went, and I was so unhappy, I kept wondering why you bothered bringing me back in the first place." She takes a deep breath. "And when we found the colony, I was so glad. I didn't want to be the only one left. I couldn't *bear* being the only one left. And now I don't have to be. I never should have left."

Andy walks forward, puts her hand on the glass. Violet doesn't touch it.

"We need you," Violet says. "We need your help."

Andy blinks, and I think a part of her understands. A part of her knows. A part of her still remembers.

"Andy," I cut in. "The crystal inside the box. What does it mean?"

"What box?"

"The box from Hl'lor," I tell her. "There's another crystal there. A Universal crystal."

Andy looks around her cell. When she moves her hands, the crystals closest to her change colors.

"You have an original one?"

"What does it mean, Andy?" Violet presses.

"It's an original crystal," she says, voice lost in wonder. "It accelerates the process. It lets Universali become."

Fuck. It could be just another crystal, but of course it isn't. It's even more dangerous than Andy and the others.

"Andy, you need to help us destroy it," Violet says. "There's another Universal out there."

Andy blinks, her eyes changing colors so quickly, I can't name them.

"It can't be," she says. "I'm the last one."

Her attention span is short, and a blink is enough to lose her.

Violet slams her hands against the glass to get her attention back. Andy's attention snaps back to Violet, her gaze cold.

"What's going to happen, Andy?"

"Nothing is going to happen," Andy says, gritting her teeth. "It's doing what it's supposed to do. It's forming Universali."

Violet exchanges one look with me. "Can you destroy them?"

"Why would I do that?" Andy says. "My planet is gone. If someone is bringing it back, I'm helping them." She lays her hands on her own crystals just to make her point. And then she points to Violet.

Violet's skin shivers, cracks showing. Violet shakes, energy seeping through her eyeballs.

"Andy," I say.

"I should've let you die," Andy whispers, her eyes fixed on Violet.

"Andy, let her go," I order, slamming my hand against the glass. "I know you're listening to me."

Andy doesn't give any sign of understanding. It's like it's all gone, and there's only power bubbling beneath her surface. Raw, unlimited power.

Violet manages to say something, so quiet that I almost don't hear it while she's choking the words out.

Andy raises an eyebrow, and Violet repeats it, a little louder.

"I'm not afraid, Andy."

"Oh yeah?" she says, a glint in her eye, turning to me until chills climb up my spine. "You should be."

Andy slams forward, but before she does anything drastic, she stops, looking beyond us. I turn around to see someone else.

Castor walks calmly, as if he has no reason to hurry. He looks at both me and Violet with a slight frown.

"I really thought I'd won you over, you know," he says first, looking at Violet. "I thought I'd made you right at home."

Violet stops struggling against Andy.

I step forward.

"I wouldn't do that," Castor says, his tone changed completely. His voice is serious and low, like a threat. "I just want the crystal."

Violet puts herself in front of Andy's cell. As if she's in danger and not us. "We can explain."

"Explanations? I don't want explanations, Violet. I don't need them from you." He shakes his head. "I needed you to lead me here."

He jerks his head toward Andy.

When Castor steps into the light, the color of his eyes changes. From light brown, they go to purple and green and orange and silver, a spectacle on their own. His skin acquires the translucent color of stars, and nebulae swirl in his cheeks. Supernovas burst above his eyebrow, and the whole universe is contained within Castor.

He's Universal.

Andy opens her mouth in shock.

"It can't be," she says, her voice trembling, "I'm the only one left."

Castor smiles at her. "Of course not, Andromeda," he says kindly. He offers her a hand. "Come on. We have a job to finish."

He takes a step forward.

"Don't move," I say.

Castor blinks. "Clover, I'm not here to fight."

I don't move. I don't believe any of it.

Andy's still shocked, shaking her head.

"That's impossible," she says. "You died. All of you died."

Castor looks at Andy. "Yes, most of us did. We separated ships. You're too young to remember. I left on the other ship, made the other way around. I came to Earth after our planet's destruction, hoping to find other survivors."

Andy shakes her head again, her body frozen into a state of shock.

"You weren't here," Castor says, his voice kind and soft. "My ship broke down in the fall, smashed against the rocks. So I decided to do what the Universals have done before—I stayed, hidden among the last of humankind. I built this place so they'd feel welcome, so that the rest of you, when you came back, would feel welcome and trust me."

He steps forward.

"Don't," I say. "Don't try."

"You can't stop me. I built all this. I waited ten years. Ten years until I felt a shiver of Universal, all the way across space. I felt Andromeda's power, seeping again. I knew she was alive. I knew you'd bring me what I needed to finish this."

"You're the one who created the crystals," Violet says quietly.

"Of course I did," Castor says. "And the barrier, with my ship, so you wouldn't leave before I got what I wanted. And the distress signal so you would come all the way over here."

Andy looks at him. "What are you doing?"

"I'm bringing us back home."

Andy snarls. She's back on edge. Castor's crystals are the ones that made Andy like this.

He steps forward again.

I'm faster than he is. I go for a full left-handed punch, and I hit Castor across the eyes. He isn't expecting a fight, and he stumbles to the ground.

Castor rises up again, but I'm quick, too. I catch his leg, forcing my elbow down on his knee. He shouts, but his struggle isn't to hit me back. I cut myself with my teeth, and I taste blood. I stumble, but Castor doesn't fight. He only advances, as if I'm some minor inconvenience he can ignore.

I jump on his back, trying to stop him from walking. He was clear on what he wanted—the crystal. I need to make sure he doesn't get it. I hold against his back, but Castor is now used to my strength, and my element of surprise is gone.

He turns and moves his elbow with might so he shrugs me off. It hits me on the side, and my lung is robbed of air. It's in the exact spot that never healed properly, and I fall to the ground.

Violet stands in front of him, but she's only human. He pushes her aside like a toy, and she flies back, her back slamming against the wall of the Arc.

He stands in front of Andy's cell.

He's not just Universal. He's more than that—he's fully grown, and he accepts his powers like Andy never did.

"Andromeda," he says.

"I thought you were dead," she replies.

"Just waiting for you."

Then Andy smiles. Sharp. Predatory. "Maybe you should've stayed dead."

Getting up again, I try to go for his neck, try to hit his head so he drops to the ground. Castor struggles against me, and I jam my thumb against his eyeball. He screams. In the struggle, he steps over Violet's ankle, and I hear the crack, as if everything inside her is breaking. I try to get him away, but I'm not strong enough. Castor turns, his attention fully on me, and pushes me back. The shoving is pure strength, and I fly back across the ship, slamming against the glass.

I'm not going to win this fight by myself.

I can't win against him.

So I do the only thing I can.

I jam my hand to the controls, and I open Andy's cell.

CHAPTER 38

The glass dissolves like mist.

No one moves, holding their breaths.

Then Andy steps out of her cell, almost unsure. The power curls over her right fist, emanating from her skin, her hair rising as she faces Castor. I nudge Violet, who nods silently at me as we step back very slowly. I need to grab the crystal from Hl'lor and make sure it doesn't reach Castor's hands. That's all I need to do.

"Andromeda, you can't hurt me," he says. "I'm on your side."

"Your crystal made me like this," Andy says.

"Yes," Castor agrees. "I made you remember your powers."

Andy looks down at her hands. I've never seen her like this

before—not with this untamed, raw strength that seeps from her like madness, turning her ideas upside down. Her eyes are wide as she takes in the surroundings and her own crystals.

I'm not fooled.

"I understand," Andy says. "And I thank you."

Then she shoots lightning straight at Castor.

The Arc shimmers with the use of her power, and Castor is thrown back against the wall. It's enough of a distraction that I bolt with Violet toward the lab, half carrying her, running for my life. I can still hear the fight in the background, but I don't look back. I don't have much time. None of us do.

I scramble through the door of the lab, and I find the box with the crystal where Avani put it back. I trace the pattern like I did before, and it opens with ease. The crystal sits inside, but I don't have time to think or take precautions. I grab it. The shard is barely the size of my palm.

"We need to go," Violet says, biting back the pain of her ankle.

"Can you walk?"

Violet grimaces. "I have to, don't I?"

Something shatters in the background.

"We have to go through them," I say.

"Okay." Violet nods as if it's no big deal. As if I'm not suggesting we cross a battle made for titans. "Let's go."

I put the crystal in my pocket, and we head back to the front of the Arc. Andy's standing over Castor's fallen figure, her hair strange shades of orange and pink. Her hands are pure light, but

Castor doesn't look like he wants to fight. Not looking good for him. I just unleashed a monster.

Which doesn't really bode well, since I don't know how to stop her.

I'm hoping Castor does. I'm not sure what is worse. Dealing with him or her.

"Andromeda, listen to me," Castor says, still on the ground. "We need to get the crystal. We need—"

His words are drowned by another strike that comes from Andy's hand. She's distracted. I sneak by with my back to the wall, Violet by my side. Castor is thrown back by Andy's power; she's holding him in the air like he's nothing but a puppet. Castor is a full-grown Universal who must have thousands of years of experience.

But Andy is one very angry teenager.

I'm pretty sure I know where this is going.

I nudge Violet with my hands so we move faster. We're almost through the door and on our way back to the forest when I feel the atmosphere turn suddenly heavy.

"Where do you think you're going?" Andy calls out.

Her head turns to us. Her eyes are like glowing orbs. I can see red dwarfs in her pupils. It's strange and haunting and beautiful how her power can be.

"Andy, I—"

"I don't want your excuses," Andy says, her gaze fixed on Violet. "You locked me up."

"You aren't yourself."

"I'm myself," she replies. "A part of me. The part of me that knows my power. That knows what I am capable of doing."

Andy steps forward, facing Violet. I can't move. My eyes dart between them.

Andy raises her hand, and Violet's feet float a few centimeters above the ground. Andy holds her there.

"I told you I was breaking out of that cage," Andy hisses. "It was only a matter of time."

"Andy, this isn't you," Violet says. Her voice cracks, and I know that Andy is squeezing the life out of her. Her eyes water, and she gasps for air. "Andy, please. You need to remember."

"I remember enough," she says. "I think Castor is right. It's time we begin again."

I realize what Violet is doing. She's gesturing to the door with her eyes.

In her lips, I read the word *go*.

She doesn't have to tell me twice.

Maybe Andy is after me; maybe Castor is. Violet can't buy me enough time to get away, but I need to get this crystal far from everybody. That's my sole mission.

My heart pumps in time with my feet as I exit the Arc and run through the forest back to Unity. I need to tell the others. My legs ache with the adrenaline as I speed, my vision blurry, still clutching the crystal in my hand so it doesn't get to the wrong hands.

I hear noise behind me but can't afford to look back. I break clean of the forest through Unity, the cabins in the near distance.

The first thing I spot is Sputnik. When I look back, I can almost feel the presence of Andy behind me, coming after the crystal.

Sputnik barks as I meet her.

There are no places to hide anymore. I run and stumble, falling to the ground and scraping my knees. The crystal rolls from my pocket.

Sputnik runs forward and sniffs it.

Then she eats it.

CHAPTER 39

My dog just ate a crystal that could bring about the end of the world.

"Are you serious?" I shout at her. "Spit it back."

Sputnik wags her tail. I stare at her, unable to grasp the reality of what just happened.

"Come here."

She trots forward.

"Spit it out!" I order, tackling her to the ground with a thud.

I open Sputnik's mouth, but there's no sign of it. She struggles against my grip, because I've done this a hundred times before when I needed to check what exactly she was eating, holding her mouth open. I check inside her mouth, trying to avoid her snapping teeth as she withers and thrashes. It's like fighting a dinosaur.

It's no use. It's gone straight down.

Great.

Just great.

"Okay, now what?" I ask her as if she can give me an answer. Apparently, eating a Universal crystal doesn't really affect her. She doesn't start talking or gain special powers. A pity, really. A super powerful dog would have been useful. "Jesus Christ."

I run back to the cabins. Rayen comes bursting out the front door.

"Where's Violet?" she asks as soon as we meet halfway.

"She stayed behind," I tell her. "Castor is the one we're looking for. He came for the crystal. The one in the box."

"What happened? Is it safe?" Rayen demands, her brown eyes wide with worry. Rayen is good under pressure, and she doesn't hesitate a second before starting to think of a plan.

"Safe inside Sputnik's stomach. She just ate it."

Rayen stares at the dog. The dog stares back, thumping her tail.

"You know what? That doesn't actually surprise me," Rayen mutters. "Come on. The others—"

She's interrupted midsentence and looks out to the edge of the woods. I swing around, and I see Andy.

Behind her is Castor.

Fuck.

"I thought she was locked up," Rayen says.

"Well, you know. Difficult circumstances."

Rayen sighs, and I grimace.

"Sorry."

"Let's call the others," she says. "I'm not even sure what we need to do."

Except I don't think we need to do anything. Before Andy approaches—and she's clearly coming toward us—Castor moves his hand, and Andy flies back a hundred feet.

"What exactly are we watching right now?" Rayen asks in disbelief.

"Alien UFC," I reply. "It's pretty great if you're not standing too close."

Rayen blinks, mesmerized.

Andy gets up, unfazed.

"Should we help?" Rayen asks. "I mean, do we *have* to?"

I shrug.

Andy snarls something, and a strike of lightning hits Castor straight in the chest. He flies back to the woods.

"Okay, they're going to destroy Unity if this keeps going," Rayen says. "We need them to move. They can kill themselves for all I care, but it's kind of a bummer if they destroy the food and the houses."

Castor throws something toward Andy, and lightning strikes again. She stops the light in the middle and twists it away from her.

A piece of the roof is thrown in our direction us as Brooklyn steps out of the house.

"Whoever threw that rooftop," Brooklyn announces loudly, "your mom is a ho."

Flint sees the devastation, openmouthed. "I did not sign up for this. Any of this. I want to go home right now."

I give him a look of deep solidarity.

"What are they doing?" Avani demands. "What's happening?"

"I'll explain later," I say. I look at Sputnik. "You guys protect Sputnik. She's the most important thing right now."

"Clover, we know you love Sputnik, but is this really the time?"

"I mean literally. She just ate the crystal that can transform the Earth into Universali."

Brooklyn opens her mouth, but for once, I've left her speechless. I'd celebrate the feat if I had more time.

"I'm going to try and distract them," I say. "I'm running back to the forest. You guys make sure everyone is safe. And hide Sputnik or something. He can't know."

I run toward Castor and Andy. Both of them have power curled around their fists, ready to take the other out.

"Hey!" I shout. "You want the crystal? Come get it!"

It's the stupidest thing I've ever done. Castor and Andy both stop fighting, their eyes fixed on me.

I take off running toward the woods. My body might want to kill me, if I even survive this. The woods are like home by now, and I run, navigating through the trees with ease. I can feel both Castor and Andy running after me, and I don't know what exactly my plan is, because I have no idea how to get them both to stop fighting or, in this case, following through on some megalomaniacal alien scheme.

Sounds like just another Thursday.

I run into the forest, and an idea sparks. It can't hurt. I run back.

Back toward the clearing where we first saw the crystals.

Both Andy and Castor are behind me, their footsteps sure.

I stop when I see the crystal cluster. I can now see how the veins are sucking up the earth from inside, molding it so it becomes more alien. I step closer and don't move.

Andy and Castor stand side by side in the clearing.

Castor is the first to speak.

"You don't have it," he says.

"Of course I don't," I reply with a grin. My adrenaline is pumping, and I think I've pretty much lost all sense of self-preservation I had left, if I ever even had any to start with. "Feel free to go back to frying each other all you want."

Castor instead runs toward me, and I dodge him. He may be Universal, but I'm fast. I'm built to survive the extreme. Andy steps in front of him, though.

He turns to her and grabs her by the neck. She yelps in surprise. I see her power being drained, going from her body to Castor's hands.

He points his other hand toward the crystal, and it starts glowing.

"You can't," Andy gasps. "I won't—"

She doesn't finish her sentence. Andy's eyes start to fade from the unnatural glow to their regular blue.

I run forward and kick Castor as hard as I can. He lets Andy go, and she drops to the ground. He turns around, pushing me, and I fall back, gasping for air. He turns his attention to Andy once again, picking her up once more.

I go for his neck, trying to hit his head so he drops to the ground, snapping both his arms at the elbows. He yelps, dropping Andy. I tackle him again, but Castor's too strong, pushing me aside again. Andy's color is drained, her skin pale.

"I don't want to hurt you," he repeats to me as if this is something fundamental that I need to understand. "You can't stop it. It's only a matter of time."

"Accepting reality isn't really my thing, sorry."

I wish I'd brought Rayen's guns. I wish I'd gotten enough time to manage this fight. All I can do is stall them, and I don't know how to win against them both. I move forward again, but Castor's hands wrap me in a burst of light, hurling me to the ground.

Before I can do anything else, Castor picks Andy up, slamming her against the crystal. It's a second that lasts an eternity, light bursting from her palms and her eyes, and I'm thrown back as the whole world lights up.

A single beacon of light crosses all the way from Andy to far out in the atmosphere.

"What did you do?" I ask.

But Castor only smiles. He drops Andy to the ground, then moves over to me, and he presses his hand against my forehead.

The world goes dark.

CHAPTER 40

When I wake up, someone's holding me, and my head is cold.

I blink, trying to clear away the brightness and get away from whoever is there.

"Ouch," Brooklyn complains. "I'm trying to help here."

When I regain my senses, I notice that I'm back in the jail cell of the first day, the wood floor beneath me. My head throbs, even with the ice Brooklyn is pressing against my forehead. Then I look to my side and realize that Andy is also on the floor, passed out. It had been daytime while we were in the Arc, but now it was the darkness before dawn that seeped in through the window.

"What the hell happened?" I ask.

"Chaos broke out with Andy arriving in Unity," Avani says. "They locked all of us in."

I don't dare get up, the world still dizzy around me. Castor's fight with Andy. Sputnik eating the crystal. Andy touching the crystal in the woods, lighting up the whole way to the sky.

I look at Andy. She looks normal. As in human. Her skin is a pale marble color, and her hair has returned to its usual brown. I open her eyes, and they're pale blue once more. There's no sign of her powers anywhere, not even a small glow to her skin.

Violet's sitting next to her.

"What the hell happened?" Flint asks, his arms crossed.

"Castor showed up in the Arc," Violet says. "He wanted Andy and the crystal inside the box. I bought Clover some time to get here with the crystal."

There's a red line on Violet's neck from where Andy was holding her.

"How did you get out?"

"Castor attacked Andy," Violet says. "I think they truly don't care about us. This is between the two of them." She looks at us. "Tell me the crystal is safe."

I look at Rayen. "Where is she?"

"With Heidi, last I saw," Rayen says easily.

"What happened with you?" Violet turns to me.

"I tried to drive them away from Unity. Only partially worked. Castor slammed Andy against the crystal in the woods, and she just sent out this weird beam into the atmosphere."

Brooklyn sighs deeply. "Great. So now we're all stuck back in a tiny cell with no chance of leaving, plus everyone knows by now we're aliens."

"I'm not," Violet adds.

"Don't start," Flint snaps, glaring at her through his glasses. "We need a plan."

We grow quiet. We barely understand what's happening, each of us still sulking that we're locked up.

"So he made the crystals," Flint starts. "What exactly does he want with them?"

"He wants to reshape Earth to remake Universali," Violet says. "I think he lured us here to get to Andy."

"Is she all right now?" Avani asks quietly. "What if she wakes up—"

"I didn't have a choice," I say.

"You could have talked to us," Brooklyn says. "You just went off and made the decision on your own. Just like you've been doing since we got here."

"Hey," Rayen says, "we're not the ones causing problems."

"Oh, really?" Brooklyn's voice rises. "All of you were obsessed with finding things wrong with this place."

"But we were right about the distress signal," I tell her. "It was a trap."

"Clover, now is not the time."

"Not the time?" My voice rises automatically. "We're stuck inside a cell, Brooklyn. I'd say this is a pretty good time."

"This is not necessary," Avani interrupts us, both staring daggers at each other, but it's too late now. I'm on edge, my muscles are hurting, and I've got a headache.

And I'm tired.

I'm tired of pretending that I cared about fitting into a place where I had to constantly lie about my experiences, about what had happened, where I couldn't tell a single person what I'd been through.

"We gave it a chance, but we don't belong here," Rayen snaps. "Or what? Do you think they'll just accept that you're part alien? That everything they think about the invasion is a lie? What do you think will happen if you tell them the truth, huh?" Rayen shakes her head.

The only one who hasn't spoken is Violet, still quiet, sitting and staring at the other side of the bars.

It's exhausting that this discussion will not end.

It's no use blaming each other.

Brooklyn wipes a tear on her cheek, holding Avani's hand in her own as if it is the last thing holding her together. I close my eyes, breathing hard, just wishing that we'd never listened to the signal, never came back at all.

"Maybe it really taught us that we don't fit together," Avani says, her voice ringing clearly. "That it was just another thing that the end of the world brought, and we should let it die. Like the rest."

I face Avani, my heart squeezing in my chest, but she eyes me back, and there's nothing but truth in her gaze.

The truth that echoes within me and breaks my heart even further.

The world can end in many different ways.

"You're right," Rayen says, facing Avani. "As soon as this is done, we can each go our own way."

"Shut up, all of you."

We turn to Violet, but we were so caught up in the argument that we hadn't seen that she is on the floor, and Andy is stirring.

"She's waking up."

CHAPTER 41

Andy's eyes fly open, and we all step back.

Her eyes are not like before. They're just a regular shade of blue, almost faded. She blinks, and we hold our breath.

"Where am I?"

Rayen and I exchange looks. I learned not to trust Andy while she was inside the cell.

"What do you remember?" Violet is the first one to speak.

"We came to Earth, and then..." Andy's eyes widen. "Oh dear holy mother of rainbow roads, I touched the crystal."

"Yeah, you did," Flint says without easing up. "Do you remember what happened next?"

Andy closes her eyes in concentration, then she shakes her head. "Some of it, but I..." Her voice dies as she stares at her hands. She picks up some of her hair and looks at the color.

There isn't a single part of hers that looks Universal.

"Oh no." Andy shoots up, but her legs are weak. Rayen holds her, with her knees shaking. "I can't feel it. I can't—" She starts crying. Her tears are normal. She shakes her head again, trying to bring her sobs to a stop. "Where are we?"

Rayen is the first to answer, quickly summing up what had happened while Andy was still locked back in the Arc.

When she's done, Andy looks like she's about to have a panic attack.

"We need to get out of here," Andy says. "This can't be good. Oh God, oh God, oh God."

Violet walks over to her, putting her hands on Andy's shoulders. "Come on, Andy. Breathe."

Andy takes a deep breath she doesn't need. There's no evidence of the other, darker Andy. I'm not sure whether to be relieved or worried.

"So it's true," Avani finally says. "The crystals. Castor. All of it."

"Yes," Andy says.

"What are these crystals, exactly?" Rayen says.

"They're what made our planet, Universali," Andy replies. "Every single one of us has the capability of making them to some extent. To build houses, spaceships. They're one of the strongest materials known to the universe. They can't be destroyed."

"Man, I love my life. Don't you?" Brooklyn laughs nervously, and Avani glares at her.

"Why does Castor need the one in the box?" Violet asks.

Andy grips her shirt, pulling the hem of it tight around the knots of her fingers.

"The crystal is pure energy. You know my powers, the ones I can use to manipulate everything around me—the crystal is the embodiment of that. The Universals were born out of those crystals. We're able to manipulate the energy inside them, change the universe from that. By themselves, the crystals are harmless. But once you try to manipulate that energy... It's like trying to manipulate the big bang."

I take a deep breath, wiping my eyebrow. None of this is helping my headache.

"Castor wants that energy to terraform the planet," Flint says. "He wants that energy to transform it into Universali."

"So we're all going to die?" Brooklyn asks.

We all ignore her.

"The Universal planet was destroyed during the war against the Hostemn," Andy starts. "But that's not just it. When it died, the universe rearranged."

"What do you mean?"

"I mean the universe is always expanding," Andy explains. "It expands in all directions, at all times. And it expands because at one point, it had a center. My planet."

"Are you fucking serious?" Rayen frowns. "The literal center of the universe?"

Andy shrugs.

"It's a wonder you lasted so long with that ego," Brooklyn says. "No offense."

"None taken," Andy says. "Either way, the crystals used to shift the planetary courses so Universali would stay centered. And if Castor succeeds…"

"The universe collapses to give way to a new order," Flint finishes. "With Earth at the center of the universe."

A year ago, none of this would have made any sense to me. Now, I accept it naturally, like my brain has been trained for this type of situation.

"So if he didn't need the crystals but grew them anyway, what are they for?"

"On our planet, they grew naturally. They lodged into the surface or anything that covers it and changed what was beneath."

I guess where Flint is going before he finishes his sentence.

"So hypothetically, if you threw a crystal deep into the Earth, it would lodge itself there?"

"Yeah," Andy says. "It would."

"The mountains," Violet replies. "That's where he's going. If he can somehow open a hole inside…"

"Oh, very well," another voice says, outside the cell.

We turn to the door where Castor has just walked in. He has the same human face as before. Andy's eyes are fire as she sees him.

"Castor," she says. "I didn't know you were alive."

"Don't act so surprised, Andromeda," he says. "Aren't you glad you're not the last one anymore?"

"What do you want?" Violet asks.

"I wanted to see how you were doing," he replies. "Is that so hard to believe?"

"What did you do to me?" Andy asks, shaking her head and getting up to face him. "I can't feel my powers."

"You won't for a while. I'm sorry," Castor says, and he sounds genuinely apologetic. "I needed the extra charge so the crystals would work faster. Your power has energized them. Once I get the original, the process will work perfectly."

"You can't do this," Andy replies. "This whole planet is going to die."

"It's not going to die," Castor says. "It's going to be reborn."

"You're going to destroy it," Andy accuses him. "Please, you must remember—"

Castor's eyes flare in anger.

"Remember what, Andromeda?" he asks. "You were a child when you first came here. You barely remember anything from Universali. You're not one of us. Not truly." He looks at her. "But you can be. It will be whole again."

Andy shakes her head. "You're wrong."

"Join me, Andromeda," Castor says, ignoring the rest of us. "We can bring Universali back. We can restore our race to what it was. We can make the universe whole again."

Andy hesitates, opening her mouth.

"Leave her alone," Violet says, pushing Andy back.

"Wouldn't you like to see it? To feel at home?"

Andy doesn't answer. Violet stands in front of Castor, and I'm sure she would try to punch him if we weren't all locked behind these bars.

"It's wrong," Andy spits. "You know the rules."

"You broke the rule," Castor replies. "You brought someone back. Energy is supposed to dissipate. No interference. But we both know that's wrong. You understand, don't you?"

Andy doesn't answer. Her eyes skip to Violet, then back to Castor.

"It's time we change those rules. What I'm building is going to be another Universali. Bring back what it was, before the Hostemn, before the others. We can be so much more."

A chill climbs up my spine. The Universals as pacifists were terrifying. The Universals as something else... I can't think of a word to describe it.

"I waited so long for you to bring it," Castor continues, his tone low. "I knew it'd call to you. That somehow, you'd find it. It's the way the lines are written. You brought it so we can finish this. We can build our planet again."

Castor reaches out, and I feel the power surging through the room. It's suffocating, intoxicating, contaminating the atmosphere as he raises his fingers. The strange magic that spreads the universe thin, the power of creation as Castor controls it. Andy's eyes turn a bright blue, stars reaching across her irises.

"I led you here to bring us home," Castor says, "Let me bring us home, Andromeda."

I wait for what seems like centuries. This is what real power feels like. I can't move, and I can't breathe while he's here, and I know he would end it, like the rest of the universe, just by playing the notes to a song.

"You can't do this," Andy whispers as Castor lets go, and everything bright in the universe is gone. There are tears welling up in her eyes.

"Tell me where the crystal is," Castor says, turning to me. "Tell me now."

I don't reply.

"It's no use fighting," Castor says. "I can feel its presence, and I'll find it soon enough. It'll end, one way or the other."

"You'll have to hurt me first."

Castor shakes his head. "I don't want to hurt you," he says. "I don't want to hurt any of you. I'm only changing things."

"Yeah, and our planet dies along with it," Brooklyn mutters. "Nice change."

"It's only a consequence of the actions," Castor replies. "The energy will dissipate. It'll rebuild. Equal energy and balance."

Andy sets her jaw.

"We will stop you," she replies.

"You won't," he says, not unkindly. "It'll all be fine, I promise."

Suddenly, there's a commotion outside. There are shouts that echo from the only window we have, and Castor frowns. He turns his back without saying anything and heads out the door.

"What's happening?" Brooklyn asks.

Rayen goes to the window, reaching out with her hands so she can prop herself on the ledge. The others follow, and all open their mouths. I move, shoving Avani aside so I can take a look.

What I see outside makes my stomach lurch.

A single ray of light blue crosses the sky, decelerating. Others follow, a meteor shower.

"It's a..." Flint starts, but he can never finish the words.

But I can. I remember seeing them on that first day. A lifetime ago.

"Spaceship," I say.

CHAPTER 42

We stand there looking as it crosses, and there's no doubt in my heart of what it is, even though I can't see it properly.

"It backfired," Andy says, and all of us turn to her.

"Is it really a spaceship?" Avani's voice is quiet. Meeting aliens when you're in space is expected, because to them, you're also strange. It's different when it's here. When they're coming again.

"When Castor tried to drain me of my powers, instead of just boosting the process, I think something else happened," Andy says. "I think I've broadcast our location to everyone in the entire universe."

"Ours as in…?" Flint asks.

"Ours as in Universal," Andy says, looking up to meet my eyes. "Every single one of our enemies will be coming here."

Brooklyn blinks, opens her mouth, shuts it again. She sighs. "So let me get all this," she starts. "Castor is trying to make the crystals work faster so he can transform the whole of Earth back into Universali, which will literally kill every single person left on this planet, and now the aliens are coming all the way over here to kick your asses. Am I missing anything?"

"No, I think that's pretty much it," Andy replies, unaware of Brooklyn's evident sarcastic tone.

"We're all going to die," Brooklyn says cheerfully.

"We're not going to die," Violet snaps.

Unfortunately, Violet's promise doesn't look too good. The bars of the cell are made of strong metal that none of us can bend. Rayen tries to pick the lock, but eventually, her pin breaks, and we're still sitting inside with no hope of getting out.

Flint keeps an eye on the window, and he sees when other silver trails cross the night sky and land near us. It's an hour before we hear the screams.

Rayen gets up again. "Shit," she says. "Can you see what's happening outside?"

Flint climbs on her shoulders to see better and says, "Damn. Aliens."

Somehow, that sums up all of my life in the last year and a half.

"What kind?" Andy asks. "We need a plan. Where the hell is the crystal?"

"It's going to be hard with the aliens around," Flint responds. "Looks like—"

He doesn't finish his sentence. Suddenly, a tremor goes through the ground, and he falls over Rayen, landing them both on the floor. The earthquake spreads, shaking the cabin, and I hold on for dear life, my heart hammering inside my chest.

Violet turns to me. "Clover, where did you hide it?"

"I didn't hide it," I say. "Sputnik ate it."

Violet and Andy stare at me openmouthed.

"Don't look at me like that. I couldn't stop her," I tell them. "I don't know how long we have before he finds out."

"Not long. Castor will be able to sense the crystal's energy and track it," Andy says. "You need to take Sputnik and get the hell out of here. Get the Arc, and then—"

"The Arc can't leave, not with the barrier still up," Avani replies. "We're stuck."

Andy takes a deep breath. "Castor's ship," she breathes. "He's using it to broadcast the barrier. If we find it, we can take it down. Then we're out of here."

I nod. It doesn't sound like a solid plan, but it's the closest thing we have. "I'll go get Sputnik," I say. "You guys distract Castor if you can. Andy, we need you to find that ship."

The screams outside grow exponentially, and there are heavy thuds on the ground. I close my eyes, imagining what it looks like outside. The alien invasion, once again.

I open my eyes and meet Andy's gaze across the cell. She knows what they're after. And we have to stop them.

A second later, I hear the noise of something rattling near the door.

Thankfully, it's my father who steps in, looking disheveled but with the keys.

Violet jumps from her seat. "You have to let us out of here."

"There's something going on outside," he says, out of breath, "and we don't—"

"Aliens," Rayen completes for him. "We know. Let us out."

He looks between me and my friends, and then his eyes fall on Andy. "What's going on?" he asks.

"It's a long story," I say. "One I can tell another day. We need to get out of here now. And people need to stay inside the cabins."

"But the aliens—"

"We'll take care of it."

Marcelo shakes as his fingers put the key inside the lock and the cell opens. Violet is the first out, and the others follow. I pause at the threshold.

"What's happening, Clover?"

I purse my lips, not knowing where to begin.

"Honestly, I don't think you'd understand."

"You can try."

He looks sincere when he says it. I've got nothing else to lose. Not right now. If we don't stop Castor, our planet will be gone in the next couple of hours.

Everything I know and love will be gone.

"We were the ones who stopped the alien invasion," I say, my voice low. "We left the planet after it ended, going through space. But we heard a distress signal, and we came to investigate.

Andy, our friend, is an alien, and Castor is the same species as her. He used the signal to lure Andy so she'd be able to boost some terraforming crystals to turn Earth into their dead planet, and if we don't move fast enough, Earth is going to die." I take a deep breath. "Also, I have some alien DNA."

I pause, hoping I covered it all.

"I don't understand half of what you just said," he finally says. "You can tell me all later. I believe you."

I smile, and he smiles back.

"Thank you," I tell him. "For everything."

He reaches out, and his hands touch my face. It's a gesture that echoes Abuelo, that comfort I once felt.

He wraps me into a hug, and I let him, hugging him back tight.

"Get everyone to safety," I tell him. "Make everyone sit inside their cabins, and don't let them leave." I step away.

"Where are you going, Clover?"

I look back at him. "I stopped an alien invasion before. It's time to do it again."

I run out of the cabin, ready to fight.

CHAPTER 43

Everyone is panicking outside.

There are no signs of aliens nearby, but there's reason behind their panic. It's been ten years since these people faced this kind of danger. Ten years is a long time. Time enough to forget what it's like, living on that edge, that fear that sets deep within your bones and robs your lungs of air.

But I know this fear like I know my own mind, and I'm not bending to it anymore.

My father starts herding people toward the cabins, but I don't spot Sputnik or Heidi anywhere.

"Where's Castor?" I ask him.

"Haven't seen him," he answers.

It's no use asking. Castor's after the same thing we are. We just need to get somewhere first.

"Andy, go to the Arc," I tell her. "Access the Universal files and see if you can track the other ship. I'm gonna find my dog."

Andy nods.

The ships keep landing on the edge of the forest. The good thing is that if they're coming after Andy, they're coming after Castor. The aliens will hopefully buy us time.

"Split into pairs and cover the forest," Rayen instructs. "At least one good shooter in each group. Whistle three times if something goes wrong."

"And boy, is it going to go wrong," Brooklyn says.

Rayen glares at her.

We split into groups, and most of them move toward the forest. Andy disappears into the woods, and I keep checking that the others in Unity have made it back safely to their cabins. There's panic all over town, but I don't let it get to me. I've lived through this once already. I'm surviving whatever comes next.

While the rest are going to fight the invasion, I open every single cabin in Unity, searching for Sputnik. I don't find her. I bust open doors and windows, searching through scared faces, but I don't linger. My father tries to keep people calm, following in my footsteps, reassuring the others that everything is under control.

"What do you need her for?" he asks while we search the cabins with provisions for the winter.

"She's important" is the only thing I can say.

Finally, after what feels like hours but can't be more than minutes, I go back to Heidi and Castor's cabin.

It's quiet when I walk inside.

The floor creaks when I come in, and the windows have been barred completely, the light seeping in through the cracks. There is a desk, a chair, a couple of archives. There are notebooks spread over the desk, all written in different symbols. Pages and pages of senseless scribbles, written notes in the margins, and what looks like drawings.

There's nothing in the cabin that looks organized.

It's also small.

It looks pointless, to build a cabin this size, only to keep the administration of the colony here. It can't be all there is to it. I look down and notice a carpet. I kick it away.

There's a trapdoor right beneath us.

I look back at my dad. He raises an eyebrow, picking up an old rifle that was forgotten in the corner. Then he nods.

I open the trapdoor with a bang and jump out of the way.

Still nothing.

I lick my lips, looking at the stairs.

I descend and notice the walls are made of solid wood. It's a reflection of the rest of the cabin, but this room, unlike the one above, is organized. There are neat piles of notebooks and papers, and there are cell phones and computers that don't work anymore. A huge map is spread over one of the walls, but it's not of Earth. It's a series of concentric circles, from the size of a small ring to one that takes the space of half the wall. It's a star chart.

When I turn around, cold metal grazes the back of my neck.

"Don't move," Heidi's voice says.

I raise my hand immediately.

Sputnik barks.

"Sputnik!" I exclaim.

The pressure on my back lessens, and I slowly turn around. Heidi is still holding a gun, pointed right at me.

"Clover?" my dad calls.

"It's fine!" I call back to him. Sputnik whimpers, running up to me and brushing her fur against my legs. I raise my eyes to Heidi's. "I'm not going to hurt you."

Heidi doesn't falter.

"You're with him," she says. "I saw what Castor can do. No one else was paying attention, but I saw it. I saw him tear the roof apart with only the light from his hands."

Her eyes are calm, sure. I know why she has survived the invasion before.

She's like me.

"Please, put it down," I say, trying to keep my voice calm. The last thing I need is my dad coming here and making it worse. "I was just looking for Sputnik. I don't want to hurt anyone."

"How can I tell you're not lying?" Heidi asks. "It's all you've done since you arrived here. All of you."

"Castor lied, too."

Heidi doesn't even blink. "I want the truth."

"I told you the truth," I say. "We came here because of a distress signal."

"Not from west."

"No," I say. Then I point up. "From up there."

Sputnik nudges me again, and I try to step back, but Heidi's grip on the gun is tighter than ever. She keeps it trained on me.

Heidi is not going to hesitate.

The same woman who said I was brave to keep living, who said I didn't have to be afraid. The same woman who helped me see that there was something after the end of the world.

Something worth fighting for.

Better.

Something worth *living* for.

"What are you?" she asks.

"I'm just..." My voice falters. "I'm surviving."

Heidi buckles back, her gaze lowering from mine. I'm supposed to be scared, to beg for my life. I'm not afraid of these things anymore.

"I'll tell you everything," I say to her. "But I need to stop this invasion, right now."

Heidi lowers the gun, her eyes glistening with tears. So are mine.

I grab Sputnik's collar and haul her up. "Come on, girl. Come on."

It's quiet upstairs.

When I come up, though, Castor is holding my father against his body. My father doesn't move.

"That was a clever trick," Castor says quietly. "There aren't too many places to hide the crystal. It calls to me. I'll take Sputnik now."

Sputnik doesn't move.

"You won't hurt him," I say, but I can't say for sure.

"One human life to end at my hands seems like a fair price to pay," Castor replies. "I haven't done it in all these years. I never wanted to fight. It's not my people's way. Give me Sputnik. I won't hurt her."

I take a step forward, and Castor's choke hold tightens. My father's face starts turning red.

"Clover—" he starts.

I shake my head.

"Don't do this," I tell Castor. "Please."

He extends a hand, the other still choking my father. His eyes start to flutter, and a knot closes up in my throat.

Slowly, I hand Castor Sputnik's leash.

Castor lets my father go immediately, dropping him to the floor. I run to him, and in a blink, Castor has picked up Sputnik with his superhuman strength and is out the door, running fast.

I kneel on the floor next to my father. He gasps for air, his hands clawing at his throat. He sits up, taking deep breaths. My body won't answer my commands. I try to take a breath, but I'm barely holding on.

Castor has Sputnik.

It's over.

My father closes his eyes for a moment, shaking his head. Then he laughs, a nervous, fluttery sound that's half amusement, half desperation.

"I can't believe this is happening," he says to me. "It feels surreal. Just like the first time."

"It doesn't get any better."

He opens his eyes and searches my face with a concerned expression I've seen before in my grandparents.

"So what is it like?" he asks. "Being up there?"

My heart clenches in my chest, and I'm taken back to the first time I saw the Earth from above. The moment I knew all of it would be worth it and if I were to die, I'd be okay with it.

"It's beautiful," I say. "More than you can imagine."

My father nods, regaining his breath. I try to hold back my tears, my desperation growing inside me. I need to find the others. I need to tell them that Castor has the crystal, that I couldn't stop him.

"I've got…" I say. "I've gotta go."

"It's going to be fine," he says.

"Why do you keep saying that?"

He shrugs. "Because once you say it enough, you believe in it. You stopped an invasion once. Now it's saving what's left of us."

It's easier to see what it means here next to him, what this whole world means. It's not just about the planet and the trees and the buildings and humanity. When I scale it down to just me and my father, I can see the whole world.

A tear slips from my face. He kisses my forehead.

"Go, mija," he says.

I go save the world.

CHAPTER 44

Outside, the world is ending.

It's a feeling I'm surprisingly used to. I find the gun Rayen has hidden and head into the woods where I can hear the oncoming battle of the aliens following Andy and Castor.

I need to find the others and tell them what happened.

My footsteps echo in the woods as I move toward the mountains, listening for where the sounds are coming from. The spaceships landed just beyond, and I can see Unity as a quiet little village behind me.

I hear nothing but the breathing of the forest around me.

And then I hear them.

Something my DNA understands better than I do myself.

It's that small sound of hearing my enemy approach, my body ready for impact.

I have no fear left within me.

The first alien drops within ten feet of me.

It's a species I've seen before. Its body is made of clay, four arms spread on shoulders that are too large for its torso. Its three legs spin down the mountain path, unused to the tree roots and the uneven ground. It's too large and violent to be here, and I don't wait.

My first shot hits its head, and the creature makes a shrieking sound that echoes the birds in the trees. The alien turns around, trying to identify its prey, but it's on its own here. On a strange planet, seeking its enemy.

I take another shot, this time for the chest, and then I run, swipe my rifle against its head to knock it out to the ground. It grabs me easily with one of its enormous hands, and I swipe the rifle again. The clay shatters, revealing an underlying layer that looks like tree bark. The creature shrieks again, and I go for its eye, the gaping hole in the middle of its head. It falls back, stuttering on the ground, and I latch myself onto it.

I can't defeat this thing on my own.

I see a flash among the trees, and Flint comes down the mountain to help. He aims at its head, and I duck. The creature howls.

The alien goes down but not without a fight. Its four arms are struggling against me, and I roll back, grabbing the gun.

Flint shoots again for its head. The creature swings its arm around, planting its feet ahead, sinking to the ground. The mountainside shakes around us, dropping rocks and tree branches, and Flint and I duck for cover.

The rocks slide in every direction, the trees shaking off leaves onto the frost-covered ground. My breath comes out in smoky coils. The terrain stops shaking, and then I nod to Flint.

I jump in front of the alien, and Flint sneaks behind its back. He swings his rifle over the creature's third leg, toppling it to the ground. I aim for the chest and then keep shooting as I go higher. Each shot makes my shoulders draw back, but I remain steady. Every time I shoot, it's the sound of a tree cut off, the clay of the alien falling.

When I get to its eye, the alien disintegrates. It falls into pieces of clay and rock until there's nothing but rubble.

Flint wipes sweat off his brown and cleans his glasses. "Why can't there be nice aliens?" he asks.

"We are nice," I tell him.

He shakes his head. "What happened? We didn't see Castor, and—"

"He got away," I cut him off. "He has Sputnik. We don't have much time."

Flint pales considerably. "Let's go."

We run up the mountain toward the Arc. It's our only hope now. I don't know where Castor is going, but if we can follow him, there's still time to stop it.

When we get to the Arc, the only person already there is

Andy. She has scratch marks on her face that haven't healed, her eyes a dull shade of blue.

"Castor didn't show up," she says.

"He has what he wants," I say, summing up what happened in the cabin to her. Andy listens, shaking her head. "We were also followed by weird aliens that look like ill-formed Power Ranger monsters."

"Oh, Grrronters," Andy replies. "They're cute."

"Why are they your enemy, exactly?" Flint asks.

Andy shrugs. "It's safe to say that most species hate the Universals freely. And simultaneously want what we can do."

I pat her back. "You feeling better?"

She shakes her head. "Still can't access my powers. And I feel tired. Is that how humans feel all the time? I just feel like dropping down to the ground and sleeping for a week."

Flint and I exchange a look and roll our eyes.

Flint taps the map of the crystals. "Where does he need to go with it?"

Andy looks at the map. "I'm not sure. It's the Universali symbol of power. It's just missing…"

She types a command to the computer, and a location right at the center shows up. "It's like a line. The center connects all the others. If he puts the original crystal there, it forms a net. He spreads Universali."

"Great," Flint mutters under his breath. "We have his location. We call the others, we go to him."

At that moment, Rayen walks inside the Arc. "What the hell happened?" she asks.

"Castor has Sputnik," Andy says.

Rayen pales considerably. "Is she…is she d—"

"I don't think he'd kill her," Andy says. "At his core, he's a pacifist. He fought us, but he didn't try to kill us. Just stuck us in jail."

"So he's willing to commit genocide but doesn't want to kill one dog?" Rayen frowns deeply. "Space Hitler much?"

"He doesn't see it that way," Andy says. "He won't technically be killing anyone. The crystal will."

"That doesn't sound right, but I'm not questioning anything at this point," Flint says. "We need to go after him before he gets the crystal from Sputnik."

"Great plan," Rayen nods. "Let's go. Where are the others?"

That's when we realize Violet, Brooklyn, and Avani haven't made it to the Arc.

Fuck.

We all head outside, but the forest is quiet.

Rayen makes a circling gesture with her fingers, and we all grip our guns harder, making our way back to the forest, the tension far from leaving my body. We follow the path we came along, listening for anything out of the ordinary, listening for the sound of invaders and battle.

"All right, they've been through here," Rayen says, pointing to footsteps. "Now if they veered left—"

That's when we hear the scream.

We start running toward the sound. When we get to the clearing, there are five Grrronters facing the three girls. Except Brooklyn is on the ground, bleeding, and Avani is with her, trying to stop the blood.

As if we're one single unit, we start moving. Rayen stands back-to-back with Violet, and I shout, drawing the attention of the creatures to me. Andy stands in front of the fallen girls. Flint and I cover our circle around the clearing and start getting ready to shoot.

Rayen gives the sign, and just like magic, we swing. Rayen first, shooting the first Grronter in the eye, making it stumble back. Flint drops to the ground and uses his rifle as a baton, swinging it over the third leg, making the alien fall. Violet drops the second alien, shooting it in the chest, and I do the same as Flint.

When the last Grrronter drops in a pile of tumbling clay and rock, I turn to see Brooklyn. She is clutching her side, which is torn open. The sight makes me want to throw up, but I hold on.

It's like Adam all over again.

I freeze, my mind going into a panic. I can't deal with this. I see Adam, blown into bits and pieces of dust until there's nothing left of him.

Brooklyn's on the ground, and I can't move. I can't breathe. I can't do anything at all.

"Help me get her up," Avani says, and Brooklyn coughs up more blood.

Violet nudges me forward, and I try to regain control over

my muscles, but even then, my brain is still screaming inside my head. Brooklyn is going to die.

Brooklyn is going to die.

"Clover!" Flint shouts, trying to make me snap out of it. He touches my back, and his touch solidifies my world again—it brings me back to my reality, and not just inside my brain.

I start helping, even though I can't feel my own hands. We improvise a stretcher for Brooklyn, and all of us help carry her back to the Arc.

All the while, my brain still screams, and I pray, under my breath, over and over again.

Not again. Not again. Not again.

CHAPTER 45

Brooklyn is put inside the Arc's healing incubators.

We all stand together in the infirmary. I try to get myself together, to get my muscles to stop shaking and make my breath regular, but it's hard.

Not again.

I can't lose someone else.

I just can't.

The machine beeps with Brooklyn inside, the incubator glowing blue. Avani is next to it, her hair tied in a bun as she concentrates. Finally, after what seems like days but can't be more than a couple of hours, the incubator opens its glass door. I get up, too fast, my knees wobbly. Flint catches me so I don't fall, and I need his help just to approach the machine. He pretends this is normal, and so do I.

"She's going to be fine," Avani says, relief flooding through her voice.

"Of course I am," Brooklyn mumbles, opening her eyes. "You can't get rid of me that easily."

"Stop talking. You need to rest," Avani snaps.

"I'm not dying," Brooklyn announces, convinced. "I mean, eventually, yes. We're all going to die. There will come a day when we'll perish. But it is not this day."

"She's quoting *Lord of the Rings*." Rayen sighs, shaking her head. "She's fine."

Brooklyn has a couple of scratches on her face and a wrap around her torso, the incubator still showing her vitals.

We stand quietly, shoulder to shoulder, and it's the first time since we got back to Earth we've been like this. United.

Avani looks up from Brooklyn. "I'm sorry," she says. "I mean, we might have solved this sooner if we weren't so determined to stay here."

"It's not your fault," I say. "Anyone normal would have wanted to stay."

Rayen shoves me with an elbow.

"It's true," Flint says. "Maybe we all needed to do a little better."

"I wouldn't trust anyone else with saving my life," Brooklyn says. "Except you guys. That has to count for something."

"I wouldn't trust anyone else with communicating with aliens," Flint replies.

"Well, I wouldn't trust me, either, but thank you for the sentiment," Brooklyn says with a laugh, and then she coughs up more blood.

"Quiet, for heaven's sake," Avani snaps at her. "Are you incapable of doing the only thing you're supposed to do?"

"It's against my principles."

Avani smacks her in the head and not gently. I laugh, and I'm relieved that everyone is safe. That we're not losing anyone this time. It's a strange relief, but I don't think I can bear another loss. I can't bear for someone else to be left behind.

I'm tired of people dying.

I want people to live.

"I'm sorry," Violet says. "I was so caught up in all this. I missed the Earth. I missed having a place where everyone didn't think I was strange, where no one looked twice at me." She takes a deep breath. "I wanted what all of you had. Being special. Being able to fight the aliens and survive out there. And when I didn't, I wanted to take that away." She swallows.

"Being special is overrated," Flint says, squeezing Violet's shoulder.

"I just…" Violet stops herself. "This is where I'm supposed to be. Here. With everyone else. Not out there, in space. And if you guys decide to go back, I'm not going back with you." She looks at all of us. "You're my family. But it's not my place in the end." Violet looks at Andy, who looks back at her. "After you brought me back, I kept wondering and wondering," Violet says, "if I am the same as before. I couldn't tell. From the moment you healed me, there was something different. Maybe I'm not the same as I was before, and I'm never going to know for sure. You should have just let me die."

Andy winces, and I can't think of anything to ease that pain.

But of course, it's Brooklyn who has the answer.

"Shut up," Brooklyn says. "This is *my* dying moment. You can't steal it. You had your dying moment before, and you didn't die, so now it's time you move on. Let me have mine in peace."

Violet opens her mouth, but Brooklyn glares at her.

"Look, I get it," she says. "It's a deep philosophical question. It's something that'll haunt you for the rest of your life, because Andy brought you back, reconstructed you, and something reconstructed is not the same as before. It never is. But guess what? We all change either way. We're all alive, and we're all changing. You're never, ever going to be the same. It's what makes you human."

Andy puts her arms around Violet, and Violet leans in against her shoulder.

"So did Brooklyn say something that's not completely senseless?" Flint pipes up. "This is new."

"Fuck you," Brooklyn says.

And then we all laugh.

Because again, we're right here. In this world that we don't understand and that was supposed to belong to us, but we're not quite there yet. And all that matters is that we're right here, together, linked through shoulders and hands and hearts. That nobody else could separate us even though they tried, because right here, with these people, I have my family.

I'm home.

That's what home means.

Not blood. Not a planet. Not anything that's tangible. It's just that feeling that will follow you, that no matter how far you go, it'll let you know where you are when you get there.

And looking at my friends, I know that wherever the journey takes us, I'll always be home.

Violet looks up. "So," she starts, "time to save Earth? Again?"

We sigh collectively.

We already saved the world once. We can do it again.

CHAPTER 46

The plan is pretty simple.

At least that's what we tell ourselves. The simple truth is that we don't really have a plan.

"All right," Violet says, getting to the navigation room. "We follow Castor down to the mountains, but he's already ahead of us. At any given moment, he's going to get the crystal. Where is he exactly?"

Flint points it out on the map. I hadn't really looked the first time, but now I see it—the location is right in the middle of the Rockies. We're flying deep into the mountain range.

"The Arc won't land there," I say. "At least not inside. And that's where he's going to be, right? He has to connect the crystal to the Earth."

Andy nods. "Yeah, we'll have to follow on foot. Fight our way in."

"With the aliens following? That's ridiculous. They're all after you already," Avani replies.

"Unless…" I start saying and then stop in the middle of my sentence, calling up the distress signal again. "We use the distress signal against him. He was sending it from his ship."

"And?" Brooklyn frowns.

"The aliens are going to follow *him*," I say. "It's a distraction. He fights the aliens, and we steal the crystal back."

"It surprisingly makes sense," Violet says.

"I've been known to make sense once a year," I reply with a cocked eyebrow.

She glares.

"All right." Brooklyn claps her hands. "Off we go, then."

Everyone turns to her.

"You're not going," Avani says. "You've just been trampled by aliens."

"Of course I'm going. You never know when an alien is going to need to be talked to death," Brooklyn replies.

No one really has the patience to argue with Brooklyn.

"So, plan," Violet says, turning our attention back. "We find Castor's ship, let the aliens take him, get the crystal. Hopefully, bring down the barrier."

"Aye aye, captain," Brooklyn says.

Violet glares at her. "Once we're there, it's likely we'll have to split up. I think we're ready to go. Brooklyn, you should stay behind."

"Aw, shucks, you've convinced me," Brooklyn says. "Let's get moving, you assholes."

She doesn't need to say it twice.

We scramble to our usual places, everyone sitting down and ready. Rayen takes the usual armament, distributing alien guns and equipment to everyone. The distress signal beeps toward us. I take the wheel, and the Arc's motors rise into the air of the cavern, and then we're out, out to the mountains, silver crossing the sky ahead as I follow the distress signal.

The mountains get larger around me, the wild taking over deeply. The trees are close together, the woods too dense for me to make a good landing. I manage to get a strip at the base of the mountain.

"We're here," I say quietly.

We're not the only ones.

Through the tops of the trees, there's a glimpse of another blazing fiery trail crossing the sky. Another ship lands near, and everyone in the woods is heading for the same target. I download the distress signal to our GPS devices and distribute them around the room.

"All you have to do is get to the source," I say. "Whoever gets there first, find Sputnik, and then we're bringing down the barrier."

Violet goes out first, and the rest of us follow. The woods have an eerie feeling to them—it's colder than I thought it would be, and it might even snow. I close the ramp of the Arc. It hurts to leave it behind, but there's no way we're heading inside the mountain with a ship this big.

"Follow the plan," Violet says, turning to us. "We head in, head out. Don't confront Castor if you see him. We can't fight him—we can only delay him. Our priority is getting the crystal away from him."

"Let's go," Rayen says. "Look alive."

"That's gonna be hard," Brooklyn groans.

The climb is quiet and fast. We don't waste our breaths with chitchat. There's just the sure sound of our footsteps as we head up and one or another bird that chirps in the woods.

And then there's an echo in the woods, a sound of something unusual.

"They're following us," Andy whispers as if reading my mind. "Three of them."

"Good," Rayen says. "Let them follow."

We step up the pace, and I start to hear them behind us every time we move. Brooklyn is a little slower, but she pretends she can get through this, and none of us want to tell her otherwise.

When we've climbed several feet and I see the first cave, I point it out.

"Must be a series of tunnels," I say. "Probably how Castor got inside."

I'm not keen on climbing into unknown caves, but there's no other way to get inside. The distress signal is still strong, pointing toward the mountain.

"Get to the caves," Rayen orders. "We pick a better battleground to confront them."

I start running, and everyone else follows. The footsteps and the noise behind us get faster, too, but then I'm helping Flint climb over the rocks, entering the mouth of the cave, and Avani and I swing Brooklyn up. Rayen is the last to come, and she stays close to the ground, watching as our enemy closes in.

Rayen spots them first, and she points toward the glow of light.

As darkness falls, I see them clearly. Round balls of light with what looks like lightning inside them as they rush toward us. Their shapes transform as they get to the mouth of the cave, forming semi-humanoid bubbles that are still transparent.

"What are they?" Brooklyn asks Andy.

"I don't even know," Andy says, shaking her head.

The mouth of the cave is cavernous, and I wasn't wrong—there is indeed a series of tunnels that must lead inside. We'll have to rely on our instincts to get there.

"Split up," Violet orders. "Head to Castor's ship."

We nod, and the hunt begins. I get Rayen, Brooklyn, and Andy on my team, and the rest follow the path on the right. We start running, going deeper inside the paths of the mountain, getting lost ourselves. Andy dictates the way, and it's almost like she's being led there by an unknown force.

When she takes us to a dead end, we turn around, and two aliens are standing in front of the path. They are strange, gray bubbles, and the surfaces of their skin burst into smaller bubbles like a bath bomb.

They start making noises, and we all look at Andy.

Andy listens, waiting, and even Brooklyn seems to have a good idea of whatever they're saying.

"What is it?" Rayen asks as she waits, her rifle ready at her shoulders.

"Oh, the usual," Brooklyn says. "Come with us and we won't hurt you! We hate your species! Honestly, whatever." She waits, and when Rayen does nothing, she waves her hand. "You can start shooting now."

She doesn't need to say it twice. Rayen aims for the middle of the bubble, and it bursts with a strange sound that shakes the cave's walls. But instead of killing it, all it does is free the lightning inside. I try shooting again, but it doesn't work—there's no stopping the energy as it approaches.

Andy gets in front of it, and in a second, she's zapped up with energy. It boosts through her body, an electric current that shakes her to the core, electrifying her hair. I watch as it passes through her, still playing on her skin, and Andy turns to us with wide eyes.

"Guess that's what it feels like to go through shock therapy," she says. "I don't think these things can actually harm us."

Brooklyn shrugs, and Rayen puts the guns away. The other bubble alien does nothing as we step again through the cave and go back to tracking our beeps, and the lightning only proceeds to follow us as if trying to give us yet another shock.

"Move!" Brooklyn orders. "We're busy teens trying to save a dog!"

The aliens are unable to stop us.

The tunnels spread and slowly become larger. This is the work of centuries, and I'm not even sure how Castor would get a whole ship through here. The base of the mountain is close, and I can almost feel it as we approach, the warmth that radiates out from the center. A wave of heat rushes toward us, passing over everything inside the tunnel.

Rayen's device keeps beeping.

"We're close," she says.

Another step takes us to the mouth of the tunnel. I walk forward, and down below, almost at the center of the mountain, inside a pool of heat, there's a ship.

It's exactly like the Arc but smaller. Its silver shine looks polished, and the floor is cracked, and water is seeping through. The ship, though, looks strange—its wing is half broken, metal and wires showing. The front itself is unmarked, but the ship is clearly broken.

There's a treacherous path that goes down the mountain, but none of it provides cover.

"Here goes nothing," Rayen mutters.

She starts climbing down, and I follow her, helping Brooklyn. When I step down on the base of the mountain, I notice how warm it is—almost like the mountain is roaring and fighting against us.

Rayen looks around, but there's no sign of anyone else except us. Maybe Violet and the others haven't made it yet.

Rayen looks back at Andy. "Ready?"

Andy nods. "Whatever it takes."

"Good."

We enter the ship through the open ramp.

At first, everything is quiet. It looks empty, the panel clean and buttons all ready. It's a ghost of the Arc. Everything is covered in a layer of dust, and the atmosphere inside breathes stale. It's eerie, cobwebs hanging from the ceiling.

"I have a bad feeling about this," Brooklyn says.

"Split up?" Rayen suggests, and I nod. "Find the navigation room. We can bring down the barrier."

Brooklyn and Rayen take one side of the ship, and Andy and I take the other. I move, holding my gun tight, and Andy is right behind me. I'm not sure what we'll find.

"Can you feel anything?" I ask, not daring to raise my voice above a whisper.

"No," she replies. "It's strange. I really can't feel—" She quiets, closing her eyes.

"We keep going," I say. "Sputnik?" I ask, almost afraid but hoping she'll bark back. Instead, there's only silence.

We take the right side of the ship, moving from room to room. There are bunks and a lab here, too. It's empty and quiet to the point where the silence is deafening, and all my footsteps echo through the ship. I find the navigation room, but there's nothing there. I swipe my hand against the dusty surface, and the ship lights up. The computer is flickering, the numbers all wrong. Castor did say he was stranded here, but there's no reason why something like this would have stopped working.

I hit on another button, feeling the hum of the motor. I click on the distress signal, see it beeping on the screen, calling out to the whole universe. I lean on the panel, examining what's wrong. The ship didn't just crash and stop working. It was… dying. Like its energy was being sucked up. I knit my eyebrows, looking for the computer and the diagnosis.

That's when I see a shadow across the room.

I turn, pointing my gun, and there he is. I turn around, looking for Andy, but she's gone.

"What do you think is going to happen if you shoot, Clover?" Castor asks, voice quiet. "You can't change how this is going to go."

I shoot anyway.

The alien gun rips a hole through his chest, and I can see his insides leaking onto the floor. Castor stops for a second, gasping, but in a moment, he's whole again, as if it's nothing.

I raise the gun again.

"Where's Sputnik?" I demand.

"You'll live," he says. "You're part Universal, too. Can't you feel it? The crystals call to you, too."

"This is my planet," I reply. "You aren't going to destroy it."

He approaches, and I'm frozen in place. My hands shake as I try to break his control, try to fire the gun again, but instead, my mind only hears the distant song of the crystals.

The songs of Universali.

"It's going to be fine," he says. It's in his body's cells, ordering me to stay in place. Ordering me not to fight back. "Everything is going to be like it used to be. Don't you want that?"

"I don't want to forget."

His voice is soothing and calm. Like the song that's playing in my mind, like the planet that is going to sleep so it'll wake up and become something else.

"I'm turning it all back," he says. "It'll be like nothing ever happened."

I can't move, even as I fight his control. The threads of the world hold me together here, and Castor touches my forehead with his fingers.

And then I'm sent spiraling through black.

CHAPTER 47

I wake up with sweat lining my back.

The linen sheets have been changed, and they smell of the soap Abuela uses to wash my clothes. It takes a minute for me to settle down and see where I am. I get up, padding across the wooden floor, and look outside. It's a June morning, bright as they come, with the sky clear and the cornfields stretching to the horizon and the mountains.

I frown.

"Clover!" Abuela shouts from downstairs. "Clover, you're going to be late!"

I skip my way downstairs, paying attention to that one step that always creaks. I show up in the kitchen in my pajamas. Abuela is making breakfast.

"Eat," she orders, pointing to an omelet. "You should've changed your clothes. You know you shouldn't stay in pajamas all day. They get dirty."

I sit down, pulling my hair backward. There's something I can't identify in the atmosphere, something that feels strange that I should remember. The eggs are delicious, and Abuela doesn't need to order me twice.

Abuelo opens the door of the kitchen, cleaning his boots off before coming in.

"Buenos días, bella durmiente," he says with a smile. "You sure you still have time to take your old grandfather out with the airplane?"

I smile back at him. "Sure I do."

I finish eating my breakfast, running back upstairs to get dressed. The smell of the mountain breeze swings through the window, and the Beechcraft is waiting for us outside. When I pad downstairs again, Abuela is rearranging my bag.

"Is everything packed?" she asks. "Did you get the socks? Did you get the water?"

"Sí, Abuela."

She eyes me suspiciously. "I don't like that tone."

"It's the only tone I have," I answer her. "Look, I'll be back soon. I'm just going to take a quick ride."

She tsks, disapproving, but lets me go anyway. Abuelo waits for me outside next to the plane, his sunglasses already on.

"It's a good morning for flying," he announces, and I couldn't agree more.

There's a certain easiness as I hop inside the cabin and start the plane. When the plane takes off, there's just the slightest pit in the bottom of my stomach. I start flying over the cornfields, heading for our neighbor to check on the cows. When I look at the horizon, I see the mountains, and I frown again. There's something I should remember about the mountains.

"What is it, Clover?" Abuelo asks.

"I think I dreamed something last night."

"What was it?"

"Aliens."

He gives a hearty laugh.

"That's interesting. What movie did you watch last night?"

I frown. "I can't remember."

"You're just tired," he says. "And excited about the trip."

I nod in agreement, but there's something else about the dream that I should be remembering. The wind sings through the corn, whistling its usual tune. I make the rounds with the plane in silence, enjoying the view ahead.

When I land, I feel an ache inside my chest, something burning, and I can't breathe. I put a hand to my heart, and Abuelo looks at me, concerned.

"Are you sure you're feeling all right?" he asks. "Estás diferente."

"It's nothing," I tell him quickly. "It's the dream. It's still bothering me."

"Dreams are dreams, mija," he says. "Leave them where they belong." He taps a finger against my temple.

"Something is wrong."

"Better go inside and drink some water."

I agree, and we head to the house. Abuela is there cleaning the living room, and Abuelo grabs a glass of water for me. I gulp it down, feeling my brain suddenly clear. I cannot remember the dream, and I wish I could just put it aside. But there's something in my brain that's trying to fight back.

"¿Con fiebre?" Abuela asks, putting her hand against my forehead.

"It's nothing, really," I protest. "I haven't slept well."

"Of course you haven't. You went to sleep with your hair wet. I have said a hundred times, you get a migraine from these things." She proceeds to talk for ten minutes about the dangers of sleeping with wet hair even when it's summer and how I should always blow-dry my hair before going to bed.

I've heard this at least a hundred different times. I cough.

"Do you want me to get the Vicks VapoRub? It'll help you breathe better."

"I just had a nightmare, that's all," I say, cutting the sermon short, ignoring the symptoms of my body. "It'll be fine."

Her frown deepens. "Maybe you should rest instead of going on this trip."

"Abuela, you've tried to dissuade me, like, thirty different times."

"Sí, because I know what's good for you and maybe—"

A knock at the door interrupts her. Abuelo goes to open it, and in the doorway stands Noah.

My heart does a leap when I see him, and I feel a wave of relief. Noah is here, and he's fine. He isn't dead.

I frown. Why would he be dead?

"Morning, Mr. and Mrs. Martinez," he says in his most polite voice. He sees me sitting on the chair, a glass of water in my hands. "Hey, is everything okay?"

I nod. God, why did I think he was dead? What's happening to me?

"It's all good," I say. "Let's just go outside for a second."

Noah nods, accompanying me back to the porch. My grandparents' eyes follow me with concern. They know I'm acting weird.

We sit on the steps of the porch, and I look at the cornfields with the scarecrow in the distance.

"We can cancel the trip if you want," Noah says. "I mean, your grandma would be overjoyed."

I smile. "That's not it. I just had a really strange dream."

"About me?" He winks.

"Yes," I say, "I think you died in it."

He goes quiet and then takes my hand. "I'm not dead. I'm right here."

"I know," I reply. It's what's bothering me.

I feel it, deep in my soul. Something strange. Something I should know and pay attention to. But this is just another regular day at the farm—where I go flying with Abuelo, Abuela complains about something or other, and Noah shows up. We're supposed to be going on a trip to the caves, and yet I can't seem to be happy about it.

"Hey," Noah says, cupping my chin in his hands and turning my face so I look in his eyes. "It's fine, Clover. It's just a bad dream."

Something flashes in his eyes. They're the usual blue-gray, but the eyes don't belong to him. They belong to someone else.

Adam.

I frown again, trying to grasp the memory, but it's gone in a second like it was never there.

"We can definitely cancel the trip if you're not feeling well," Noah says. "You look awful."

"Thanks, you ass."

"In my defense, you're always mean to me first," he pronounces. "It's why I'm your only friend."

But he isn't. I'm sure he isn't. There are more people. People whose names and faces are forgotten. People in that strange dream.

"Clover?" Noah asks.

I get up suddenly. There's something wrong. I'm sure there is. My memory has always been perfect, bordering on scary.

I walk forward to the cornfields, grabbing one of the leaves. It slides under my thumb, its texture grated. It feels real. I go back to the house, and the wood there also feels real. I put my head through the door, and both of my grandparents look back at me. My heart aches looking at them.

"¿Está todo bien, Clover?" Abuelo asks.

I nod. My throat closes up.

"Te amo," I say, and they smile back.

"Te amo también," Abuela says.

They sit there quiet. It's just another regular day for them.

No, it's not just regular.

It's a perfect day.

The weather, the sky, the farm. My grandparents, quiet in the living room. The flying. Nothing is out of place—no one is shouting or fighting, and nothing is wrong. And I remember that sometimes life used to be like that, that it was this tiny little place in the corner of the universe with the people I loved the most, and nothing was ever wrong.

Tears well in my eyes, and Noah rushes toward me.

"It's okay," he says in a whisper. "Hey, look at me. It's okay."

I look up to meet his blue-gray eyes that most definitely do not belong to him.

"Don't cry," Noah says. "It's just a really bad dream."

And then he kisses me. His lips are warm and soft against mine. They taste of sunshine and better days.

They taste of things I'll never have again.

I break away, pushing him back gently. This wasn't what I wanted, but I understand it now.

"I'm sorry," I tell him, cupping his face in my hands. "I'm sorry I didn't love you back the way you loved me. And I'm sorry that it took me so long to figure that out."

"Clover, what are you saying?"

My voice is more urgent. I'm not sure how long this will last. "I'm sorry I left you behind. I'm sorry you died that day, and I'll never forget it. I'm just so sorry."

I'm crying now, letting my tears fall. I catch a single glimpse of my grandparents still in the living room. I could choose to stay here, but I can't bear to say goodbye to them again. If I do, I'll never have the strength to leave.

Noah wipes away a tear from my cheek with his thumb. He starts slowly fading, becoming translucent.

"Are you going to be okay?" he asks.

I start remembering as the things around me fade. First the mountains, then the cornfields, then the plane. It's nothing but a dream. A sweet, good dream, where everything turns out fine.

I have more to life than just a dream.

"I am," I tell him with sincerity. "I'm going to be just fine."

Noah's smile is the last thing I see before the scene vanishes around me.

I'm left standing in the ship, all by myself.

CHAPTER 48

My first instinct is to look around for the others.

I'm still in Castor's ship, but there's no sign of him. I shut off the distress signal, and the ship responds, the image crumbling like it was never there. I can hear noises outside and step forward to look through the window, and sure enough, Castor is outside, fighting against the oncoming wave of invaders. I can't even distinguish what's happening in the battle.

With Castor distracted, it's our chance to grab the crystal.

We don't have much time.

"Sputnik?" I call, but there's still no answer. I run around the ship, searching for any sign of life.

The first person I stumble on is Flint. He sits in a corner, his eyes distant and vacant. I go to him, touching his hands, but they are cold. His eyes are glazed over, and he's muttering to himself.

"Come on, Flint," I say. "It's time to get up."

He doesn't move. I'm not sure how to wake him, and I squeeze my fingers tighter around his, hoping the heat is enough. I'm scared that if I try too hard to wake him, he won't wake up at all.

"Flint, wake up." I snap my fingers loudly in front of him. It doesn't work.

Then someone else comes forward and slaps him.

The effects are immediate. Flint jostles awake, his eyes wide, and turns to Brooklyn with a frown. "Hey! What was that for?"

"Stop dreaming about your weird *Star Wars* fan fiction," Brooklyn says. "We've got a planet to save."

"Ouch," Flint says. I don't know if he's more hurt by the slap or Brooklyn's comment. "What exactly *was* that?"

"Castor's powers," I reply. "Making us see paradise so we'd want to stay there."

"Wow." Flint blinks. "What did you see?"

I shrug. "My grandparents. You?"

Flint turns to Brooklyn. Brooklyn grins like a demon.

"I hate you," he says to her.

"You're predictable," Brooklyn says. "And don't worry, all of us would rather be watching *Star Wars*."

I help Flint get up, and he adjusts his glasses.

"What did you see?" Flint asks.

"The usual," Brooklyn replies. "Home with my parents, going to college, all of it."

"But you woke up by yourself," I say.

"Well, basically, One Direction started playing at this party, and then I remembered that they split up, and thus it couldn't be a perfect world with this memory. The pain was just too much, and it shattered my illusion."

I only look at her.

"What?"

"I love you, Brooklyn."

"I love you, too," she says with a grin.

We move along the ship, going room by room.

"I'm going back to the panel," I say. "Castor's still battling the aliens outside. If I can get this ship to work, maybe then we can get out—"

But I never get to finish my sentence. Something outside causes the ship to shake, and the whole thing starts falling down. I run, and Brooklyn and Flint follow me outside. As we step out onto the ramp, the earth below us shakes. I'm thrown to the ground, and the ship falls farther into an open crack.

Beyond the crack, down below, there's something deep and red.

"Tell me that this isn't—"

"A volcano?" Flint completes. "Sure looks like it."

"Why can't anything be normal?" I moan. "I'm so exhausted."

"There, there." Brooklyn pats my back.

Then I hear a bark. "Sputnik!" I call out, and she barks back.

I run toward the sound.

She's chained to the side of the ship. She licks my face as soon as she sees me.

"Come on, you goofball," I say. "Stay still. Gotta break you out of here."

Sputnik does as she's told. I point my gun at the base of the chain, and it breaks off easily. Sputnik shakes out her fur, trotting forward.

"So?" Flint asks, eyeing the dog. "Did you poop it or not?"

Sputnik wags her tail.

"You know, it's almost comforting to know that if Castor manages to destroy the world, he had to dig through dog shit to get it," Brooklyn says. "Feels like Earth is still fair."

I pat Sputnik's head, glad to get her back. My heart swells a little, and it eases my own worry. Now all we gotta do is find the crystal and stop the end of the world.

Easy.

"We should hurry up," Brooklyn says. "Looks like we got some company."

Brooklyn is subtle when she says "company." What she means instead is a horde of aliens in the caves. There are extra sets of arms, aliens made of clay and bark and silver and so many other things I don't recognize. I recognize some of them from our travels, but all of them are here for one thing only.

Castor hasn't gotten below yet, fighting off the aliens.

"Come on," I say. "We gotta find the crystal."

I don't need to say it twice. Brooklyn dives inside Castor's ship again with Flint this time. I check the damage to the ship—the wing is completely broken. I'm not sure we'll be able to get out of here with it.

It'll have to be the hard way.

The only problem is, there's a horde of aliens standing between us and getting out of this volcano. Castor shoots another bolt of light across the aliens, but none of them are hurt. It only drives them farther, more mad as they try to get to the Universal.

Then, slipping through the alien crowd, I spot Andy.

She doesn't look like a Universal. No supernatural glow comes out of her eyes and hair, and she slips among the rest of the aliens unnoticed.

"Where the hell are the others?" I ask her.

Andy shakes her head. "No idea. Do you think we have a way out?"

I point to the alien army.

"Great," she mutters. "Did you find Sputnik? She still has it?"

"I doubt it," I reply. "I don't think Castor would just have left her here if she did."

Another earthquake rumbles in the ground, and I grasp the ship so I don't fall to the ground. The ship turns, slowly descending as the ground shifts and reveals something else.

There's another crystal formation here, right in the middle of the volcano, crystals spreading over the hot magma. They're

Castor's crystals, deep blue and purple and black, their edges sharp. On top of the formation, it looks like there's a piece missing.

The place where the original crystal goes.

On the ground next to it, there sits a box, exactly like the one we found on Hl'lor.

Andy sees the same thing I do. We both run toward it as the rest of the cave explodes into a burst of light. Castor's shout echoes through the cave, and the shimmering wave that hits the aliens makes them all drop to the ground, unconscious. I feel the wave hit my bones, but it does nothing to me.

Castor heaves a sigh and turns to us.

"Did you really think that distraction would work?" he asks, his tone calm.

I tense.

Andy steps forward. A hundred fallen aliens all around us and the two Universals in the middle, with the fate of the galaxy between them.

"Castor," Andy says, loud and clear, "there's still time. We can change this."

"You can't stop it, Andromeda," Castor says. "There's no more time. Can't you feel it? The Earth calls for it, too."

As the ground rumbles beneath my feet, I sense it.

The ground shakes again, and the box is still down there, in the chasm.

I'll have to grab it.

Behind me, the others emerge from the ship, Sputnik with

them. None of us dare to move. We're fast, but one move from Castor and it's over. All he has to do is put the crystal in the right place. I look at the others. Rayen, Violet, Avani, Brooklyn, Flint—all unmoving.

I catch Flint's eyes, gesture toward the chasm and the open volcano below with the crystal formation.

Flint sees it and nods.

I inch closer.

Andy and Castor keep staring at each other.

I slide down the chasm, one inch at a time. The ground shakes again, and I let myself slide closer. The temperature rises hot and burning, crawling its way up my clothes, my body dripping with sweat. While the earth shakes, I hold on.

Just a few more feet.

My hands reach the rock.

I can see the crystal. I'm almost there.

Almost there.

Another earthquake hits, and I'm thrown back. I scream, grasping for a place to hold as I free-fall through the abyss, feeling nothing at my feet.

Nothing but empty air.

A hand grasps me, and I hold on as Andy pulls me up, my hands shaking and my muscles aching. But it's that second where she makes the decision that changes everything. Castor dives for the box, jumping to the chasm below, and in his hands, there's the crystal.

He takes it out, his face illuminated by the glow.

Suddenly,
the
world
just
stops.

CHAPTER 49

Everything changes when the crystal is in Castor's hand.

Time becomes meaningless. I don't know where and when I am. It does not matter. Everything hangs in the air in particles, waiting. Waiting for the universe to take a breath and rearrange itself. The Earth has stopped in place, suspended.

A song echoes inside me.

Castor holds the crystal right next to his own crystal formation.

The crystal is pure. There is no evil intent in it. No good, no evil. It simply is. In his hand, it ceases to be an object, and it becomes a destiny. It changes the entire world.

The colors reflect the transparency and the silver shine of the stars. It bursts in colors I don't comprehend with my irises, pink and blue and red and black. It's orange for the hope of rebirth. It's yellow for the streaks of the sun that will light the way. It's blue for the act of missing home, and it's green for what was left behind.

The colors shift in his hand, and he shakes, taking in the power of the crystal. Taking in what it can do.

My friends descend into the chasm with me. We all stop in front of Castor's crystal. We all feel its power, mesmerized.

It calls us. It calls us from within our bones.

It whispers to me, *let me bring you home.*

I try to shake its powers off me, but there is nothing in this universe that exists as long as this crystal does, where Castor is grasping its energy, shaping it to his intent. The crystal mutes everything else, as if no one should dare to exist in the same place as it does. Even Andy, eyes wide open, feels its calling.

In Castor's hand, it stops being harmless. It awakens.

"It'll remake everything," Castor says, turning to Andy.

He's peaceful. That's how I feel, too. The crystal brings peace and purpose. It's an ancient calling fulfilled.

When Castor places it with his own crystal, its energy will burst. It'll remake the Earth. It'll complete its ancient calling.

Castor holds it in his hand, trembling.

"No," Andy says, but her voice is not sure.

Castor smiles. Slowly, he stretches the crystal over to Andy so she can feel its power for herself.

Andy reaches out for it, and when she touches it, I see the universe as the Universals want to remake it.

Earth is reborn in its own way, crystals everywhere. It spins as the new center of the universe as beings of outlandish strength and wisdom fill it. The stars glow above us, the atmosphere thin and the galaxy just beyond our reach if we're willing to touch it.

Castor's tears are falling freely.

"This is what I'm promising you," he says. "No more destruction. No more dead planet. We deserve to be here, Andromeda. We fought hard for it. We deserve to exist, to go back to the way it was before."

He presses the crystal harder into her hand.

"We can go all the way back," he whispers. "Before we were destroyed. Before we were sent to this planet, before anything else. It won't have to hurt anymore. We won't have to be the last ones."

It's not about hurting anymore.

I understand this now. We can't go back. We can't wipe the alien invasion from our history. I wouldn't wipe away all I've been through, because then I'd forget all I learned.

Maybe it will never stop hurting. I remember Adam and Noah and my grandparents, the ache they left behind. It's never not going to hurt. But going back to the way it was before won't fix anything. Going back means becoming less of ourselves.

In a flash of clarity, I'm the one who reaches for the crystal. I lunge for it, grabbing it from Castor, but he's quick, too. He grips me by the neck, raising me against the crystals he made. They cut into my back, their edges sharp, my blood soaking them.

The crystal starts slipping from my hands, little by little.

Castor presses me farther into the crystal.

Andy rams against Castor, and he drops me, the crystal clattering to the ground. It's no use. Her powers are gone, drained to fuel the crystal and Earth's transformation.

"No," Andy says, pulling Castor away. "It's not our way!"

"You broke the rules, Andromeda," Castor says. "You brought Violet back. I should break them, too."

Castor lunges for the crystal, but I'm faster than he is. I kick it away from him, my back feeling like a hundred different needles have plunged through it. The smell of the blood scents the atmosphere, and I blink away tears of pain.

The crystal spins, and Violet tries to reach for it, but Castor is already there. There's a light bursting from his hands, and then Violet is smashed against the ground, head thrown back.

She doesn't move.

I reach for it again despite the pain. Castor is faster, though.

When the earth shakes, the platform between me and my friends cracks.

The screams echo inside the cave. We split up. Brooklyn jumps to Avani, pulling her forward. Flint stumbles on the platform just as Rayen reaches for him. The earth cracks open around us, stranding us on different levels as Andy and I stay down below.

They start moving back, Brooklyn holding Sputnik's collar. There's nothing they can do but watch. It's petrifying. If we fail, they're going to watch our destruction without being able to do anything.

All that's left on our platform is me, Andy, and Castor.

The crystal formation rises in the middle, ready to finish what has been started. All Castor needs to do is put the crystal in its place.

Castor lunges again, but Andy puts herself in front. Castor twists her arm, and Andy yelps, and I crawl despite the heat, despite the pain, just to get to that one shard. My fingers grasp against the crumbling rock, my skin bristling against the ground. I reach for it just as Castor pulls my ankle back.

I scream.

Castor bends to pick it up just as Andy slams into him, her starlight blood covering her clothes, bringing them both to the ground. The crystal clatters against the ground, driven to the edge. I push myself forward to grab it as it falls deeper into the earth, but then I'm falling, falling, right to the edge of the chasm.

Andy lets go of Castor and reaches over to me.

"Hold on," she says, her face torn with the struggle. She's not as strong as she's always been, and it takes every muscle to keep me in place. "I'm just—"

My fingers grasp against hers.

When I look below, there's just magma, burning my skin and my lungs, every breath a struggle. My palms are sweaty, slipping from Andy's fingers.

There's the crystal, right on another edge.

Castor jumps to the other platform.

I can reach the crystal only if I let go.

Andy widens her eyes as she realizes what I'm doing. I open my palms and let myself slip, let myself fall. Andy yells, and the heat wave is stronger when I hit the other platform.

My body slams against the ground, my back numb with the pain.

Castor's on the other side of the platform. We're way below everyone else, close to the center of the Earth. Andy's bent over the chasm, looking down with fearful eyes. Above her still, on another platform, are my friends and my dog.

I get up.

It's me and him.

One last chance.

"Think about it, Clover," he says, holding the crystal in his hands. "Think about this. You can be remade. There won't be any more bad memories. No more pain."

But the thing I've learned is that this pain can be good.

It's a part of who I am. I wouldn't be here if it wasn't for all that happened. I wouldn't have my friends with me. I would have never met Sputnik or gone to space. I learned to deal with that loss. Not just to survive it. To accept that it's a part of who I am and who I'll always be.

I'd rather have this than be empty, to pretend nothing happened.

I reach for him and the crystal and punch him. He stumbles back, and I snatch the crystal from his hands.

I feel its power in my palms as it reaches for the other crystals.

I can feel it as it looks for a place to lodge itself, to let it happen, to mold everything again.

I grasp it in two hands and break it.

Nothing happens.

I try again, putting all my strength to it, but there's nothing. Castor looks at me and laughs.

"Did you really think you could destroy it?" he asks, his eyes reflecting the fire below us. "You went through a great deal of trouble to keep this from me, but it's indestructible. It's Universal, like me. You won't stop us."

I hit it against the ground, but the crystal shocks me with pain and then soothes me, trying to lull me into submission. Trying to reach for the part of me that's Universal and knows that it wants to go home, too. For that one small part of my subconscious that longs for no more pain.

Andy's crying, shouting about something, and I look to my friends, all petrified, all unable to stop this type of destruction. And when I look up, Violet, awake.

Our eyes meet.

She's not Universal like us. She's immune to the song that sings in our bones. She's human, entirely human.

She's made from the same energy as the crystal.

I look at Castor, and then I throw it in her direction. It echoes the last time, but instead of being about death, it's the opposite.

It lands, and Castor widens his eyes. Violet hesitates, picking up the crystal.

She holds the fate of the universe in her hands.

"You're too much like me," Castor shouts to her. "I know you, Violet. I know what you've been through. You've been remade, and you aren't sure where you belong."

Violet's eyes water. There's a crack underneath her skin where the same energy as the crystal glitters. When she holds it, it shows. The same place Andy touched her when she first brought Violet back.

"You can belong here, Violet," Castor says. He doesn't need to reach out again to the crystal. All Violet needs to do is walk forward and place it on his own crystal. "You deserve it. No more pain. It'll be like nothing ever happened. You deserve to be okay. I know you want to go home."

Violet looks back at Castor.

I take a breath that lasts a century.

"Yes," she says. "I want to go home."

Violet breaks the crystal in two.

CHAPTER 50

The energy inside the crystal explodes like a supernova, throwing all of us back. It burns through existence as it's unmade, and Violet still holds the pieces, absorbing the energy.

She was unmade before.

This is just another unraveling, and the crystal bursts from her in a wave of light. In her hands, the crystal glows less and less. The energy that comes out of it is the same energy as emanates from Violet.

They're one and the same.

Violet and the crystal.

Castor climbs up to her, but it's useless. He can't stop what she's already started. The energy is woven around Violet like a shield, like the universe is rearranging.

Castor finally reaches her. Violet looks up, her eyes swirling with power, distant, her hair rising in the air, her feet floating above the ground as she stretches like an unearthly god.

"Violet," Castor calls. "Listen to me. It calls to Universali. Use this power. Let the crystal speak. You can feel it."

Violet looks down at her glowing hands, at the power seeping through her veins. One move from her and she can use this power to change everything. One move and she powers the crystals on her own if she wants.

"Yes," she says, and her voice echoes like the hundred faces of the crystal, each of them ringing through the cave. "I can."

"Bring us to Universali," Castor says.

"No," Andy says, loud enough that Violet—or the crystal inside Violet—snaps its attention back to her. "Violet, you need to let go."

Violet says nothing, facing Andy. Fragile Andy. Almost human Andy. With her freckles, her nose a little too big for her face, and her wide blue eyes.

"Do it," Castor orders, his voice angry. The crystal still sings of another planet, another reality. It begs to remake. "Universali calls."

Violet looks to Andy. Andy smiles. The moment seems like it lasts forever while the two girls look at each other.

"Take us home," Andy says.

Violet blinks.

She only moves a hand—it's all she needs as the power of the crystal fills her. She points a hand at Castor's chest, and a wave of light spreads over him. The crystal dissolves completely in her hand, the energy spreading like a wave, and everything comes to a standstill.

It sings of Earth.

The power is given back to the universe, seeping back where it belongs, spreading through galaxies and planets until it reaches the universe's edges. The energy is there, waiting to be molded.

I remember what it felt like, the first time Andy did it. It's exactly like that. Violet using the energy to remake everything.

Violet lowers herself and puts her hands to the ground, and suddenly, all that power, all the glowing, bursts out of her in a single explosion.

But instead of the songs of a second before, the songs of the Universal planet and the echo of the crystal Castor left behind, Violet makes the energy transform into something else.

When the energy spreads, I smell the pines of the forest close to home. The asphalt road that stretches through the country, the mountains that bend the horizons into shape, the clear water of the rivers. The taste of mint and home cooking and the breeze that blows through my hair when I'm climbing in an airplane. The sounds of the squirrels and critters running and Sputnik's distant bark. The energy is all of this at once, echoing the place Violet wants. Dissolving the energy into what we love. Into what we belong.

The crystal takes us home.

Violet falls to the ground.

When she opens her eyes, they're back to normal.

No sign of the crystal. No sign of any different energy at all.

"No," Castor says. "No. No. This can't be."

He looks at his hands, bleeding silver. The crystal in the background fades, and its energy stops sucking into the Earth. It's harmless now.

"No," Castor repeats.

Andy reaches out a hand for him. There's a trace of power in her, as if Violet breaking the crystal put it back where it belonged. It remade Andy, like Andy had remade Violet. Andy's hair unfurls in its deep black, her skin a mesmerizing purple.

"Give me your hand," Andy says. "I can help you."

"This is not what I want," he says, looking at his hands in horror. "This is not how it's supposed to be. Universali is the way."

"Come on," Andy says, reaching out for the last of her species.

But Castor doesn't grasp her hand. He only looks at his cluster of crystals again, faded and powerless. Just like him.

Castor runs, leaping back onto the other platform, ignoring us, turning his back on Andy. The ground beneath us shakes, like the volcano is still ready to explode. Castor goes back inside the ship, and I listen to it awakening.

It's weak, though. It shakes and turns as Castor tries to lift off, and Andy shouts after him, her voice an echo. She starts going for the ship, but Violet puts her arm out to stop her. Castor lifts his ship off the ground, and I realize what's going to happen before I can do anything to stop it.

The ship sputters to the edge. Castor is still determined to leave, to find something else, another answer, another crystal, another way out. The ship falters, breaking apart, dying in his hands.

Plunging straight into the abyss.

Andy screams.

The fire engulfs the ship whole, leaving nothing behind, completely swallowed by the earth. I can only look, half dazed, as it vanishes beneath the surface.

Castor fades into the earth like he was never here at all.

Andy's shoulders shake, and I put my arms around her in an embrace, feeling my back laced with pain.

"Come on," I whisper to her. "Come on."

Slowly, we climb back up, through the platforms. The volcano seems placated around us. When we're finally back in the cave and the upper platforms, I run to Sputnik, burying myself in her fur.

"He didn't take my hand," Andy says, heartbreak in her voice.

Even then, she was ready to forgive. Castor was desperate with grief. Desperate and heartbroken, living in a world where he couldn't figure out his own place. Not being able to move on.

It's what killed him in the end.

I turn around, and the rest of the aliens have vanished, too. No sign of their bodies. Everything around is completely still.

"Where did they go?" Rayen asks, her voice barely louder than a whisper.

We all turn to Violet.

She blinks, uncertain. "I think I repelled them. With the crystal."

Andy grips her shoulders, her fingers digging into Violet's skin. "I'm sorry," she says. "I'm really sorry. I should've asked you."

Violet nods. "I know."

They embrace each other. There's relief all around us as we look at one another, the emptiness around us strange, when only a moment before it was chaos. The relief helps the realization dawn.

We saved the Earth.

We did it.

"How the hell did that even work?" Brooklyn sighs, dropping to the ground.

Avani looks like she's about to complain but then simply sighs and sits down on the ground, too.

"I don't know," Violet admits. "I thought I felt something from the crystal at first. But then I understood. It was…energy, like mine. I was remade, and the crystal remakes things. We're made of the same thing. So I remade it in another shape. Sent the energy back to the universe."

Universali would have destroyed the Earth.

Instead, Violet used the energy for creating. For giving back. For setting things right.

It was never about wiping out what was in the past. It's about creating what's here, right now. Giving us another chance, fighting to the last moment for us to be here. For our home.

I realize I'm crying when Violet wipes one of my tears away with her thumb.

"Clover broke," Brooklyn announces.

"Shut the fuck up," I tell her.

We break out in laughter. Half of it is still nervous, the sound strange to our ears. Half of it is relief, the stress dissipating into the air. Castor has just died, preferring death to living in a place where he had to battle what he was left with, still refusing to confront it and let go. A part of me knows that it could easily have been me.

That's the real thing about being human.

I can feel it all at once. I don't have to pick. I can be sorry for Castor and still be glad that his plan didn't work.

"Should we go back?" Flint asks after we've all caught our breaths.

"In a moment," Brooklyn says. "I think after saving the world a couple of times, we deserve some rest."

I keep hugging Sputnik, and I'm glad I don't have to get up yet. I know that when I do, there's work to be done. There's more waiting for us outside.

I look up and meet Violet's eyes.

"How are you?" she asks.

"Shaken. You?"

She looks at her hands. They are the usual light marble color. Her hair is the regular shade of gold, her eyebrows thick, and her eyes back to their normal blue.

She looks whole.

Violet, with all that energy held inside her, unmaking universes.

"I'm human," she finally says.

And that's enough.

It's enough for all of us.

CHAPTER 51

The barrier was destroyed with Castor's ship.

It's strange how things can be simple.

We go back to the Arc, landing it in the middle of Unity. We leave the ship, battered and bruised but still holding on to one another.

My father is the first one to greet us. He comes toward me with a hug, and Sputnik runs to him, barking, making us all laugh for not giving her the attention she needs. I bury my hands in her fur, and everything is right again. We saved the Earth. We saved the dog.

I don't let the lump in my throat bother me.

Heidi is right behind my father. There are not a lot of people outside, like they're still afraid to come out. I walk tentatively toward Heidi, waiting to see what she has to say. The gun she pointed at me still hangs between us, strange and unfriendly. My friends stop at the ramp of the ship without moving.

I turn to Heidi.

"It's over," I tell her. "The aliens are all gone."

Heidi nods. Her expression is serious, her smart brown eyes boring into mine, unflinching.

"You give your word?" she asks.

I nod. "I told you I would fix it."

"You said you'd tell me the truth."

So I do.

I tell her everything.

I talk about the distress signal and the barrier, about Andy and the crystal, about Castor and his plan to change the Earth back into his planet, about everything we did to get here, and about how we were the first to send the Hostemn away, ten years ago. Heidi's expression changes from disbelief to shock, but she realizes I can't be making all this stuff up. She's seen more than her fair share of weirdness.

By the end of the tale, she softens.

"I'm sorry, Clover," she says. "I didn't know. I was...afraid. Afraid of what would happen."

"It's okay," I say quietly. "I understand."

She doesn't need to say anything else. There are no words that can be spoken now. We're still on the edge, learning how to fix things.

"Is that her?" Heidi asks, pointing to Andy.

I gesture for Andy to come over.

She steps forward. She's still Universal, though her power seems more colorful now, as if it's mingling with Earth and happy to stay here. Shifting between Earth and Universal, because Andy is both.

"So you're like Castor?" Heidi asks, curious.

Andy nods. "Yes. He came after me on another ship, but we are from the same place. The place he wanted to rebuild."

"And you don't?" Heidi asks, an edge of tension to her voice.

Andy only smiles. "I like it here the way it is."

"You have a good heart."

"I don't have a heart," Andy replies.

I break a smile over it.

We know better.

My friends all turn around to leave. We're tired, on the edge of exhaustion. We accomplished what we set out to do. We already saved enough people. Maybe Brooklyn is right—let some of the others save themselves now. Let the others take care of it.

I'm glad I can leave this to someone else for once.

"And Castor?" Heidi finally asks as Andy steps away, back toward the Arc.

I shake my head. "He didn't make it."

Heidi nods, offering me a hug. I take it.

I don't know what was on his mind or what really made Castor let it all go. But there's hope here as we watch the sky. I think about the fact that a year ago, that was me. Someone who desperately wanted to let go but found a reason to stay. Found a reason to fight.

The barrier is gone. It's time we rebuild. It's time we re-create.

It's time we unmake, to the best of our abilities.

It takes a few days to adjust. Heidi gives us another cabin instead so we can stay by ourselves until everything is sorted out.

I go into the woods, and the crystals are still all there, though faded. The trees are bouncing back, and the signs of the alien invasion are gone. Maybe there'll come a day when we'll forget what that once looked like even.

The crystals are like scars. They're reminders of something terrible. But they're reminders that above all, we got past it. We survived.

And one morning, Brooklyn uses the Arc's generator and goes to Castor's cabin to do what she's best at. She adjusts the microphone, the sound, and everything else. All seven of us hold our breaths in expectation. Knowing what it means for it to be here.

Brooklyn starts playing a song. It's an old '70s hit, because this is Brooklyn, and it couldn't be anything else. John Denver's voice echoes through the speakers and then through Unity until there's nothing but the sound of his voice singing of home.

When it ends, Brooklyn takes a second before moving to the microphone.

"This is Brooklyn Spencer, and you're listening to the Apocalypse Radio Station," she says. "If you're listening to this, we are in a colony in Wyoming, near Yellowstone Park. We're looking for other survivors."

Then she plays another song and leaves the message on loop so it echoes through for anyone who is listening, looking for radio stations.

My father meets me outside the cabin, and he wipes away the tears that the music left behind.

"It's been so long, you know," he says. "I didn't think we'd get things like this again."

I look at the Arc, how it easily fits into the background and brought the two worlds together. Our world and Andy's.

How the message would be out there and how we were going to rebuild things from now on without forgetting the past. Finding a way to move on.

"What is it?" my father asks, looking at me.

"There's one other thing I need to do," I tell my father, and he nods.

CHAPTER 52

The plane flies along the mountainside.

It's not the same as I remember it. I can see the road and the asphalt below. My dad is the one flying the plane this time, and it allows me to pay attention to the scenery.

There is no longer a landing strip. The corn is gone, the fields spreading with tall, wild grass, turning it into an over-grown meadow. My dad steadies the plane, and slowly, we begin our descent.

He lands the plane just near the old fence.

I don't move.

"You don't have to do this, you know," he says.

I nod.

Ever since my encounter with Castor, I've been wondering

if I left something real behind. Ever since the day the aliens arrived, I started running and never looked back. Even while taking back the Earth, while going to face them, it was the only thing I knew how to do. The only way I found that I could fix this broken world and the broken me.

"I'm ready," I tell him.

I land with my feet sure on the ground. I wait for a magical moment of recognition, an ache in my heart, but there's nothing. The ground remains the same. I start threading through the grass, with my father close behind me, until I get to the house and the porch.

It looks old. Ten years have not been kind to it.

I look back at the field and try to spot the old scarecrow. I can still see a hint of it, weathered and shredded but still standing. I smile, and then I open the door and step inside.

The house still has the same smell as before. The ache in my heart is slow, as if a hand is pressing it, squeezing it between my lungs. I take a deep breath, closing and opening my eyes.

I move. Through the kitchen, where there are still old pans in the sink from where Abuela last washed them before I left. Through the living room, where I forgot to put the remote controls from the TV back inside the little box. To the bathroom and then up the stairs to Abuelo's office, where we watched the news together when the world as we knew it began to end. Then my grandparents' room, where there is no longer any trace of them, a bedroom with only the quilt to remember them by, and then my room, which is exactly the same as I left it.

I play with the telescope, still pointed to the window, a dream that seemed distant at the time. Something from my old life.

My father comes up behind me and stops in the threshold, looking at my room with the NASA posters, taking in this part of my life that is now gone.

My heart is a jumble of feelings and thoughts I don't understand. I left in a rush and never thought of coming back here, to the place where I first started.

"Come on," Dad says. "I found a couple of photo albums we can look at."

I go down with him. We sit on the sofa on another of my abuela's quilts, which she loved to make. He opens up the old album, and there are bits and pieces of a childhood I don't remember that well.

The second time I went in an airplane with my abuelo by myself. I was four. Abuelo didn't let Abuela know the first time, afraid that she'd stop him. She was angry, but in the end, she knew that I was never meant to stay grounded down here. Our trip to Malmstrom. Our trip to the NASA base when I was eleven. Abuelo and I going to the movies and watching *Star Trek*, after he'd been waiting for it to come out for years. Abuela and I in the kitchen making tamales, me with a face that would rather be on the other side of the world instead of there.

"She showed me this one." My dad points to the kitchen picture. Abuelo took that one. It's out of focus. He was never good with the camera like Abuela was. "She told me you'd always rather be in an airplane. And I was glad of that, because that's something we could have in common, even if we never met."

I look at him. "We've met now."

He smiles and kisses my forehead, just like Abuela used to.

"I spent the last ten years wondering, every day," he says. "After I survived, I kept wondering if you'd made it, too. Every single day. I looked at the pictures, and I prayed that God would let my little girl live. Wherever she was."

I take his hand and squeeze it. "I'm here now."

He smiles, and there are tears welling in his eyes. We both look at the pictures again, and I keep looking, finding myself and my family over and over again in those small clicked moments, with my father by my side.

And then I start talking.

I tell him about my school projects and the first time I decided to go to Mars. I tell him about Noah and how we met in school, about our trips, and how we used to sit on the roof together. I tell him about Noah's family and my grandparents and my feelings and the one hundred things that used to make up my life that don't exist anymore.

And my father does the one thing I expect him to do.

He listens.

I tell him about the attack, about Noah dying, and how I survived. I tell him how Sputnik found me with the gun pointed to my head, and she sat down in front of me and kept looking until I lowered it. I tell him about finding the others after a car crash, about our story together, and about Adam. I tell him that it was me fighting to stay alive, with the last shred of hope I had, with the last shred of being that I still held on to. I tell him about fighting the aliens and about running away, again and again, until the day we heard the distress call.

When I'm done, I wipe my tears away and still hold tight to his hand.

"You're here now, Clover," he says quietly. "And surviving takes a toll. It's harder than dying."

And he's right. I spent so much time trying to fight the aliens back in a suicide mission, dealing with the hurt and the trauma in the only way I could. Fighting and surviving.

But this time, I get to do something better. I get to heal.

Dad taps the photo album and points to a picture of us three. Abuelo, Abuela, and I. We're not in Disneyland or any other trip. It's a photo Noah took for us. The three of us sitting on the porch, me between them. I must have been around thirteen, awkward and gangly.

"It's this that matters," he says.

I look at the picture. It wasn't perfect. But it was completely, blissfully happy.

And it's those little things, the small quiet memories that will stay with me forever.

As long as I have those, I know I'll be okay.

CHAPTER 53

When we circle back to Unity, it's near dawn.

My father and I spent the weekend at my grandparents' house, tidying things up, picking things I wanted to take with me, and just enjoying each other's company. In the end, I decided to take only the photo album, Abuela's quilt, some clothes that still fit me, and a couple of books.

The mountainside is quiet at this hour, not like just a couple of days before when we saw Earth as an intergalactic battlefield and complete displacement of the universe. But Earth, oblivious to everything, just stays in place.

I land the plane. The feeling of the sky doesn't leave me breathless anymore. It doesn't offer me an escape as I used to think of it, but it offers me solace, which is much better.

The place is quiet when we arrive. I can hear the animals and the cattle in the distance, and I take my bag to the cabin.

"Morning," I say, putting my feet up on Sputnik's back. She tries to lick them, and I push her playfully.

"Not at this hour," Avani mumbles, putting the pillow over her head. "Why is it so early?"

I roll my eyes. Rayen wakes up, rolls over, and looks at me. "How did it go?"

"Fine," I say. "I thought it was going to be different."

I don't know what I expected when I went to my grandparents' house. I thought I'd break down and cry. I put off going back there as if I could erase a part of my past, lock it down where I couldn't access it and it wouldn't make me hurt.

But denying it for so long is what was going to break me in the end.

"I'm glad it worked," Rayen says with a smile and gives me her hand. I squeeze it back, and we just stay like that in our beds, holding hands.

"So no more mysteries," says Brooklyn. "No more secretly evil villains and no more aliens for a while except us. How is that for the end of the fucking world?"

"If another alien shows up," Andy mutters, "I'm murdering everybody."

We all break into another bout of laughter, relieved.

A beep echoes through the cabin, and I frown.

"What is that?"

"Isn't that—" Flint says, but he never finishes the sentence.

All seven of us are up and running toward the admin-istration cabin. Sputnik follows. The radio crackles to life as Brooklyn sits down in front of it, and all of us hold our breaths as she adjusts the sounds and the recorded message she's been broadcasting ever since we broke the barrier.

The beep echoes again, and Brooklyn turns the sound up, her fingers shaking just slightly as she presses the button.

"This is the Radio Apocalypse station," Brooklyn says, "and this is Brooklyn Spencer talking from Unity in Wyoming."

We wait for another crackle of static.

"Brooklyn?" a voice says. "This is Rhonda Carson, talking from Colorado. We heard your call. Over."

For a second, there's silence. Brooklyn is shaking, and she takes a deep breath before she answers.

"It's good to hear from you, Rhonda. How many of you are there? Over."

"We've got about two hundred survivors, give or take," Rhonda answers. "It's a small community. But it's family."

Brooklyn puts her hands to her mouth, and all of us exchange looks. Two hundred survivors. And if we keep on broadcasting, we can reach more people. Find other survivors.

"Thank you, Rhonda," Brooklyn finally manages. "We're so happy to hear from you. We'll keep on broadcasting to find others. That's what we're hoping for. Over."

"We're glad to hear from you, too. We'll keep in touch. Over and out."

The microphone dies with a buzz, and then Brooklyn starts

the radio again with music, the message playing again. The same message that I found and that gave me hope.

Bringing hope to all the others.

And then she breaks into laughter, and all of us join. That confused, strange feeling, the hope that grows inside our chests and reaches out to the others. The feeling that no matter what happens, we won't be alone, and we'll never have to face anything without one another. That mix of solitude and sadness and happiness and, most of all, hope. That ray of sunshine in the dark.

I look at each of them. Andy and Violet grinning at each other, Andy's eyes reflecting the same blue of the Earth that I used to see up in space. Avani and Brooklyn holding hands. Flint smiling, shaking his head, and Rayen clutching her belly, trying to hold that happiness inside her. Even Sputnik, jumping up and down, waiting for somebody to pick her up even though she's too heavy.

I couldn't love any of them more than I do now.

My abuelo used to say that there are people who belong to the earth, and others, like us Martinezes, belong to the sky.

But looking here, at this bright, brave new world, I know something else.

I belong to the Earth, too.

AUTHOR'S NOTE

Clover still struggles with depression and suicidal thoughts throughout this book. Depression, post-traumatic stress disorder, suicidal thoughts, and anxiety don't get cured overnight, and it was important for me to portray this honest truth—that the path to healing is full of struggles, but it exists.

While in *The Last 8* and *The First 7*, the story is about surviving, this note is about what comes after that. Clover seeks help, and you should, too. You're not alone in this. You get to heal.

You're brave to live.

National Suicide Prevention Lifeline
1-800-273-8255
suicidepreventionlifeline.org

Crisis Text Line

crisistextline.org

Society for the Prevention of Teen Suicide

sptsusa.org/teens

Trevor Project

For LGBTQ+ teens

1-866-488-7386

thetrevorproject.org

IN BRAZIL:

Centro de Valorização da Vida

188

cvv.org.br

ACKNOWLEDGMENTS

In the beginning, the universe was created. This has made a lot of people angry and has been widely regarded as a bad move, but it also means I got to write this book and *you* got to read it. Any interactions with aliens in regard to biology, customs, and language are merely allegorical, since we have a human vocabulary, and therefore, limited.

Here is a list of both humans and aliens I'd like to thank for getting me to this page.

My mom, who kept calling me while reading the first book and worrying about Clover and all the other stupid kids who were going to get themselves killed. Dad, who did not laugh when I asked if spaceships could have headlights because light couldn't be seen in a vacuum (seriously). Clara, my sister, for existing in general.

My agent, Sarah LaPolla, who has worked tirelessly on making my writing better and took me for really decent hot chocolate on my trip to NYC. Next time: decent coffee!

My editor, Annie Berger, who loves the Last Teenagers on Earth as much as I do and worked so hard on bringing this book into the world. Sarah Kasman, Cassie Gutman, and everyone at Sourcebooks Fire who has worked on *The Last 8* and *The First 7* and made this dream come true. Thank you, from the bottom of my heart.

Samia, Rafael, Emily: no further declarations needed. I'm with you till the world ends. Vanessa, Anna, Fernanda and Priscila, for being here. AFB, always.

Solaine, for finally handing me five stars on *The Last 8* after nine different revisions.

Iris, Barbara, Mareska, who let me complain until I couldn't feel my tongue anymore and changed my life forever. May, Tassi, Vito, V.M., Lucas, Franklin, Gabs, Rafa, Bruna, Ruan, Bruna M., for their general awesomeness and bringing that special word called friendship even more into my life.

Dana Nuenighoff and Deeba Zargarpur, for all the texts and traveling across cities to get to my launch party. Love you loads. Lindsey Hodder and Lyla Lawless, who again have done wonders for this book and helped me get it into the right shape, working their CP magic.

The SpellCheck crew—Molly Owen, Emily A. Duncan,

Adib Khorram, Linsey Miller, and L. L. McKinney, for making Dungeons & Dragons greater than it was (and also more filled with bees).

Sofia, who arrived after this book was done but still held my hand while I made my way through.

Vina, who's probably an alien and has eaten a lot of things, but never something that could bring about the end of the world. You're weird, doggo.

And finally, you. Thanks for following Clover's journey, for sticking with her friends, and most of all, for sticking with me. Thank you for being wonderful readers, and I hope I get to see you in the future. The world may end, and we may be scared, but we get to survive. We get to live. We get to hope.

May the Force be with you.

ABOUT THE AUTHOR

Laura Pohl is a Brazilian writer who lives in São Paulo. She likes writing messages in Caps Lock, quoting *Hamilton*, and obsessing about *Star Wars*. When not taking pictures of her dog, she can be found discussing alien conspiracy theories. She has not crashed any cars or spaceships yet.

You can find out more about her on her website at onlybylaura.com.

FIREreads
#getbooklit

Your hub for the hottest young adult books!

Visit us online and sign up for our
newsletter at FIREreads.com

 @sourcebooksfire

 sourcebooksfire

 firereads.tumblr.com